Troubled Waters

'Is that young American still with you?' Rodney Kenway-Potter sounded annoyed and faintly puzzled.

'Good Lord, no. He went off just after six. He wanted to go up to see the longstone and the view from the top. I put him on the path at Upper Bridge.'

'Well, where the hell is he? He was due here at seven, as he probably told you, and it's past eight.'

'Have you rung the Green Man?'

'Yes, I have. Tom says his car's in the car park where he left it when he came in from Littlechester at about a quarter to five. Then he went out again soon afterwards on foot, to his appointment with you, presumably.'

'Seems a bit odd. He said he was picking up his car and driving up to you when he came down, and was a bit anxious about being on time.'

'I call it damned odd . . . I suppose he hasn't taken a purler on the path and broken a leg or something . . . I think I'd better go along and have a look round.'

ELIZABETH LEMARCHAND
Troubled Waters

WALKER AND COMPANY · NEW YORK

First published in the United States of America in 1982 by the
Walker Publishing Company, Inc.

This paperback edition first published in 1985.

ISBN: 0-8027-3130-9

Library of Congress Catalog Card Number: 81-71195

Printed in the United States of America

10 9 8 7 6 5 4 3 2 1

To Molly, Gipi and Virginia

Other titles in the Walker British Mystery Series

CHIEF CHARACTERS

Residents of the village of Woodcombe

Rodney Kenway-Potter of Woodcombe Manor
Amaryllis, his wife
James Fordyce, genealogist
Eileen, his wife
Ella Rawlings, folklore enthusiast
Leonard Bolling, retired bookseller

Overseas Visitor

Edward Tuke, an American citizen and an employee of
Integrated Oils

Police

Detective-Inspector Deeds of the Littlechester C.I.D.
Detective-Chief Superintendent Tom Pollard and
Detective-Inspector Gregory Toye of New Scotland Yard

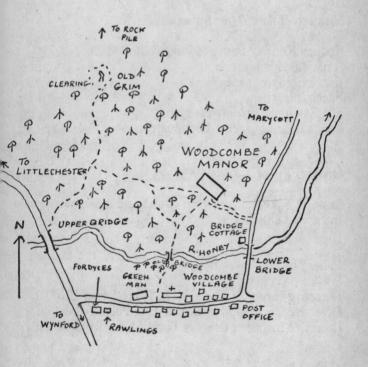

Chapter One

The Plaintiff, Mr Leonard Bolling, his Honour said, has applied to the court for an injunction to restrain the Defendant, Mr Rodney Kenway-Potter from leasing his fishing rights on the River Honey to a syndicate, on the grounds that the activities of its members have infringed his privacy and constituted a nuisance in other respects.

The Defendant, who owns and lives at Woodcombe Manor in the village of Woodcombe, also owns the fishing rights on that section of the River Honey which runs through his estate. Until approximately a year ago fishing was carried on only by himself and his family and their invited friends. He then decided to form a syndicate to share the fishing rights and provide the necessary funds for the restocking of the stream with brown trout.

The Plaintiff is the owner-occupier of Bridge Cottage, a freehold property which he bought two years ago. It is situated close to the bridge which carries a minor road from the village of Woodcombe. This road runs northwards past Bridge Cottage and the drive gates of Woodcombe Manor. The cottage has no river frontage, its garden hedge being set some ten yards back from the river bank, and its ownership does not carry any fishing rights.

Mr Bolling is a retired bookshop proprietor. He lives alone and his interests are academic. He is not, therefore,

1

obliged to live in Woodcombe or its near neighbourhood in connection with his employment, and purchased Bridge Cottage of his own free choice. Before any question of the formation of a fishing syndicate had arisen he had complained on a number of occasions to Mr Kenway-Potter that he had been disturbed by persons fishing the Bridge Pool who had looked over the hedge into his garden, and by their conversation. He complains that since the syndicate began to operate in March of this year, these annoyances have greatly increased, and that on several occasions the gate leading from the riverside path to the lane has been left open. On one of these cattle from a herd in transit came through and—er—began to eat his hedge. An even more serious disturbance, he claims, is caused by the parking of cars on a grass verge at the side of the lane, about fifty yards north of his cottage.

As is well known, fly fishing is frequently carried on after dark. Mr Kenway-Potter freely admits that members of the syndicate do arrive by car after dusk, and may not leave until midnight or later. Mr Bolling asserts that this constitutes an intolerable nuisance.

These, then, are the grounds on which the Plaintiff bases his application for an injunction against the fishing syndicate formed and operated by Mr Kenway-Potter.

Judge Higson's small dark eyes flicked saurian-fashion over his captive audience. He clasped his hands together and rested them on the papers in front of him.

How many members constitute this fishing syndicate, he enquired rhetorically? Six, including Mr Kenway-Potter himself. His wife does not fish, and his two children are now adult and not normally in residence at the Manor. The Manor fishing is divided into six beats which rotate on a regular basis among the members. Therefore only one member at a time will be fishing the Bridge Pool in the immediate vicinity of Bridge Cottage. As a fly fisherman myself I know that noisy companions would effectively put an end to successful sport. At the same time

2

it is possible that a member of the syndicate fishing one of the other beats might look in on the Bridge Pool beat and ask whoever was there if he had had any luck, but certainly would not be encouraged to linger and carry on loud and lengthy conversation. With regard to the cars, the maximum number arriving on the same occasion would be five, the average number fewer.

Judge Higson made another brief pause, this time to pour a small quantity of water from a carafe into a tumbler from which he took a few sips.

If you live by choice in a rural area, he reminded those present, you will enjoy advantages greatly appreciated by many people, including, presumably, Mr Bolling. But you also have to accept certain disadvantages. One of these is the noise inseparable from certain rural activities. I refer to such things as the frequent comings and goings of farm tractors, and the whine of circular saws in areas where forestry is carried on. Fishing is a typical rural pastime, and, it may fairly be said, one of the least obtrusive. Moreover, in the case of fishing for brown trout, the branch of the sport with which we are here concerned, the permitted season extends only from March the fifteenth to September the thirtieth: just over half the year.

In view of these facts, I have arrived at the conclusion that the activities of the syndicate formed by Mr Kenway-Potter to fish the Woodcombe Manor waters cannot reasonably be held to constitute a nuisance to Mr Bolling. The application for an injunction suspending its operation therefore fails, and costs are awarded to Mr Kenway-Potter.

The next case was called.

*

Bolling v Kenway-Potter had come early on Judge Higson's list for the day, and its swift despatch enabled the successful defendant and his supporters to foregather

3

in Woodcombe's pub at lunch-time.

The Green Man was a family-run village inn with no pretensions about it. The landlord, Tom Wonnacott, had taken over from his father, and carried on the latter's resistance to the inducements of entrepreneurs to enlarge the premises into an eating-out resort for the car owners of the neighbourhood, complete with chef, subdued lighting and canned music. A stout oak door, in a deeply recessed porch, led into a large rectangular room with a bar at the far end. Wooden benches and tables flanked the walls. These were whitewashed and decorated with a record-breaking stuffed trout in a glass case taken from the River Honey in '02 by Rodney Kenway-Potter's grandfather, a pitted darts board and a number of framed photographs of local teams and events. Behind the bar were shelves lined with bottles bearing well-known labels, with barrels of local beers and cider standing on the floor below them. Bread and cheese were always available on request, but cooked meals were only provided for occasional residents.

On the morning of the court case the bar was unusually full. The door was propped open to the warm April sunshine and elderly patrons with their beer mugs and pipes occupied the benches on each side of the porch. As the cars from Littlechester drew up they were greeted by the raising of tankards, the outcome of the case having already reached Woodcombe by bush telegraph. Leonard Bolling's Woodcombe rating, never high, was at an all-time low. Foremost among the local grievances against him were the facts that he had never crossed the threshold of the Green Man, and his habit of supplying all his needs in bulk from the Littlechester Cash and Carry instead of patronising the village shop.

Once inside, Rodney Kenway-Potter proceeded to stand a comprehensive round of drinks. A tall man, greying a little at the temples, with a wide smile, and a trick of screwing up his eyes as he looked at you with his head slightly on one side, he was displaying the traditional British attitude of not kicking a man who was down.

'Of course Bolling's basic mistake was thinking that he could settle in a place like this and have everything his own way,' he said. 'There's got to be give and take when everybody knows everybody else.'

There were sounds of general agreement.

'He ought to have had a flat in one of those faceless blocks in a quiet part of London,' Amaryllis Kenway-Potter, Rodney's wife, said. 'The sort of place where you don't know your neighbour by sight and there's a permanent deathly hush over everything.'

'And where you're eventually discovered as a month-old corpse,' Bill Reynolds added, a member of the syndicate and a consultant surgeon at Littlechester General Hospital. 'I must push off. I've got a clinic at two. Good show, Rodney. See you on Friday evening if the weather's O.K.'

He went off. Derek Blathwayt, another member, was uninhibited.

'Bolling is a right bastard,' he remarked concisely. 'The sooner he clears out, the better. I shouldn't think he'd have the nerve to hang on after this . . . Same again, please Tom . . . What the devil's up now?'

A new arrival was holding forth excitedly. . . . A chap from Ford's, a Littlechester Estate Agency, was putting up a 'For Sale' notice in the garden of Bridge Cottage.

''Asn't wasted much time over shiftin', 'as 'e? Must've known 'e'd never get 'is ruddy injunction, Bollin' must've,' Bert Manifold, a local builder's labourer asserted.

The general reaction was that Woodcombe would be a lot better off without Leonard Bolling.

'Niver a dull moment these days,' Tom Wonnacott commented, leaning on his bar counter. 'Not with the goin' to Court, and the rumpus last night'—

5

'What rumpus?' Rodney Kenway-Potter asked. He and his wife had spent the night with friends in Littlechester in order to be on hand for the County Court hearing next morning. 'Football fans? They were kicking up the hell of a shindy in the city yesterday evening after that surprise win over Longstaple. Quite a lot of arrests apparently.'

An indignant chorus confirmed that the trouble had been the ruddy fans right enough. Two carloads of them had fetched up at Upper Bridge and continued their celebrations there.

'Proper sozzled,' Bill Morris, Rodney Kenway-Potter's forester told him. 'It'll take me the best part o' the afternoon to clear up the muck they left and get the two "Private Fishing" notices out o' the stream where they chucked 'em along o' bottles and crisp bags and whatever.'

It appeared that having exhausted the possibilities of Upper Bridge the fans had packed into the cars and roared into the village at about half-past eleven when decent folk were in their beds. Those capable of using their legs had got out and gone round tipping the dustbins, which had been put out for the weekly collection, into people's gardens, and the glass front of the case in which public notices were put up had been smashed. There had been yelling and shouting like animals and language you wouldn't soil your mouth with. Finally the cars had driven off towards Littlechester, but hadn't got far as one had swerved off the road into the hedge just as the police, summoned by a series of 999 calls from Woodcombe, had arrived on the scene.

The Kenway-Potter family had lived at Woodcombe Manor for five generations and in times of trouble it was customary for village residents, whatever their political allegiance, to look to the current head of the house. Rodney listened to the somewhat confused account of the disturbance, asked a few relevant questions, and under-

6

took to approach the Chief Constable about police patrols on the main roads leading out of Littlechester after home matches.

'And if anybody wants to claim from their insurance company and would like any help, come along up,' he concluded, 'I'll be at home this evening.'

There was a partial exodus as his wife offered to go and inspect the damage. In the comparative calm Rodney's ear caught an unmistakeably American voice in conversation with Tom Wonnacott at the bar counter. The landlord replied to an enquiry that he'd have to put it to the missus, and vanished through a door leading to the domestic quarters of the Green Man. A young man half-turned and surveyed the scene behind him. He was of medium height with dark hair worn fractionally on the long side and had a thoughtful intelligent face, and was impeccably spruce in fawn trousers and a light blue jacket.

'On vacation over here?' Rodney asked.

He got a friendly grin.

'My firm's sent me over on an assignment at the London branch, and part of the deal was a week's leave for taking a look around.'

'I hope you feel it's been worth it?'

'I'll say it sure has,' came the enthusiastic reply. 'And that doesn't just go for the top places like Westminster Abbey and Stratford-on-Avon, but for everywhere I've been. You folk breathe history over here. I'—

He was interrupted by the reappearance of Tom Wonnacott with the information that the missus would be pleased to fix up the gentleman with a bed for the night, and could lay on a bit of supper if wanted. This matter having been settled satisfactorily, the young American returned to a nearby table and resumed his consumption of bread and cheese and beer while observing his fellow patrons with interest. It was his first experience of a village pub in its function as the community centre and he

7

was intrigued. The general outrage at the fans' invasion made him wonder what Woodcombe would make of night life in certain areas of London and New York. The British class system seemed to be functioning, although at the same time everyone appeared to be on effortlessly easy terms, and there was an instant closing of ranks against hostility from outside.

Rodney Kenway-Potter finished his drink and glanced towards the open door of the pub, but there was no sign of his wife's return. He propped himself against the bar counter and took up the conversation again.

'What's brought you down to these parts?' he asked. 'We locals think it's one of the most pleasant bits of the U.K. but we don't get all that many overseas visitors.'

'I've come down to call on a Mr James Fordyce who lives in this village. He is a genealogist, and we've been in correspondence about tracing my family. He's been held up and won't be back till this afternoon, so I thought I'd put up here at this pub and go over to Littlechester before contacting him at five o'clock.'

'This is interesting,' Rodney said. 'You're in luck over James Fordyce. He's a damn good genealogist and a very decent chap, too. He's got me hooked on researching into my own forebears... Your name is?'

'Tuke, sir. Edward Tuke.'

'Tom, halves of Green Man Special for all three of us, please. Have you heard of anybody called Tuke in this part of the world?'

'Thank you, sir... No, I can't say as I have,' Tom Wonnacott replied, carefully filling three tankards. 'I was listenin' to what the gentleman was sayin' and searchin' in me mind, but I'm sure there's nobody o' the name around here.'

Edward Tuke explained that he had not expected to discover any family connections locally, but had come to meet Mr Fordyce and get him to take on the job of tracking them down.

'A buddy of mine back home put me on to him,' he went on. 'A guy who knew his folk came from Little-chester, and Mr Fordyce has found a record of them going right back to the sixteen hundreds. I promised I'd go there and take some pictures of the historic centre for him if I could make it.' He paused, and eyed Rodney Kenway-Potter speculatively. 'I guess your family's been around here quite a while, Mr ...?'

'Kenway-Potter, Rodney. Well, no. Not all that long really as families go in these parts. My people came from Lancashire, up north as we say. They cashed in on the Industrial Revolution, manufacturing your American cotton. When they'd made their pile they began to fancy themselves as landed gentry. The Woodcombe Manor estate came on the market and they bought it. It was a good long way from the smoke of the mill chimneys, you see.'

'Then that big house in the trees up on the hill's yours?' Edward Tuke asked with interest. 'Would it be what you'd call a Stately Home?'

'Good Lord, no: it's not nearly big or grand enough to be classed as a Stately, and there's nothing of much interest about its history. It's just a pleasant Queen Anne house—that's early eighteenth century—and fortunately hasn't been much mucked about since... Look here, Mr Tuke, come up and have supper with us this evening, and see it from the inside. I'm keen on family history myself, as I said just now, and you might be interested in the lines I'm working on under Fordyce's tuition... There's my wife at the door. She'll be delighted to meet you.'

'That's very, very kind and hospitable of you, sir, and I'm honoured,' Edward Tuke said with appreciation, getting hastily to his feet as an unobtrusively elegant woman in early middle age came towards them. Rodney Kenway-Potter introduced him.

'Mr Tuke's here to see James Fordyce about doing a

search for him,' he told her.

Bowing over her hand, Edward Tuke repeated his thanks for the invitation to Woodcombe Manor while telling himself that he had struck real British class.

'How lucky that my husband happened to meet you in here,' Amaryllis said, smiling at him. 'Come along about seven if you're through with Mr Fordyce, and we can have drinks and show you the house before we eat. I'm afraid it'll be rather a scratch meal: we've been away for the night and are only just back. Have you had time to look round the village yet? Local patriotism, of course, but we think it's rather attractive.'

'It sure is,' Edward Tuke agreed fervently. 'And this pub's great. Just what I thought a real country pub would be like. There's only one thing missing.'

'What's that?' Rodney asked.

'Why, it's just that there's only a plain board with the name on it hanging outside: no picture. I've seen real eye-catchers at some of the pubs where I've been since I came over.'

The Kenway-Potters looked at each other.

'Interesting, isn't it, that he's got on to it?' Rodney commented. 'You've hit on an old superstition in Wood-combe, Mr Tuke. I'm afraid my wife and I have got to dash off to a lunch date with friends in the next village, but I'll bring Ella Rawlings over. She's our expert on local history and folklore. Just hang on a minute.'

He hurried towards a woman sitting alone at one of the tables further down the room. Edward Tuke glanced quickly at Mrs Kenway-Potter, hoping that she had not noticed the passing dismay in his face at the prospect of a possibly lengthy holdup of his departure for Little-chester. To his relief she was watching her husband's pro-gress and then proceeded to consult her watch. He thought she looked tired and rather distraite, and he hoped that being suddenly landed with an unknown and unexpected guest was not the last straw. As Rodney

10

Kenway-Potter came hurrying back with the woman who had been sitting by herself his heart sank. He recognised a familiar type: the dedicated sort with an obsessive interest. Added to this she was ungainly, with one shoulder slightly higher than the other, had a large expressionless face and was wearing a shapeless green jumper over a thick tweed skirt.

'Mr Edward Tuke—Mrs Rawlings,' Rodney Kenway-Potter was saying hurriedly. 'She's a mine of information on the village, as I told you. See you this evening. Drive straight along the village street, past the church and turn left over the bridge. Our drive gates are a couple of hundred yards further on, on your left . . . I'm coming, Amaryllis, we'll just about make it with luck.'

'Till tonight then, Mr Tuke,' she called over her shoulder as her husband hurried her off with his hand under her elbow.

Resigning himself to his fate Edward Tuke offered Mrs Rawlings a drink.

'Thank you, no,' she replied, planting herself purposefully at his table. 'I'm afraid I haven't much time. It's one of my days on the Mobile Library van, but I'm always glad to meet a fellow folklore enthusiast. Have you published in America?'

'I'm afraid there's been a bit of a misunderstanding,' he told her, conscious of unexpected relief. 'I really don't know anything about folklore. I just casually asked Mr Kenway-Potter why this fine pub hasn't got one of those painted signs outside. I mustn't take up your time.'

He looked up to find himself under keen scrutiny from a pair of sharp dark eyes.

'If you weren't subconsciously aware of the past, Mr Tuke, you'd never have asked that question. The answer goes back two thousand years and more. This is the inn sign that ought to be hanging over the door.'

As she spoke Mrs Rawlings extracted an envelope from her handbag and passed it across the table. Edward Tuke opened it and took out a photograph of a startlingly repellent face. At first glance it reminded him of the masks worn by devil dancers in a documentary he had watched on television. But a closer study suggested a basically human quality, even though sprigs of what looked like hawthorn were sprouting prolifically from the corners of the staring eyes and ravenous sensual mouth... It's as though two kinds of life were fighting like hell to come out on top, he thought, and realised that he was finding the photograph in some way disturbing. Irritated by the discovery he fell back on flippancy.

'A sign with a face like this on it certainly wouldn't be a viable commercial proposition, I'll grant you. It would put folks right off their liquor. Who is the guy, anyway?'

'The Green Man of Woodcombe, Mr Tuke. Green Men are familiar figures in medieval folklore, symbolising the process of regeneration in nature. Fertility symbols, if you like. But the Woodcombe Green Man is more than this. Much more.'

She had lowered her voice and paused dramatically. Edward Tuke looked up, met the intent eyes in the expressionless face and began to feel embarrassed.

'The original of this photograph is one of the bosses in the nave roof of the parish church just down the road,' she went on.

'Funny sort of thing to have in a church, you'd think,' he reacted.

'Perhaps the safest place for it, Mr Tuke.'

He stared at her incredulously. This was a real crank: not just one of the dedicated sort of females.

'In a clearing up at the top of the Manor Woods there's a standing stone, ten feet high, hewn out of granite. There's no granite nearer than fifty miles. It was brought here by the men of the Bronze Age. When the Saxons came in the seventh and eighth centuries they called it Old Grim, their name for the devil, and kept clear of it. But in the fifteenth century a stonemason went up one

12

night for a bet, saying he'd give Old Grim a face.' Mrs Rawlings paused again.

'What happened?' Edward Tuke asked in an attempt to speed things up. 'Can you still see it? I'll have to go up and have a look this evening.'

She tapped the photograph.

'He came down crazy with terror saying that Old Grim already had a face: this one. And he carved what he had seen on the boss I told you about . . . I must be going, I'm afraid. Goodbye, Mr Tuke.'

She got up so quickly that she was already on her way to the door before he was on his feet.

'Excuse me, sir.'

He turned to find Tom Wonnacott beside him and received an unmistakeable wink.

'Takes all sorts, don't it, sir? If you'd care to see your room, the missus'll be pleased to take you up. Just step this way. When bar's closed us comes and goes by the door round to the back.'

The bedroom was low with massive oak beams and a sloping floor. The lattice window was set so low in the immensely thick wall that it was necessary to kneel on the floor in order to see out adequately. In reply to a question from Edward Tuke Mrs Wonnacott, small, plump and rosy-cheeked replied that folk said the Green Man was more than three hundred years old, but nobody knew for sure. She hastened to add that Tom had put in a bathroom just across the landing, the water was scalding hot day and night, and visitors always said the bed was real comfortable to lie on. Edward Tuke assured her that he had never seen a bedroom he liked better, and went down to his car to get his suitcase. After unpacking the contents he left for Littlechester. As he drove up to the main road a car coming from the Littlechester direction turned into the village, its only occupant being the man at the wheel.

At first the road took a winding course through woods,

13

rising gently but steadily until it finally emerged into more open country at the crest of the long hill. Edward Tuke pulled into a lay-by, got out of the car and crossed the road to a gate. He leant on it, his forearms resting on the topmost bar, and surveyed the wide landscape spread out beneath him lying tranquilly in the spring sunshine. He saw a vast pattern of fields broken here and there by clumps of trees, isolated groups of farm buildings and occasional irregularly-shaped villages in most of which he could detect a church tower. The road he had been following seemed to become more purposeful from now on, straightening out and taking a more direct course towards a distant blur on the horizon which, he thought, must be Littlechester. The whole landscape seemed to be held together by an irregular network of narrow green lines. Country lanes, he concluded, inter-linking the villages and farms and sunk between hedges now bursting into leaf.

But it was the mosaic of fields that particularly fascinated him, as it had done when he gazed down from the aircraft on the homeland of his forebears when arriving in England ... the endless variety of their colours and shapes and their preposterously small size. As he contemplated them now he tried in vain to relate sweeping curves and mysterious acute-angled projections to the dictates of geology, slope and aspect. A phrase from the information so portentously imparted by Mrs Rawlings recurred to his mind: 'in the seventh and eighth centuries the Saxons came.' Land-hungry people on the move, of course, like the flood of immigrants flowing ever further westward in the U.S. during the nineteenth century, heading for the most fertile tracts. But down the generations since the Saxons established themselves there would have been wars, new laws, buying and selling of land, marriage settlements ... hence the incredible patchwork spread out before him. This landscape's got a human quality he thought, something quite lacking in the vast rectangular

14

fields back home in the Middle West worked out mathe-matically in a land registry office. The present pattern's rooted in the past of English people. My people, what's more.

American-born son of English-born peasants, he was aware of having reached the moment of decision. He would come back for good. Back to where his roots really were and take British nationality. Marry an English girl and raise some English kids...

★

The car which Edward Tuke had met on leaving Woodcombe turned into the short drive of a bungalow at the western end of the village. The man at the wheel was James Fordyce, the research genealogist with whom the young American had been corresponding. He was a man in his middle fifties with a narrow face and intelligent hazel eyes under bushy brows. His wife had opened the doors of the integral garage and he ran his car straight in. He unlocked the door into the kitchen and carried in his suitcase and a number of cardboard folders, each bearing the name of a client for whom he was carrying out a search. His wife Eileen, was, as he knew, out at the monthly meeting of the Women's Institute's local branch, but she had left a note for him propped against the tea caddy.

'The K-Ps got away with it, of course,' he read in her large childish handwriting, 'but guess what!!! Len Bolling's clearing out!!! A For Sale board (Ford's) went up this morning. He must have known he hadn't a hope against the K-Ps and fixed to go anyway. Oh, James, *couldn't* we buy Bridge Cottage? *Do* ring Ford's and find out what he's asking. I'm *sure* this place would sell all right. What *heaven* to live in that super little house! Back as soon as I can make it. Cake in tin. Love. E. P.S. A young American's coming to see you at five, worse luck.'

James Fordyce read the note with a wry smile. Did Eileen really believe that he didn't know her motive for wanting the move? Already she was visualising herself in the enhanced social status of living virtually on the doorstep of the Manor, and the opportunities for frequent contacts with the Kenway-Potters which this would bring. He read her snide opening remark again. It was pathetic, of course. Behind it lay the unconscious social and intellectual inferiority complexes which had coloured her attitude to life ever since he had committed the supreme blunder of marrying her, an attractive young secretary twenty years his junior.

For Eileen it had meant translation to a sphere for which she was wholly unequipped, and for him the realisation in a matter of weeks that any building up of genuine companionship between them had been a pipe dream on his part. An honest thinker, he accepted responsibility for the situation and had stood by his bargain, providing her with security and a comfortable home and falling in with her wishes when he felt it possible to do so. And he was fairminded enough to admit that the marriage had not been a dead loss. It was still possible to describe her as attractive, she was a competent housekeeper and usually cheerful in an immature way. It would never have entered her head to be unfaithful to him, or to suspect him of extra-marital relationships, although she often commented with tiresome facetiousness on his frequent absences from home. She enjoyed the status of being married to a clever man but he was well aware that his real self was a closed book to her.

Still standing with the note in his hand memories of her effusiveness when encountering the Kenway-Potters brought a sense of discomfort. He wondered briefly if she had the remotest idea of why he, too, was attracted to the idea of moving to Bridge Cottage. He crumpled up the note, dropped it into the wastepaper basket and took the folders into his minute study. Some correspondence

16

awaited him on his desk. He sat down, glanced through it, and dealt with the only letter needing immediate attention. It took only a few minutes to consult his diary and write a postcard offering an appointment. This done he sat deep in thought for several minutes. Finally he got up, unlocked his filing cabinet, and deposited the folders under the appropriate initial letters. He had always kept papers connected with his searches under lock and key. As he relocked the cabinet he remembered Eileen's indignant protests when she discovered this practice after they were married. His attempt to get across to her the concept of professional ethos where confidential information was concerned had been unavailing.

His immediate objective was to have a good look at Bridge Cottage, even if only from the outside. It was just possible that Leonard Bolling had decided to make himself scarce. Gone to see his solicitor, perhaps, or even to look at a house somewhere else. Almost certainly one could find out about his movements by dropping in at the village post office-cum-shop, unofficially known as the Information Bureau. He left the bungalow and walked along the street which was almost deserted. The postmistress and shop owner was seated behind the counter, knitting vigorously while keeping an eye on the open door.

'So you're back again, Mr Fordyce,' she greeted him, putting her knitting aside and getting to her feet. 'My, but there's been some pretty doings here in Woodcombe since you went away. Mr Kenway-Potter in court, and football hooligans smashin' the place up last night, drat 'em. Bring back the birch, that's what I says. And now that Bolling's off, and a mighty good riddance, too. There's been a man over from Ford's puttin' up a For Sale board: you can see it for yourself if you take a look. And there's an American gentleman puttin' up for the night at the Green Man, but I expect you know that, seein' that he called at your place round about midday.'

James Fordyce, attuned to village life, allowed five minutes for his further briefing on the state of the nation.

'Well,' he said at last, 'you've put me in the picture all right. At any rate people will be able to fish in peace now. Mr Bolling's gone to ground in Bridge Cottage, I expect?'

'That he hasn't, Mr Fordyce, not him. He was off one-twenty in that blessed van of his, drivin' through the village bold as brass. Lookin' for a new house like as not, and the further away the better, I says.'

'All this has made me forget what I came in for,' James Fordyce told her. 'Stamps, as usual. I want to post this pc before Dick Stone comes to clear the box.'

'Robbery or daylight robbery, sir?' Mrs Trotman asked, getting out her stamp book and referring to the current charges for first and second class postage.

'Make it ten of each,' he said, producing his wallet.

After stamping his postcard he managed to extricate himself and went outside to post it. He then turned right and walked the short distance to the junction of the road leading to Woodcombe Manor and over the hill to Mary-cott, the next village. Here he turned left, reflecting that it would soon be common knowledge that he was interested in Bridge Cottage. However, the same report would circulate about all the other local residents who would be unable to resist coming along and having a look. He arrived at the crest of the single span stone bridge, leant on the parapet and critically surveyed the little house.

It had been built, he knew, about a century ago as a modest dower house for the Manor, and had remained Kenway-Potter property until Rodney's father had sold it during a period of financial stringencies in the thirties. Mercifully the architect had eschewed Victorian Gothic and produced a simple two-storied small house in keeping with both the village as a whole and the Manor itself. It was well-proportioned with good windows and its mellowed red brick and white paint combined to

18

produce a very pleasing effect. There appeared to be four main rooms in the front of the house, facing south, and James Fordyce remembered noticing an extension built out at the back and some outbuildings. He looked at his watch. It was only just after three. Bolling must have gone off pretty quickly after his lunch, so it looked as though he had some definite programme for the afternoon and would not turn up again just yet. Walking on, James Fordyce arrived at the garden gate. He walked up to the front door and rang the bell twice. No one answered it, and he circumnavigated the cottage, peering in at the ground floor windows with an eye to the possibility of a reasonably secluded study for himself. He then inspected the outbuildings and finally returned to the road. He stood for a few moments looking up at the rose-coloured chimneys of the Manor just visible above the trees, and finally began to make his way along the path on the north bank of the little River Honey.

When he approached Upper Bridge some time later there were sounds of activity which included bursts of vigorous hammering, and he came upon Bill Morris engaged in re-erecting the 'Private Fishing' notices and clearing up the litter scattered about by the football fans. James stopped to chat and heard an even more forceful account of what had taken place. Finally he went on again and returned to the bungalow by way of the Littlechester road, letting himself in as the grandfather clock in the sitting room struck four. After consulting the yellow pages he rang Ford's, the Littlechester estate agents. He had been put through to the partner who was handling the sale of Bridge Cottage when he heard his wife's foot-steps coming hurriedly up the garden path. The front door burst open and he raised a hand enjoining silence, mouthing the word 'Ford's'.

At thirty-four Eileen Fordyce still retained much of the attractiveness that had captivated him ten years earlier: the fresh pink and white complexion, the heart-shaped face with its big expressive blue eyes, and the naturally curly hair worn short and kept golden with only minimal assistance from her hairdresser. Only the small mouth was now a little hard and wary in repose, raising doubts in the mind of the critical observer about the genuineness of her spontaneity. Now she dashed across the hall and pressed close to her husband, craning her head towards the telephone receiver in an attempt to listen in. James rested his hand lightly on her shoulder and went on with the conversation. This was now about the selling prospects of the bungalow, and Eileen quickly lost interest. She squeezed his arm, murmured 'tea' and went off to the kitchen.

'No problem,' the Ford partner was saying, who had sold James the bungalow five years earlier, when a legacy from an uncle had enabled him to give up a senior post in the Area Income Tax Office and devote his whole time to his hobby of genealogy. 'I remember your place perfectly well. It's well-built and the lay-out's unusually good. Not too much garden. Just the job for a Littlechester commuter. We'll get the particulars out right away and I'll put your offer to Bolling. I'll send a chap over tomorrow morning to have a look around and he can bring you an order to view Bridge Cottage at the same time.'

'I can't buy unless I sell, you know. A lengthy bridging loan at current rates just isn't on.'

'Mr Bolling,' the estate agent said, 'is in one hell of a hurry to move, no doubt realising that he's made a bloody fool of himself. In other words, keener on a quick sale than haggling over price'....

As James replaced the receiver Eileen ran towards him from the kitchen and stretched up for a kiss.

'The wretched W.I. meeting went on and on,' she told him. 'I thought I'd never get away. Oh, James, now you've contacted Ford's, is there *any* hope of Bridge Cottage? Len Bolling's asking the earth, I suppose? Tea's up. You must be dying for it.'

20

Repressing his irritation at her habit of bandying current catch phrases picked up from television programmes, James followed her into the kitchen and sat down at the table.

'Let me tell you,' he said, as she began to pour out, 'the Bridge Cottage kitchen isn't a patch on this one.'

Teapot in hand, Eileen stared at him incredulously.

'You can't possibly know,' she said. 'You've never been inside the place. You're trying to put me off.'

'Admittedly I've never been inside,' he said, ignoring her last remark, 'but one can always make a recce from outside, you know. After I got back and found your note I went along to the Information Bureau on the pretext of needing stamps. After being briefed by Mother Trot on the past eighteen hours or so, it was easy to find out that Bolling had gone out in his van at about two. So after ringing the bell and getting no answer, I risked a good snoop through the ground floor windows.'

As he talked, the expression on his wife's face was transformed from resentment to rapturous delight.

'You absolute old sweetie!' she exclaimed, her eyes shining. 'Fancy you doing a thing like that? Oh, *do* tell me what it's like. When can we go over it? Don't you have to have an order to view, or something?'

She listened enthralled to his account of what he had been able to see, and the gist of his conversation with Ford's.

'Does he think it will be difficult for us to sell?' she asked anxiously.

'He seemed quite hopeful, I thought. Of course, it's a dicey business selling a house at the moment, but he thinks Littlechester commuters might be interested ... Look, if this American is coming at five, I must go and read up the correspondence. What's he like?'

'Awfully young. Funny to be so interested in your family history at his age. Rather a serious type. You'd never think he was an American until he starts talking.'

Back in his study James unlocked the filing cabinet and took out the Tuke folder. After glancing through the two letters he had received from Edward Tuke he read the notes that he had made in London. They apparently provided him with much food for thought. He sat motionless, staring out of the window and frowning. From his knowledge of Americans he had assumed that his prospective client would arrive by car, and made no move on merely hearing the gate click and steps approach the front door. The next moment a soft American voice made him spring from his chair and hurry to rescue his caller from Eileen's over-effusive welcome, only pausing to push the pages of notes into a drawer.

'Bit cramped in here, I'm afraid,' he said, escorting Edward Tuke to the study, and indicating a small easy chair. Sitting down at his desk he swivelled his office-type chair round and faced his visitor. As Rodney Kenway-Potter had done, he liked what he saw: spruce, serious-faced young man with a touch of British formality about him. He reflected that Eileen's perception could be quite acute on occasions.

'I'm sorry I didn't manage to get back earlier Mr Tuke,' he said. 'I hope I haven't held you up?'

Edward Tuke reassured him.

'I didn't reckon to turn up here until this afternoon myself, but managed to get a clear day and made an early start. I've been taking a look round Littlechester since lunch and wouldn't have missed it.'

'You're putting up there, I expect?'

'No, I'm staying right here in Woodcombe. I liked the look of your Green Man and thought I'd try a real old British pub if the landlord could fix me up with a bed.'

'Well, you've hit on a good specimen. The Wonnacotts will make you comfortable all right, and Florrie—Mrs Wonnacott—lays on excellent grub. Plain, but the real old British sort, like the beer.'

'Going in there for a drink turned out a lucky move in

another way,' Edward Tuke told him. 'I've been asked up to a real old British home for some supper tonight: Wood-combe Manor.'

James Fordyce looked up quickly.

'I'd no idea you knew the Kenway-Potters.'

'I don't. I'd never met them till this morning in the Green Man. Mr Kenway-Potter got talking and gave me the invitation. Very friendly, I thought, and so was his wife when she came in. It's the big red house up in the woods, isn't it?'

'Yes. They're very hospitable, and it's an attractive house with some good pictures and furniture, if you're interested in that sort of thing. . . . Well, since you've got a supper date, Mr Tuke, we'd better get down to business, hadn't we?' James Fordyce swung his chair round and picked up the Tuke folder from his desk. 'Briefly, this is the position, I take it? Your father emigrated to Canada in 1948 and after moving on to the U.S.A. in 1950, married your mother, the daughter of English immigrants called Brown, in 1951. You were born in 1952. In 1953 both your parents were killed in a car accident. You were taken over and brought up by your mother's elder and unmarried sister, Miss Helen Brown. She died last year, and her parents—your maternal grandparents—had predeceased her. You want me to try to trace both your parents' families. All correct so far?'

'That's all quite correct, Mr Fordyce. It feels a bit lonesome not having a soul who's your own kin.'

James Fordyce turned over the correspondence in the Tuke folder.

'Well, to do—or try to do—these searches for you, I need every bit of information you can give me as a starting point. Let's begin with your mother's family. You say her parents were both English emigrants. Unfortunately Brown is one of the commonest English surnames. What can you tell me about them?'

'I know they came over after the 1914–18 war, just after

23

they married, and both of them were from farming families, my grandfather from Somerset and my grandmother from Norfolk. He'd been in the war and got wounded, and she'd nursed him in an army hospital. That's how they met up. Her maiden name was Melford.'

'This looks like being a nice straightforward search,' James Fordyce said, writing rapidly. 'It ought to be fairly simple to find some connections for you on both sides of your mother's family. Now, about your father's family? Where did he come from?'

On getting no answer, James Fordyce's upward glance detected reluctance.

'Don't mind bringing a skeleton or two out of the cupboard, Mr Tuke,' he said. 'Most families have them, you know.'

'The trouble is I've damn all to bring out of the cupboard where my father's concerned. I don't remember him, of course. You know how smart kids are at picking up things without anything actually being said, though. I understood that my mother's people hadn't liked him or wanted the marriage. They never talked about him, and if I asked questions they'd clam up. Change the subject: you know. Pretty well all I could ever find out was that he'd come over in '48, and had a job in Winnipeg, and then moved across into the U.S. where my mother's people were farming, and got another one there. He was a salesman for one of the big car makers and once asked my aunt—the one who raised me—what part of the U.K. he came from, and if he had relatives over here, but all I could get out of her was that she thought he had come from Longshire and that she'd never heard him speak of any relatives back home.'

'What conclusion did you draw from this reluctance to talk about your father?' James Fordyce asked, after a pause.

'I reckoned he could have been in some sort of trouble and decided to clear out of the U.K. It wouldn't have

24

been all that difficult back in '48, with the war only just over. I've wondered if Tuke was his real name, come to that. Maybe a passport in another name was pretty easy to come by if you knew your way around.'

'Do you think that your mother's parents had found out something discreditable about him?'

'No,' Edward Tuke replied, slowly but emphatically. 'I don't. They wouldn't have had the know-how. They were decent simple folk. No, I think they felt he wasn't the solid sort of chap with a family back here that they'd have liked their daughter to marry. And then, they blamed him for her death in the car crash, you see. The car went into a skid on a wet night, and there was evidence that he'd been driving the hell of a lick... Tell you the truth, Mr Fordyce, there's something at the back of my mind that I've never been able to bring out, but somehow I can talk to you ... I've wondered if he was a deserter.'

'From the British armed forces in the Second World War, you mean?'

'Yea.'

'Why do you mind so much about this possibility?' James Fordyce asked.

'Aw, hell—it's difficult to explain! I'm legally a U.S. citizen, of course, and didn't they din it into me when I was a kid. Maybe it was a kid's cussedness, but as far back as I can remember I told myself I was British. Read all the books I could get hold of about the U.K. And I made up my mind I'd come over here when I grew up and see it. And the thought that my dad might have ratted from the British army when Britain was right up against Hitler just sticks in my throat.'

'Now you're over here,' James Fordyce asked after a further pause, 'how do you feel about this country?'

'Even more than I thought I would. So I'm coming back. I've applied to the firm for a transfer, and there's no problem, they've told me. So that's why I want to link up with my people, if you can track them down for me.'

James Fordyce sat silent for a few moments, turning over the papers in front of him.

'It's only fair to tell you, Mr Tuke, that these searches you want me to undertake for you, and especially the one into your father's family and personal history will take time and cost you quite a bit.'

A smile lit up Edward Tuke's composed young face.

'No problem, Mr Fordyce. I've waited twenty-eight years to get moving on this, and I reckon I can wait a bit longer. And the money's O.K. I'm pulling down a decent wage packet with Integrated Oils, and Aunt Helen left me all she'd got. It came out quite a tidy bit.'

'Very well, then,' James Fordyce replied. 'I'll go ahead. How much longer are you going to be over here on this trip?'

Edward Tuke outlined his immediate plans. Suddenly he glanced at his watch.

'It's just turned six o'clock. Say, would I have the time to go up and take a look at this famous old stone in the woods before I go along to the Manor? A lady Mr Kenway-Potter introduced me to in the pub this morning told me all about it. A Mrs Rawlings.'

'Good Lord!' James Fordyce exclaimed with amusement. 'Really K-P shouldn't have let her loose on you. She's got a folklore fixation. She's our neighbour, and descends on us at intervals with some extraordinary old yarn that she's unearthed... Yes, to answer your question you could make it all right, and the view from the top of the ridge is well worth seeing. Where's your car?'

'Back at the pub. When I come down I'll pick it up there and drive round to the Manor.'

'Right, then. Let me show you where the path starts up. It's only a couple of minutes' walk from here: quicker than going to fetch your car.'

Leaving the bungalow together they walked the short

distance to the main road and turned right towards Upper Bridge.

'This little river's the Honey,' James Fordyce said. 'It's a quite good trout stream and Rodney Kenway-Potter owns the fishing rights here. If you cross that stile on the left bank and take the path going up on your left it'll bring you out at the longstone. From there it's a short distance to the top.'

'O.K.,' Edward Tuke said, 'and thanks a lot, Mr Fordyce, for taking me on. And I mean that. We'll be in touch.'

They shook hands. He vaulted over the stile, gave a parting wave and started up the path at a brisk pace, making his way upwards under the shimmering light green of trees just breaking into leaf. The early evening sun came slanting through the branches, shafts falling on drifts of primroses and wood anemones. He paused briefly to track down a delicious elusive fragrance and traced it to a clump of wild violets. Bird song came cascading down from overhead, and he had the sensation of breasting a sea of pure enjoyment. The path steepened as he gained height. Suddenly he emerged into a clearing and stopped dead in his tracks. A pillar of rough weather-beaten stone lay prone on the ground, pointing to the direction from which he had come.

*

James Fordyce walked slowly home, reviewing his conversation with Edward Tuke.

As he expected, Eileen was impatiently awaiting his return. Over the years since their marriage he had developed a satisfactory technique for meeting both her demands for attention and his own need for solitude. During supper he gave the subject of their possible purchase of Bridge Cottage and its implications his undivided attention, taking her views seriously and contributing his own in a form geared to her understanding. Then, when the meal was over, he remarked that he must get the information young Tuke had given him sorted out while it was all fresh in his mind. Back at his desk, he assembled the original correspondence with Edward Tuke, the notes that he had made during their conversation, and those which he had brought back from London. For half an hour he sat mulling over them, at intervals leaning back in his chair and staring unseeingly at the back garden of the bungalow. Suddenly the telephone rang. He got up with a grunt of irritation to go into the hall. As he expected, Eileen was already taking the call.

'Here he is!' she was saying gaily. 'It's Rodney,' she mouthed to her husband, wide-eyed with excitement. 'Could it be about the cottage?'

He took the receiver from her unresponsively.

'Hallo, old man' he said. 'Congratulations on the outcome of the case. What can I do for you?'

'Is that young American still with you?' Rodney Kenway-Potter sounded annoyed and faintly puzzled.

'Good Lord, no. He went off just after six. He wanted to go up to see the longstone and the view from the top. I put him on the path at Upper Bridge.'

'Well, where the hell is he? He was due here at seven, as he probably told you, and it's past eight.'

'Have you rung the Green Man?'

'Yes, I have. Tom says his car's in the car park where he left it when he came in from Littlechester at about a quarter to five. Then he went out again soon afterwards on foot, to his appointment with you, presumably.'

'Seems a bit odd. He said he was picking up his car and driving up to you when he came down, and was a bit anxious about being on time.'

'I call it damned odd ... I suppose he hasn't taken a purler on the path and broken a leg or something ... I think I'd better go along and have a look round. Amaryllis is here if he turns up.'

'Like me to come with you?'

'No, don't bother, thanks all the same. Not at this stage, anyway. I'll ring you later if the chap doesn't materialise.'

He rang off. Puzzled and faintly disturbed James disillusioned Eileen on the subject of Rodney Kenway-Potter's call and went back to his study, disregarding her exclamations of surprise. Unusually for him he found it difficult to concentrate on the problems presented by the Tuke search, and finally decided to knock off for the evening. At this point the telephone suddenly rang again. He had been subconsciously expecting another call from Rodney, and this time managed to arrive in the hall before his wife.

'James, the most bloody awful thing's happened,' Rodney told him hoarsely and without preamble. 'I found Tuke in the river. Drowned. Just downstream from the old bridge.'

'In the *river*?'

'Yea. Those blasted yobs had chucked the warning notice about the bridge being unusable into the water, like the others.'

'But how on earth did he drown in that depth of water?'

'Hit his head on a rock. Must have concussed himself. His nose and mouth were submerged. I dragged him out and tried artificial respiration, and chaps from the pub took turns but it was no go. Dr Bryce is here and an ambulance is on the way. And the police, of course.'

'Shall I come round?'

'Do, for God's sake. Get here before the police start pushing everybody about. I suppose you were the last person to see him alive, anyway.'

'Right. I'll come up.'

As he put down the receiver James turned to see Eileen looking aghast, her hand to her mouth. He gave her the bare facts and started for the front door.

'James! Wait! I'm coming too. Amaryllis will want

someone with her. I'll get my coat.'

His habitual self-control snapped suddenly.

'Stay where you are,' he ordered peremptorily. 'This isn't the moment to go forcing yourself on them. There's nothing you can do.'

A second later the door slammed behind him. Eileen stood staring after him, biting the joint of her right thumb.

Chapter Two

On a June morning, six weeks after Edward Tuke's death, a conference was in progress in the Chief Constable of Buryshire's office at Littlechester police headquarters. Those present were Superintendent Newman and Inspector Deeds of the County C.I.D., and Detective Chief Superintendent Tom Pollard and Detective-Inspector Toye of New Scotland Yard. A request for the Yard's assistance had been made on the previous day.

'So that's about the length of it,' Robert Gregg, the Chief Constable concluded. 'And proper Charleys we feel taking the case as cleared up as far as it ever could be, and then having to send you people an S.O.S. after all this time when the trail's stone cold.'

Pollard, who had taken to him on sight, grinned back, reclining in his chair with his long legs stretched out in front of him and his hands clasped behind his head.

'Thanks for a masterly run through,' he said. 'You people have absolutely nothing to blame yourselves about. You took all the obvious and proper steps to establish who Tuke was and exactly how he died. Without third-degree methods you couldn't force the sozzled football fans to admit they'd chucked the "Bridge Unsafe" notice into the river. The "Death by Misadventure" verdict when the inquest was resumed for the second time was the only possible one. No one could have foreseen the anonymous letters which followed, nor the publicity they sparked off in the Press and through the media.'

The Chief Constable stated his news on multinational consortia with special reference to Integrated Oils, the late Edward Tuke's employers, and their apparent ability to poke their noses into a member country's properly and legally conducted affairs. There were assenting noises.

'I know it's all in there,' Pollard said, indicating a formidably bulky file, but may I recap briefly to clear my mind? Here goes. Edward Tuke, aged twenty-eight and employed by Integrated Oils, comes over to the London office on a specific job. It is his first visit to the U.K. He takes the opportunity of contacting Mr James Fordyce of Woodcombe, an established genealogist, who had been recommended to him by a pal in the U.S., with a view to getting his family history traced. He finds that Mr Fordyce has been delayed in London, and won't be able to see him before 5.00 p.m. He books a bed at the Green Man, the village pub, and runs into Mr Kenway-Potter of Woodcombe Manor in the bar, who asks him up to supper that evening. He spends the afternoon sightseeing in the city here, and turns up for his appointment with Mr Fordyce at 5.00 p.m. He leaves soon after six o'clock to have a look at a prehistoric monument at the top of the Manor Woods before going on to his supper fixture with the Kenway-Potters at seven. He never turns up for this, and is eventually found drowned in the river which runs through the Manor grounds, apparently having tried to take a short cut across it to the car park of the Green Man to pick up his bus. A conspicuous notice, partly blocking the entrance to the foot bridge he used and saying that it was unsafe had been pulled up and chucked into the river, just like the "Private Fishing" notice further upstream where the football fans had rampaged the night before. Obvious conclusion: the fans dunnit. Only they just won't come clean, either about the warning notice or the aforesaid prehistoric monument, a hefty longstone found prone on the ground on Friday, April the twenty-fifth . . . Have I got it right so far?'

The C.C. and the local C.I.D. officers assured him that he hadn't missed a thing.

'Right. Well, I suppose we might call everything up to this point Stage One,' Pollard went on. 'Stage Two opens with the resumed inquest on May the second, and the unsatisfactory but inevitable verdict of Death by Misadventure. There is then a lull until Tuesday May the thirteenth, when you people get an anonymous letter telling you to find out who it was in Woodcombe who had had it in for Tuke. A week later another arrives, saying that Woodcombe people aren't going to stand for a coverup. All the signs are that the letters are from a joker or a crackpot. Then, on May the thirtieth a letter of similar type arrives at the office of the *Littlechester Evening News*. The whole affair becomes a story to the national Press and the media, and a burst of paternalism towards young Tuke surges in the breast of Integrated Oils, his grandiose and influential employers...'

'Leading,' cut in the Chief Constable, 'to Stage Three: The Yard Takes Over. No hard feelings towards you personally, Mr Pollard, I assure you. We're flattered at someone of your status being sent down. No need to say that we'll lay on any help you ask for.'

'I just happened to be unemployed at the moment. That's all there was to it. And at the moment at least it certainly isn't a takeover. Just a second opinion on whether there's anything to take. As to your help, we'll need lashings of it. Our local knowledge is nil at the moment. Would it be possible for you to lay on an escorted tour of Woodcombe and the immediate neighbourhood?'

'No problem. Inspector Deeds here is your man. He's done most of the actual fieldwork. I suggest that he drives you over to Woodcombe when you've had something to eat. You won't want to patronise the village pub and be surrounded by goggling natives.'

'That'll be fine. Many thanks. Just before we break up, there's one more point I'd like to raise. Am I right that no trace has been found of any contact between Tuke and a

33

local resident except what appears to have been a correspondence with Mr Fordyce on genealogical matters?'

'Not a vestige of one,' the Chief Constable replied. 'The correspondence with Fordyce is in the file. He was recommended to Tuke by a friend in the States and had never met him until April the twenty-third. There seems no reason to disbelieve Fordyce's statement about this, and in any case it's borne out by the correspondence.'

'What sort of a chap is Fordyce? I know it's all in the file but I'd like your personal reaction.'

'He's fifty-five, a very decent scholarly punctilious sort of chap. He was in the Inland Revenue Office here for about fifteen years and lived in a flat in the city. He married a girl quite a lot younger than himself. She's about thirty-five now. They moved out to a bungalow in Woodcombe five years ago when he came into some money and retired early. Genealogy's always been his hobby and he's made it a second career. I can't imagine him being involved in any funny business.'

'Tuke was invited to supper by a Woodcombe resident though, wasn't he?'

'Yes, but there seems no doubt that it was just the outcome of that casual encounter in the Green Man, the village pub. Just a touch of Lord of the Manor there, don't you think, Super?'

Superintendent Newman agreed.

'Mr Kenway-Potter lives at Woodcombe Manor, Mr Pollard,' he explained. 'The Big House, you might say. He's a public-spirited friendly type, and it would be just in character for him to offer a bit of hospitality to a young foreigner turning up out of the blue.'

'He's the fourth generation of Kenway-Potters to own the Manor and the estate,' the Chief Constable added. 'His career's been entirely orthodox: public school, army for the last years of the war, agricultural college, and then home to run the estate and be a director of the family hotel chain. Plenty of lolly but doesn't live it up. Married a distant cousin. Two grown-up children. Not a whisper of a dubious connection with someone in the States or anywhere else.'

★

Inspector Deeds had remained discreetly silent during the conference unless addressed by his superiors. However, Pollard had noted that he missed nothing. He was not much above regulation height but gave the impression of a physical toughness and an active mind. Early thirties, Pollard decided, and destined for higher things. He drove out to Woodcombe with expertise coupled with just a dash of panache. For once Toye, whose passion was cars and everything connected with them and who usually suffered agonies when driven, made no disparaging comments later. The police car drew up smartly just beyond Upper Bridge and the three men got out. Pollard stood for a few moments contemplating the stiles leading to the fishermen's paths on both banks of the river, and two PRIVATE FISHING notices just inside them. These were in bold black lettering on white boards secured to posts driven into the ground. He saw that about fifty yards downstream the Honey made a slight curve to the right, and that the disused footbridge and its warning notice were not visible from where he was standing.

'Inspector,' he said suddenly, 'do you personally think that the football fans pulled up that notice further down?'

As he spoke he looked round and met a steady gaze from a pair of intelligent grey eyes.

'No, sir.'

'I'd like to hear your reasons.'

'Well, sir, to begin with all of them were Littlechester lads, and none of them had relatives or friends living here in Woodcombe, so they wouldn't be likely to know the place well. As you can see for yourself, the warning notice

35

is out of sight from here, and it was half-past eleven and a dark night. To my mind there's reasonable doubt that any of them knew the footbridge and the notice existed, and they all swear they didn't. Then they were all under the influence. It came out through counter-checking their statements that three of them were dead drunk and never got out of the cars. The others went on the rampage, drinking and chucking bottles and whatever into the river and two of them were pushed in by the others. They admit that they had no end of a job pulling these notices down and chucking them in. I can't believe that after all this they'd have started off in the state they were in along that path or up to the top looking for more damage to do, and in the dark, too. Much more of a lark to make for the village and stir things up there. And when it came to questioning them you couldn't shake a single one of 'em. Except for the three who never got out of the cars they all pleaded guilty to being drunk and disorderly, and to causing wilful damage. But each one swore ten times over that he'd never gone more than a few yards beyond this bridge. So as far as Mr Tuke's fall went we had to leave it at that, and the verdict was Death from Misadventure.'

'Thanks, Inspector. That's all very clear and helpful,' Pollard said thoughtfully. 'Tell me one other thing. Are these two paths along the banks rights of way?'

'Not in the legal sense, sir. The Woodcombe Manor Estate owns both banks and the fields on the right-hand side of the river up to the gardens of the village houses. We asked Mr Kenway-Potter if the paths were used much by walkers and the village people, and he said no, but that he'd no objection so long as they didn't disturb anybody who was fishing or do any damage. Sometimes he gets requests for parties to go up and see the ancient monument affair up near the top of the woods. The path starts just a short distance along the left bank there.'

'And that's where Mr Tuke was last seen as far as we know, by Mr Fordyce, the genealogist who'd brought him along to show him the way?'

'That's correct, sir.'

'Right. Let's go up ourselves.'

It was an oppressively warm afternoon and the path was little more than a stony track which became steeper as it gained height. Pollard was soon convinced that the football fans could never have made it in their sozzled state, even if they had discovered in the darkness the place where it started up from the river bank. Inspector Deeds who was leading the way bore left round a fine full-grown oak and they emerged into a clearing.

The longstone had been re-erected. It was a rough grey granite column about ten feet high. At about three-quarters of the distance from its base it had a curious twist which gave the eerie impression that it was struggling to wrench itself out of the ground, while its weathered top inclined slightly forward. Toye, a staunch evangelical churchman, surveyed it disapprovingly and remarked that anybody wanting to see a heathen idol wouldn't need to go any further. Inspector Deeds contributed the information that there used to be a lot of superstition about the stone, and that he had got the impression that there were still some people in Woodcombe who wouldn't be keen on coming near it after dark.

'Well, somebody didn't jib at coming,' Pollard said. 'I can't believe the job was done in daylight. Digging the thing out must have been a pretty hefty business too, which suggests an able-bodied person.'

'As a matter of fact, sir, toppling it would be much easier than you'd think. I came over as soon as Mr Kenway-Potter phoned in to report the damage, him thinking naturally enough that it might link up with the football fans and indirectly with Mr Tuke's death. I was surprised to see that the stone hadn't been bedded deep into the ground. It stands in a hole only about eighteen inches deep and it's kept upright by being packed in tight with bits of rock. You'll find a photo in the file. All anybody'd have to do would be to cut away the turf round the base and loosen the rock packing on the downhill side. When you'd got enough of 'em out the big chap would begin to heel over, and a good shove would topple it, seeing how hefty it is. And Mr Kenway-Potter said that it had developed a bit of list downhill, anyway.'

Pollard and Toye both expressed their astonishment. Toye, who was practical and good with his hands, asked what would be the best tools for the job.

'Well,' Inspector Deeds replied, 'I'd clear the turf with a spade, and loosen the packing stones with a pickaxe by choice till I could get 'em out by hand. But if you'd all the time in the world I reckon you could manage with a trowel.'

'Whoever it was wouldn't have wanted to be around any longer than he was obliged,' Pollard said. 'Given a spade and a pickaxe, how long would it have taken, do you think?'

'Say an hour, sir, for a chap used to handling tools of that sort, and double that if he wasn't. And you'd need light, of course. First light comes early towards the end of April: well before folks get moving, so time shouldn't have been much of a problem. And nobody much comes up here as a general rule, except Bill Morris, the forester.'

'When do you think it was done?'

'Almost certainly in the early morning of Wednesday, April the twenty-third, sir. It would have been a good time to choose because Mr and Mrs Kenway-Potter were away for the night of April the twenty-second, staying with friends in Littlechester to be on time for the County Court hearing next morning, and nobody would be sleeping in the Manor. You could come along the drive with no risk of being seen or heard. According to a Mrs Rawlings, a lady living in the village who's keen on prehistoric remains and whatever, the stone was upright on the early evening of the twenty-second. She came up for a stroll and to have a look at it after her tea. The damage wasn't discovered until early on the Friday morning when Bill Morris came this way.'

Pollard asked if there were any point from which one could get a good general view of the village, and Inspector Deeds led the way to an outcrop of bare rock on the west of the slope above the clearing. They climbed this and stood gazing round them. Regretfully Pollard turned his back on a superb panorama to the north and concentrated on the lay-out of Woodcombe below. Under the Inspector's guidance his eyes moved from the roof and chimneys of the Manor to those of Bridge Cottage. He learnt that this was the residence of Mr Leonard Bolling, the plaintiff and loser in the fishing syndicate case, and that it had been put up for sale even before the court hearing. He raised an eyebrow but made no comment. The post office-cum-village store, the village hall, the church, the Green Man with its car park adjacent to the churchyard, the Fordyces' bungalow and the junction of the village street with the main road were successively pointed out.

'Fine,' Pollard said, after a long hard look. 'It's all quite clear in my mind now. O.K. by you, Toye? Right. I don't think we need actually go through Woodcombe. Inspector, but I'd like to retrace Tuke's route down to the bridge before we go back to Littlechester. Presumably he didn't go down the way he came up, or he would have gone round by the road. It's no distance to the Green Man car park, is it?'

Inspector Deeds agreed that it was not much longer than by the short cut Edward Tuke was apparently trying to take.

'There's a track branching off on the left from the one we came up by which takes you to the Manor,' he said, 'and a little way along it there's one on the right going straight down to the footbridge. They're very little used these days, and easy to miss, you'd think, especially the one to the bridge. It looked to us as though Mr Tuke may have stayed up on the top longer than he meant to, enjoying the view. Then he could have come to, and realised that he was running late for his supper date, and thought that he'd cut straight down to the footbridge—you can just get a glimpse of it on the way down—and cross the meadow to the Green Man. He may not even have used the two tracks: just made a bee line for the bridge through the wood. It's mostly beech around here and there's not much undergrowth. He'd have been in a hurry, and with it getting a bit dimpsey and the notice gone, it's easy to see how he might dash on to the bridge and never notice the gap.'

'There's another possible explanation, of course,' Pollard remarked. 'He met somebody up here who deliberately misdirected him.'

The three detectives looked at each other in questioning silence.

'The footbridge itself next, I think,' Pollard said.

Inspector Deeds led the way down by the little-used tracks to the single-span bridge. He had learnt from Mr Kenway-Potter, he told Pollard, that it had been built in the middle of the eighteenth century to provide a short cut on foot from the Manor to the parish church and the village. Its collapse not long after the First World War had been mainly due to the unsuitability of the site. While the north bank provided a foundation of hard rock, the ground on the south side was much softer, and in the course of time the south pier had started to settle. This process was aided by the gradual deterioration of the mortar used in the brick facing which eventually affected the keystone of the arch. Occasional serious floods brought down fallen trees and other debris which battered the piers, and eventually the southern part of the arch had collapsed into the river.

'Mr Kenway-Potter said that his father didn't see any point in rebuilding the bridge now that it was quicker to go round by car, but, as a precaution, warning notices that nobody could miss were fixed at both ends,' Inspector Deeds concluded.

Pollard studied the notice board facing him which partly blocked access to the bridge. It was about three feet square and mounted on a post for which a socket had been made. Bold black capitals on a white ground stated BRIDGE COLLAPSED. DO NOT CROSS. He tried to pull it up and found that he could manage this with a good hard tug.

'Is this the one that was chucked into the water?' he asked.

'Yes, sir. The lettering wasn't damaged as the paint's waterproof. There's an identical notice over there on the other side with its back to us. It's been fixed to block the way to anybody coming up the steps which lead down to the path over the meadow. The ground level's a lot lower on that side, as you can see.'

Pollard studied the remains of the bridge. The arch had a low stone balustrade on each side. The collapse had taken place just south of the crown of the arch, and it was not immediately obvious from where he stood. It was easy to understand how an active young man, sprinting down the wooded hillside, could have dashed on to the bridge in the gathering twilight without taking in what lay ahead, and been unable to stop himself in time. There was a drop of about twelve feet on to quite large pieces of masonry which were still lying on the stream bed, and it was on one of these that Edward Tuke had apparently landed head first and fatally concussed himself. And it was a secluded spot, almost hidden by trees and bushes from the village houses. Pollard glanced along the fishermen's paths on both sides of the river. According to Deeds they were little used. Most Woodcombe people would have been at their evening meal between six-thirty and seven o'clock, and members of the fishing syndicate unlikely to have arrived, even if they had decided to exercise their now undisputed rights that evening. He noticed how narrow concrete paths had been built up round the

41

bases of the piers to facilitate their movements. He looked questioningly at Toye.

'You couldn't bank on the chap going headlong,' the latter asserted, habitually cautious.

'What's your opinion, Deeds?' Pollard asked.

'Well, sir,' the young inspector replied, 'to my mind it's a matter of what you said just now, up top. If you'd taken up the notice, and advised Mr Tuke to use the bridge knowing he was in a tearing hurry and the light was going, I'd say the chances of him coming to grief were pretty high. And it's not as though anybody else was likely to be about. Well worth a try if you'd got it in for him.'

'I agree with you both,' Pollard said thoughtfully. 'Dicey, isn't it? Very difficult to prove criminal intent.'

'Meaning criminal intent on the part of somebody who wasn't one of the fans?' Toye asked.

'Yes. Even if they—the fans—did chuck the warning notice into the river there's ample evidence that they were stoned, so they couldn't be charged with intent to murder. But I'm inclined to agree with you, Inspector, that they didn't do it. The evidence brought against them is purely circumstantial, and you might even say that on balance it's slightly in their favour.'

Inspector Deeds was gratified.

'You know,' Pollard pursued, 'if they didn't, in theory it should be possible to clear them. If they were cleared beyond any doubt the coroner would probably want to re-open the inquest, and the anonymous letters might turn out to be a really important lead. I expect you people down here had arrived at this point before we turned up?'

'Yes, we had, sir, but we were still at the stage of considering priorities when the Home Office called the C.C. about you coming down and taking over. The problem was where to begin. Any able-bodied person could have pulled up the notice and you'll have seen that the hedges on the south bank give plenty of cover. There are people living right on the spot like Mr and Mrs Kenway-Potter and Mr Bolling. Mr Fordyce made no bones about having walked along the north bank on the Wednesday afternoon, and he met Bill Morris who was putting up the "Private Fishing" notices again, and collecting the bottles and whatever that the fans had chucked around at Upper Bridge.'

'One thing about this alleged case,' Pollard commented, 'is that there's no shortage of potential suspects. From geography to history, I think. In other words we now start tackling that massive case-file with a weather eye for anything that would eliminate the ruddy fans.'

★

As they drank refreshing cups of tea in the small private office provided for them at Littlechester police headquarters, Pollard and Toye took stock of its facilities. There was a good solid table, three upright chairs, a telephone, a typewriter, and a generous supply of writing materials. A window, open at the bottom, overlooked the car park. Having drained his third cup, Toye thrust out his head and shoulders to study the parked vehicles to better advantage.

'I'll let you know when I'm knocking off for supper,' Pollard remarked caustically, pushing the tea tray to one side and drawing the file towards him.

Toye's torso and head re-entered the room. There was the vestige of a grin on his pale solemn face as he sat down on the opposite side of the table.

'What do we start on?' he asked, contemplating through his large horn-rimmed spectacles, the mass of papers in front of Pollard.

'With the anonymous letters, I think. At least they're out of the ordinary.'

The Littlechester police technicians had sandwiched the three letters and the envelopes in which they had arrived between thin sheets of glass secured by sellotape. The letters were on greaseproof paper. Their contents had been inscribed in uniform featureless block capitals with a sharp, but fairly soft pencil. A report from the forensic laboratory stated that the perfect regularity of the lettering could only be accounted for by the use of a stencil. It added that stencilled alphabets not infrequently formed part of children's educational toys. The addresses on the manila business envelopes were in the same block lettering. The only recognisable fingerprints on these were those of the police constable who had sorted the mail on its arrival. The greaseproof paper had only been handled by someone wearing thin rubber gloves of a type in common use.

The postmarks were also disappointingly unhelpful. All three missives had been posted in Littlechester and sent by second-class mail. They had been franked by machine and merely gave the date but not the time of posting.

'Beyond the fact that it points to a local, there's not much help here,' Pollard said. 'We'd better get down to the bookwork proper. Here goes: the initial 999 call from Mr R. Kenway-Potter of Woodcombe Manor at 20.37 hours on Wednesday, April the twenty-third, reporting a drowning fatality in the River Honey on his property . . . There's the hell of a lot of it.'

A quick glance through the contents of the file showed that everything was there, meticulously recorded in chronological order: the immediate steps taken by the police on their arrival at Woodcombe, the preliminary statements made by Rodney Kenway-Potter, James Fordyce and Tom Wonnacott, and the opening and adjournment of the inquest on Edward Tuke. There followed detailed accounts of the questioning of the eleven football fans, the information on the deceased's antecedents obtained from Integrated Oils, and from the U.S.A. by way of the F.B.I., and reports of interviews

44

with everyone known to have had any contact with Edward Tuke, both in Woodcombe and on his brief visit to Littlechester. In addition there were brief biographies of the Kenway-Potters, the Fordyces, the Wonnacotts, Mrs Rawlings and Canon Hugh Allbright of Littlechester Cathedral. None of these had a police record. Finally there was a report on the resumed inquest and its verdict of Death by Misadventure.

Details of the arrival and contents of the anonymous letters followed, and of the publicity sparked off by the third. In conclusion there was a brief statement about the takeover by Scotland Yard.

As an appendage there was an account of the dispute between Rodney Kenway-Potter and Leonard Bolling over the formation of the fishing syndicate, and a verbatim report of the proceedings in the County Court. The fact that Ford and Co., estate agents of Littlechester, had been instructed to put Bridge Cottage on the market on the day before the case was heard was duly noted.

They got down to the job, working along their usual line, both reading each set of documents independently, and making a note of anything that struck them as significant. By half-past seven they had finished with the interrogations of the fans. Pollard threw down his biro and stretched.

'My brain's flagging,' he said, 'I must refuel. Let's knock off for grub and a breather.'

Rooms had been booked for them at the Three Crowns, a nearby hotel. They ate in the grill room with the local evening paper for company. It had contrived to fill out its front page with the bare fact of their arrival and a photograph of Pollard. There were surreptitious glances from other tables. When they had finished their meal Pollard went to ring his wife at their home in Wimbledon. As always when he was working on a case they used a motoring code, and he told her that he did not yet know if there was going to be a car for him to try out. Jane's reply

45

was interrupted by scuffling sounds and small voices, his nine-year-old twin son and daughter having heard the bleep of the telephone and emerged from their beds for their rations of thirty seconds' conversation with him. They were then shooed away for Jane to have a final word and a promise of another call as soon as the situation clarified.

Putting down the receiver, Pollard looked at his watch and decided that he could afford to have a stroll around for quarter of an hour. Toye, who believed in reading newspapers thoroughly, had installed himself on a bench in the forecourt of the hotel with the *Littlechester Evening News*, and agreed that he, too, felt like a bit longer break.

A narrow passage flanked by small expensive-looking shops brought Pollard out into the Cathedral Green. He walked across it for a closer inspection of a magnificent rose window in the west front. It was now nearly nine o'clock and he was surprised to see a couple who were obvious tourists emerge from the building. He tried the door through which they had appeared. It swung open to his touch, and he stepped inside.

As he stood at the end of the nave looking eastward the vista before him was of such beauty that he momentarily lost all his sense of time and place. A soft blue-grey dusk had invaded the chancel and the superb vaulted roof far above him, but the screen and the great pillars of the crossing were red-gold in the sunset glow.

'I'm so sorry, but I'm afraid we close the cathedral at nine.'

The voice coming from somewhere near his right shoulder brought him abruptly to earth.

'Of course,' Pollard replied. 'I'm surprised that it's kept open so late. I happened to be passing when two people were coming out, so I thought I'd just look inside.'

The speaker proved to be a middle-aged cleric in a cassock, with gold-rimmed spectacles and a pleasant friendly face.

'We only do it in summer for the visitors,' he said, eyeing Pollard keenly. 'Forgive me, but I recognise you, of course. Detective Chief Superintendent Pollard, isn't it? I wish you were down here on happier business. I saw your photograph in the *Evening News* tonight. I can't help being interested because I had quite a long talk with that poor young American on the afternoon before he died ... yes, Chivers, we're on the way out,' he added, as a second cassocked figure came up with the jingle of a bunch of keys. 'Everything all right? Fine. Goodnight.'

'Good night, sir.'

The next minute Pollard and his new acquaintance were outside, a key was turning in a lock and bolts were being shot home.

'I expect the local C.I.D. got on to the fact that you had this conversation with Mr Tuke?' Pollard enquired tactfully.

'Oh, yes, indeed. They were anxious to trace his movements in Littlechester that afternoon and came to make enquiries at the Cathedral as it's one of the places that Americans make for. They showed Chivers his passport photograph. Chivers is a very observant chap and had noticed him talking to me at some length by the War Memorial Chapel. They asked me if he had mentioned any acquaintances in Littlechester or round about, or said anything about his plans for the rest of day, but unfortunately I wasn't able to give them any helpful information.'

'If you were talking at some length, might I ask you what the conversation was about? One simply never knows in an enquiry like this what may turn out to be relevant.'

'Of course you may, but I can hardly believe that it will in this case. We chatted a bit about the job he'd come over to do, and what it was like to work for a gigantic set-up like Integrated Oils. He said that both his parents had been immigrant stock from Britain to the States, and that

47

he'd always had an idea that he'd like to come back permanently. I asked him what particularly attracted him in the country now that he'd got here, and rather surprisingly, he said the sense of the past which you didn't feel in the U.S.'

'Did he say anything about the Woodcombe longstone?'

'Nothing. The police asked me that. For a young American he seemed rather movingly interested in our War Memorial Chapel. It's rather fine, commemorating the local fallen in both the wars. I remember his saying what a splendid thing it was to have died for your counry, and how proud your family would feel.'

There seemed nothing further to be gained by prolonging the conversation with the cleric, who was, Pollard learnt with interest, Canon Hugh Allbright, so after a few comments on the architecture of the Cathedral they parted. Pollard returned to the Three Crowns, collected Toye, and within ten minutes they were getting down to Edward Tuke's family background and past history.

It was past midnight when they arrived at the stage of comparing notes. They found themselves in complete agreement that the top priority was to see if the football fans could be cleared beyond any doubt of having removed the warning notice on the collapsed bridge.

'It's no good our tackling the chaps themselves,' Pollard said. 'If Deeds and Super Newman who understand the local mentality couldn't get anywhere with them, we certainly shouldn't. They'd only clam up all the more. My great thought is that we concentrate on the notice. Did anyone see it *after* the fans' razzmatazz just before midnight on Tuesday, April 22nd?'

Toye replied that the same idea had struck him.

'Can you swallow Mr Fordyce's story of how he walked along the north bank on the Wednesday afternoon without noticing whether the thing was there or not?'

Pollard rubbed his eyes and sat staring at the opposite

wall.

'Yes,' he said at last. 'I can. I remember the state of mind I was in when Jane and I were deciding whether to plunge and buy the Wimbledon house. Whether it really was the right house in the right place, and the mortgage problem and so on. But there is a small point about that walk of Fordyce's that may have struck you. You've seen the lie of the land. How long would it take you, personally, to saunter in an abstracted way from Bridge Cottage to Upper Bridge?'

Toye considered the matter.

'Five to seven minutes,' he said.

'That's what I'd give it. Well, as you've seen, the local chaps made exhaustive enquiries about possible contacts of Tuke's in Woodcombe and the neighbourhood. The woman at the shop-cum-post office whom Deeds called a clacker, assured him that nobody had been in early on Wednesday afternoon except Mr Fordyce, just on three, and she'd watched him go over to have a look at Bridge Cottage. Bill Morris, who was clearing up after the fans at Upper Bridge said he hadn't seen Mr Tuke except in the pub that morning. Nobody had come along the path that afternoon except Mr Fordyce at about ten to four. Forty-five minutes seems a long time for looking at a cottage you can't get into, don't you think?'

'Yes, I do,' Toye agreed. 'What could he have been up to, though? At that stage he hadn't met Tuke and couldn't have known his plans for the evening.'

'We've only his word for it that it was Tuke himself who suggested going up to see the longstone. Fordyce could have talked him into it and advised the short cut over the bridge... Pure unsupported theorising, I know. But it's possible that Fordyce didn't hand over all the correspondnece between Tuke and himself, or give Deeds all the facts about what passed between them on Wednesday evening. He's on our list for a nice long talk, anyway.'

'So's Bolling. If I was a betting man,' Toye said in tones which utterly repudiated this possibility, 'I'd put my money on Bolling. He'd got across Woodcombe and everybody in it, and his lawyer must've managed to put it over to him that he hadn't a hope of getting that injunction. Otherwise he wouldn't have decided to sell his house and quit before the county court hearing. Knocking down that stone and throwing a notice, put up by Mr Kenway-Potter, into the the river might have seemed to him a final kick in the pants for the whole lot of 'em. I'm not suggesting any criminal intent over the notice. And as Inspector Deeds said, he lives right on the spot, and would have seen the Kenway Potters drive off, and realise by the small hours that they'd gone for the night and that the coast was clear.

'I'll grant you all that,' Pollard said. 'Whether he'd have the physical strength and know-how to bring down that dirty great longstone on his own and yank up the notice as well is another matter. Put him on the list, anyway... Look here, I feel I've about had it for tonight. We've got enough jobs lined up already to keep us going for days.

Toye, a careful planner, asked exactly what they would be starting off with on the following morning.

'Tell you at breakfast,' Pollard replied, gathering papers together. 'Inspiration may float up from my subconscious while I'm asleep. At the moment my mind's blank.'

Chapter Three

Pollard and Toye were both believers in a good stout breakfast as an insurance against the possibility of getting nothing more to eat until the evening. It was not until heaped plates of bacon and eggs and various accompaniments had been disposed of that Pollard began to outline a provisional programme for the day.

'If we're going to tackle the warning notice problem by concentrating on who last saw the damn thing in situ rather than who it was that yanked it up,' he said, spreading marmalade thickly on buttered toast, 'it's a case of going over to Woodcombe again. To the village itself this time. We know you can't see the board from the hill because of the trees and the slightly convex slope, or from Upper Bridge. The trees and bushes on the south bank would hide it from anybody at ground level in the village, but what about the view from the upper windows of houses?'

'But if anybody saw it still there after the fans' rampage and all the talk when Tuke was killed, why didn't they come forward?' Toye asked.

'Either because they'd removed it themselves during the Wednesday morning or afternoon, or because it hadn't registered with them, because when they did see it they were consciously looking at something else.'

'What about Fordyce?' Toye asked indistinctly, masticating a piece of breakfast roll.

'Quite possibly, but I don't want to start on him until we've gone all out to see if the fans can be cleared. He's a complete job in himself with all his link-ups with

Tuke... Now look here.' Pushing his plate aside. Pollard placed a knife horizontally in front of him. 'This is the stream. This teaspoon at right angles to it is the dud footbridge. These two bits of toast are the two warning notices, one at each end. Put what passes for your mind back to where we were standing, just here at the north end of the dud bridge, and looking due south. What could we see of the village?'

'The church tower and a bit of the roof, straight ahead. Just to the right what Deeds said was the pub. You could see some of the roof and some dormer windows. Just to the left of the church tower a fair-sized house with top-floor dormer windows showing. The old parsonage, I daresay.'

'Observant little chap, aren't you? Just what I saw. Well, somebody could have looked out of one of those attic windows at some point during the Wednesday Tuke died. Gazing at the woods and the Manor, perhaps, and feeling bucked that the unpopular Bolling had lost his case and was clearing out. Then there's the church tower. There doesn't seem to be a local vicar these days, but one of the churchwardens might have gone up to dislodge a bird's nest or whatever from a gutter. Or there could be a factotum of some kind. Tuke was buried here, so somebody dug the poor chap's grave. Literally, I mean. And any normal human being getting up to a good vantage point stops for a look round. You may even be able to spot the longstone from the top of the tower. My idea is that it would be worth taking anybody in the dormer window or church tower category back to their vantage point, and check on everything they can remember noticing.'

Toye rather dubiously admitted that the scheme might be worth trying.

'I can see that you're hankering after a frontal attack on Bolling, and it'll probably come to that. We'll take the preliminary step of getting the people here to liaise with the Yard over unearthing his life history. And Fordyce's too, of course. There's a gaggle of newshounds lurking hopefully. As soon as I've managed to choke them off for the moment we'll go round to the station.'

On arrival Pollard put in hand the enquiries into the personal histories of Leonard Bolling and James Fordyce, and then joined Toye in their temporary office. They spent a little time re-reading the report of Inspector Deeds' interrogation of the Wonnacotts, but it did not suggest any lead worth following up.

The car park of the Green Man was at the rear of the building and they stood for a couple of minutes looking up at the two dormer windows in the roof. Both were un-curtained and shut, and gave the impression of belonging to unused attics rather than to occupied bedrooms.

The back door of the pub was standing open, and sounds of activity inside were audible. A knock brought a small brisk woman to the threshold.

'Mrs Wonnacott?' Pollard said, holding out his official card. 'I'm Detective-Chief Superintendent Pollard of New Scotland Yard, and this is my colleague, Detective Inspector Toye. I expect you've heard that we've come down to make some further enquiries into the death of Mr Edward Tuke. We'd be glad of a few minutes with you and your husband.

She eyed him doubtfully.

'Well, sir, we know it's our duty to help the police, but after all the questions Inspector Deeds asked us, I can't for the life of me think of anything else we could tell you about the poor young man. Still, please to step inside and I'll call my husband. He's down the cellar.'

Echoing voices and subterranean thuds confirmed this statement. Mrs Wonnacott returned with a stocky grey-haired man in shirt sleeves, his face flushed from physical exertion.

'Gentlemen from Scotland Yard, Tom' she said. 'About Mr Tuke.'

Tom Wonnacott gave them good morning, and pulled

up another chair to the unoccupied end of the big kitchen table.

'He was as nice a young man as ever I saw,' he told Pollard and Toye, 'but I wish he'd never set foot in the Green Man, the trouble and worry it's brought us.'

'I can well believe that, Mr Wonnacott,' Pollard replied, 'and we're only sorry to take up a bit more of your time, but the fact is that we need your help. You see, after all the talk there's been since those letters were written saying somebody in Woodcombe moved the notice, your Chief Constable has decided that the matter had better be looked into again. That's why Inspector Toye and I are here.'

'Pack o' bloody nonsense,' Tom Wonnacott explained. 'Course it was they football hooligans pulled'n up, same as they did the Private Fishin' notices. The Littlechester cops should've tried a bit of third degree stuff on 'em. They'd own up fast enough then.'

'Could be,' Pollard agreed pacifically, 'but I'm a chap under orders, you see, so here I am. One thing would settle it for good and all. If anyone saw that notice standing in its usual position *after* the football fans cleared off on the Tuesday night and *before* Mr Tuke went into the river, the fans couldn't have done the job, and somebody else must have. See?'

The Wonnacotts absorbed this proposition and nodded in reluctant agreement.

'Well then,' Pollard went on, 'we've been considering places from which somebody could have seen the notice on that day, Wednesday, April the twenty-third. Anybody going along the footpaths, of course. From the village there aren't many points from which it can be seen because of the trees and shrubs along the south bank, but we think it might be visible from the attic windows here, and those in the house just beyond the church. Is there anybody in this household who could have been doing a bit of dusting up there, say, and glanced quite casually out of a window towards the river?'

Dusting was Mrs Wonnacott's province and she took over.

'There's not much dustin' done up there,' she said, 'seein' as the attics aren't in regular use. One's just a lumber room for odd bits and pieces, and except for puttin' up camp beds for the grandchildren if we've got a full house Christmas time, say, the other stays empty. I take a look round now and again, but if I did on April the twenty-third, that I can't say. I don't recall goin' up, that's all.'

'Fair enough, Mrs Wonnacott,' Pollard reassured her. 'By the way, *can* the notice be seen from your attic windows?'

Not to his surprise, the Wonnacotts had no idea, and the party moved up to the top floor in order to settle the question. This proved a simple matter. Because of the alignment of the Green Man in relation to the river, and the existence of a large clump of bushes to the south-west of the old footbridge, neither the remains of the bridge nor the notices at each end of it could be seen from the dormer windows. The Wonnacotts relaxed perceptibly as the prospect of further involvement with the police came to an abrupt end and refreshments were offered. Over cups of coffee in the kitchen conversation about Edward Tuke flowed easily.

'Well,' Tom Wonnacott said, stirring vigorously, 'if ever he had a contact here in Woodcombe, they never met up in this pub. He came in early, asked for a pint and bread and cheese, and sat eatin' and drinkin' and saying nothin' to nobody. Not till he got up and came to the bar to ask if he could have a bed for the night. When I got back from askin' the missus, 'e was talkin' to Mr Kenway-Potter and gettin' an invite to supper up at the Manor. And if Mr Kenway-Potter set out to land 'im in the river, I'll drink every drop we've got 'ere, and go for a ten mile walk on top of it.'

'Mr Tuke had a chat with a lady called Mrs Rawlings, didn't he?' Toye asked.

The Wonnacotts exchanged amused but tolerant glances.

'That he did, poor chap. Mr Kenway-Potter brought her over and introduced them, and then cleared off quick with his lady. She's nice enough, Mrs Rawlings, but she's got what they call folklore on the brain. Seems Mr Tuke asked why there's no painted inn sign outside and that set her off.'

'There's an old tale about it,' Mrs Wonnacott took up. 'There's an awful ugly face carved in a stone up in the church roof. Seems you find others like it in churches up and down the country. A Jack-in-the-Green or a Green Man it's called. But local folk used to say a mason carved it from a face he saw on that great big stone up to Manor Woods, and that it was the Devil's face. If that's what he thought he saw he must've taken a lot more than was good for him. Anyway, it's real ugly and nasty, I'll grant you that, so Woodcombe people never wanted it hanging on a sign outside their pub. Why, they wouldn't sit in the pew underneath it in the old days, I've been told. 'Twas said that if a pregnant woman did, she'd miscarry for sure.'

'You's think there's be a queue to sit under it these days, the way the girls carry on,' Tom Wonnacott remarked sardonically.

'Now, Tom,' his wife admonished.

Pollard grinned and put down his empty coffee cup.

'We must have a look ourselves,' he said. 'The church is our next port of call. Is there somebody around who'd take us up to the top of the tower?'

'Sammy Muggett's got the key. He goes up to fix the flag when we flies 'er. We've no vicar livin' here now, not since we joined up with four other villages in what they calls a group ministry, but old Sammy does 'is best. You'll find 'im in the cottage next but one to the church, just past the old parsonage. Gettin' on, but still spry is

Sammy.'

'Some says he's a bit simple, but he keeps the church an' the churchyard a treat,' Mrs Wonnacott contributed.

Pollard thanked the pair for their help and the welcome coffee, and assured them that he and Toye would be looking in for a drink as soon as they could make it.

'You go and rout out the estimable if limited Sammy Muggett,' he said to Toye as they walked towards the church, 'while I track down this real ugly and nasty mug that Mrs Rawlings seems so impressed by.'

His hand was on the latch of the lychgate when he paused, confronted by the church notice board just inside. It was of the common funeral type with gold lettering on a black ground and headed 'Church of St George the Martyr, Woodcombe'. He felt a small tremor of excitement. April the twenty-third, St George's Day, would be the patronal festival. No doubt the feast was observed on the following Sunday, but surely the flag would have been flown on the day itself, hoisted on the tower flagstaff by Sammy Muggett? Was there just the chance of a breakthrough here? It would depend on the sort of chap he was ... nothing must be suggested to him, of course ...

Footsteps and voices were approaching from further down the road, heralding the return of Toye with a companion. Pollard, standing at the church door, watching him come through the gate with a small white-haired chirpy-looking man whose bright eyes surveyed him with wonder.

'Mr Sam Muggett?' he asked.

'That's me, sir, Sexton of this 'ere church for thirty-five years come Advent Sunday. You two gennelmen wants to go up top? My, I never thought as I'd be takin' two Scotland Yard de-tectives up the ole tower.'

Pollard's apology for giving trouble was brushed aside. Sam Muggett assured him that the ladders were no more to him than his cottage stairs, he'd been up and down that often. He escorted them into the church, unlocked a

57

small door in the ringing chamber and led the ascent with surprising nimbleness. Pollard, who disliked heights, was glad to emerge into sunlight and fresh air. A quick glance told him that the disused footbridge and the white rectangles of the two warning notices were clearly visible. He gave Toye a warning glance.

The extensive view was duly admired, Sam Muggett indicating various landmarks.

'That there be Lower Bridge,' he told Pollard, pointing with a stubby gnarled finger. 'Bridge Cottage t'other side wur that ole bugger Bolling's bin, but 'e's orf now, thanks be ... Woodcombe Manor 'alf way up slope, and on t'other side under they rocks to that 'eathenish ole stone but us can't see 'un fer the trees. Oughter be down yur in consecrated groun', I sez, then us wouldn't niver 'ave no more trouble with 'ee.'

In an attempt to get the conversation round to Sam Muggett's activities on the early morning of April the twenty-third, Pollard asked if the flag were often flown.

'Well, Sir, we runs 'er up fer the Queen's birthday an' any big royal occasion. And she wur half-mast for Mr Churchill and for Lord Mountbatten, o' course. Then there's the festivals like Christmas and Easter Day, and our Patronal. If it falls on a weekday, we keeps 'er up over the Sunday followin', when we 'as a special service.'

'Your Patronal Festival's April the twenty-third isn't it?' Toye asked casually.

'Thass right, sir. And to think o' that poor young man meetin' 'is end that very day. A beautiful mornin' it was. I was up 'ere seven o'clock a-runnin' up the flag, and real lovely it wus all around.'

'I suppose by late April it's full daylight as early as that, even allowing for Summer Time?' Pollard asked.

'Bright as noonday it wur,' Sam Mugget assured him. 'Everythin' showin' up. Me eyes is as good as ever they wur, thanks be, and I could pick out the clock turret over to the Manor on the old stables, an' the steamroller when they wur puttin' in the water main up the Marycott road, and that dratted old bridge down there yonder with the noticeboards each end'—

'You could see the noticeboards at each end?' Pollard asked with a faint touch of incredulity in his voice.

'Why, sir, they white boards stands out a mile. Look at 'em now. I could see 'em as plain as you see me this minit. An' what's more, there wur a dirty great 'eron standin' by the board on the far bank, come after Mr Kenway-Potter's trout. An' as I watched 'n 'e took off downstream and crossed Lower Bridge, that low that Bill Sparkes bringin' the milk lorry down 'ad to brake.'

There was a brief silence.

'Mr Muggett,' Pollard said gently, 'when Inspector Deeds came round the village asking if anybody had seen the notice on the far bank in its usual place during St George's Day on April the twenty-third, why didn't you tell him you saw it when you were hoisting the flag that morning?'

In a flash Sam Muggett's expression became that of a startled child charged with an unconscious misdeed.

''E never arst me that. 'E only wanted to know if I'd been along the far bank on the Wednesday, an' I 'adn't. I wur busy with gettin' ready for Sunday. Bein' up 'ere for the flag 'ad gone clean out of me 'ead with all the conflop-tion that was goin' on about the young chap.'

'Not to worry, Mr Muggett,' Pollard reassured him. 'You've remembered now, and that's what matters.'

*

Bill Sparkes, the lorry driver, worked for a big milk depot at Wynford. It turned out to be his day off and the Littlechester police were unable to run him to earth until the late afternoon. When questioned at the station he confirmed Sam Muggett's statement about the heron without hesitation.

59

'Ruddy great bird!' he said with feeling. 'Flew right past me windscreen. I might've crashed the parapet an' landed the 'ole outfit in the river.'

Asked if he had noticed anything unusual as he drove through Woodcombe, he replied that they'd got the flag flying up on the church tower, and there'd been a bloke up there, too.

After Sparkes had gone, Superintendent Martin and Inspector Deeds agreed with Pollard that this bit of supporting evidence clinched things. The fans were out as far as Edward Tuke's death went. The Super threw himself back in his chair and lit a cigarette.

'So what?' he enquired. 'Glad it's you people and not us to make the next move. It'll mean reopening the inquest. I suppose?'

Understandably the atmosphere was slightly strained on account of the significance of St George's Day having been overlooked, and the unfortunate wording of Inspector Deeds' question to Sam Muggett.

'Bolling very likely vandalised the longstone on the night of April the twenty-second,' Pollard replied, 'and may quite well have written the letters all out of bloody-mindedness, but it doesn't look as though he removed the notice. He'd have done it during the night, probably on the way up or down when on the longstone job. Not left it until broad daylight on the twenty-third. We'll have to go at him first thing tomorrow. I'm pretty sure he's only a loose end, but the sooner it's tied up, the better.'

Superintendent Martin sardonically wished them joy, and suggested a foursome supper, but Pollard rather regretfully declined on the grounds of needing to put in some more time on the file.

'I feel an urge to celebrate,' he said to Toye when they were back in their office. 'It wouldn't be exactly tactful in front of the Super and Deeds. I'll stand you a drink, though, old man, at the posh Ring and Crozier before we go and eat at our more modest pub. Let's leave the car here, and walk. It's no distance.'

The Ring and Crozier, a four-star establishment, was in the Cathedral Close. The bar was spacious, well-carpeted and there was ample seating at small tables. Pollard was instantly recognized by the head barman and received prompt attention. Bearing a couple of lagers he headed for a small table commanding a good view of the whole room. Toye asked if he were on the lookout for anyone.

'Force of habit, I suppose,' Pollard replied. 'You never know, though.'

At intervals he unobtrusively took in their fellow drinkers. Men standing at the bar and engaged in conversation with each other and the staff interested him less than people seated like Toye and himself, and enjoying their drinks in a more leisurely way. After a time he felt certain that he was being the subject of conversation between a couple on the opposite side of the room, and that a measure of disagreement was involved. The woman shifted her position, he took a lightning glance, and registered early middle age, good features and elegance and a degree of tension. The man, who appeared to be urging some point of view, was of about the same age and had the unmistakable county gentry stamp. Presently they got up rather abruptly, and the woman led the way to the door without looking in Pollard's direction. It was held open for her, and she disappeared, closely followed by the man. Pollard looked at Toye, one eyebrow slightly raised.

'Kenway-Potters?' Toye queried, who missed little.

'Could be,' Pollard agreed. 'As we go out, I'll ask the barman if the gentleman who just left with his wife was Major Hildred Cumming-Thorpe. That would be about the right social level, I think. I'd like to—hold it, Toye.' The man had returned and was crossing the room directly towards their table.

'Good evening,' he said. 'Do forgive my crashing in like this, but of course I recognise you, Chief Superintendent. This is probably entirely out of order, but I just want to say that I'm Rodney Kenway-Potter, and if there's anything—absolutely anything I can do to help in this ghastly business, you've only got to give the word.'

Pollard had risen to his feet. They were both tall men, and their eyes met.

'Thank you, Mr Kenway-Potter,' he said. 'We'll be coming along to see you, I'm afraid, although I don't know exactly when, but I'm glad to have met you now. We've read the statements you've already made, and if by any chance you can think of anything further to add to them, it would be a help, of course.'

'I'll try, Chief Superintendent, but honestly my mind feels bone dry on the whole affair. Anyway you know where to find me. Will you excuse me now? My wife's waiting in the car.'

Pollard and Toye watched him make for the door and go out. Toye looked enquiring.

'The lady,' Pollard said, 'didn't want him to make contact. Why? Finish your drink and we'll go.'

Back in the half-empty dining room of their hotel they worked through an adequate, if uninspired meal in companionable silence. They had arrived at cheese and biscuits when an elderly foursome took possession of the next table. After they had ordered, a desultory conversation about the Woodcombe case started up. A cosy motherly voice expressed the opinion that having the poor young American drowned in your own river, and then a lot of nasty anonymous letters going about wasn't at all nice for the people living at the Manor. How many years ago was it that a kiddy had been killed falling out of a tree in their woods over to Woodcombe? Dogged by bad luck, they seemed to be.

After some discussion it was agreed that it was six years ago, back in the summer of 1974.

'People called Kenway-Potter own the place where it happened, don't they?' a male voice enquired. 'One of their own kiddies, was it?'

Pollard, sitting with his back to the speakers, helped himself to some more gorgonzola. The motherly voice said that it had been a village boy, not one of their own, she was sure of that, and something funny about him, but she couldn't recall what. At this point the arrival of starters put a stop to the conversation for the moment, and when it was resumed a fresh topic was introduced.

After a decent interval Pollard signalled to his waiter for the bill.

'Worth looking into?' Toye asked, as they emerged from the dining room.

'Unlikely,' Pollard replied. 'Martin and Deeds obviously haven't thought it worth mentioning. All the same, we'll just ask about it when we get back to the station.'

A verbatim report of the inquest and the statements made by the boy's adopted parents, headmaster and others were soon available. The death of Robin Westbridge, aged ten, in July 1974, appeared to have been a perfectly straightforward tragedy. He had been adopted by a childless Woodcombe couple, George and Mildred Westbridge, at the age of two months. The home was modest but comfortable, George having a good steady job in the accounts department of a leading store in Littlechester. The representative of the County Council's Children's Department had consistently given very favourable reports of the set up on all counts. Robin had grown up healthy, and was doing well at school where his ability was assessed as above average. He was, however, something of a loner, imaginative and a reader, fonder on the whole of his own company than of the rumbustious activities of his age group. The Westbridges had told the police that recently Robin had been inclined to go off on his own and been reticent about where he had been, but as he always turned up at mealtimes they had not worried unduly, feeling that any attempt to push him around would be all wrong for a child of his type.

On the day of his death, Robin had returned home as usual on the school bus from Littlechester, been given his customary snack by Mrs Westbridge and gone out again. The Westbridges' evening meal was at six-thirty, when George got back from work. When Robin had not reappeared by half-past eight a search of the neighbourhood was organised by the villagers. He was found unconscious an hour later at the foot of a big oak in the Manor woods. He had broken his neck and severely fractured his skull and died shortly after admission to hospital. Investigation of the tree showed that it had been frequently climbed to a considerable height, to a place where a 'tree house' had been constructed in the branches.

In his summing-up the coroner emphatically cleared the Westbridges of any suggestion of neglect or inadequate supervision of Robin. Active intelligent boys of ten, he said, could not possibly be kept on leading strings, and this meant that their parents had to accept a degree of risk. It was obvious that Robin, an imaginative and enterprising boy, had an exciting secret life, like many children of his age. In due course he would have grown out of it, but at the time it was an essential part of his development. The only possible verdict was one of Death by Misadventure. The deepest sympathy would be extended to Mr and Mrs Westbridge by all their friends and by everyone living in Woodcombe.

'Except that it happened on Kenway-Potter property,' Pollard said thoughtfully when they had finished reading, 'it's difficult to see any possible link with the Tuke affair.'

'Don't you think that the kid would have got an extra kick out of the fact that he was trespassing?' Toye suggested. 'Enemy territory, and all that.'

'You've probably got something there,' Pollard agreed. 'God, I hope the twins' exciting secret lives don't lead to something like this.'

'Two of them,' Toye replied reassuringly. 'Safety in

numbers, you know. They said that poor little blighter was a loner.'

'Bless you for those heartening words. Here, we'd better return all this info to the management and limber up for tomorrow: Bolling the Belligerent, Kenway-Potter the Rather Unnecessarily Helpful, Mrs K-P who Wants to Keep Out of It. In short, the lot.'

*

At the moment when Toye went off to return the official documents on Robin Westbridge's death, Rodney Kenway-Potter came out of the front door of Woodcombe Manor. Dusk was falling, its oncoming hastened by a low bank of cloud in the sunset sky. He walked round the house and through a half-open door into a walled vegetable garden to which the sweet peas were always relegated as leggy and untidy growers. Amaryllis was still picking industriously in the half-light.

'Give over, love,' he said. 'You can't possibly see the colours.'

'No problem,' she replied. 'I like a random mix best of all. I'm just coming in, though.'

They went back into the house together and Amaryllis vanished into the kitchen regions. Presently she reappeared, walking with caution and bearing a large silver bowl containing a mass of multicoloured sweet peas. She set it down carefully on a side table, briefly buried her face in their fragrance and began to make a few adjustments.

Rodney, lying back in an armchair with his arms folded watched her intently ... It's beauty based on bone structure that lasts, he thought. That lovely brow and chiselled nose, and the set of her head on her shoulders ... A few crow's feet and the odd line here and there don't matter a damn ... nothing does ...

'That'll do,' his wife said, taking a step backwards and

surveying her work. 'I shall spoil the whole thing if I go on fiddling.'

She sank into a chair facing Rodney's and silence descended. It had become protracted when she suddenly broke it.

'Roddy, of course you must go to that meeting at County Hall tomorrow morning. I can't think why I suddenly made such a hassle about that Scotland Yard man coming. If he turns up without ringing first and you're not here, well, he must come again, that's all . . . It's the way this wretched business has flared up again when it all seemed over and done with' . . .

'My dear, I don't wonder the prospect of yet another copper asking the same questions gets under your skin. It's all my bloody fault, anyway. If only I'd never asked young Tuke to come up to supper'

'You will go to the meeting, though, won't you?'

'O.K., I will then, if you're quite sure about it. You're looking a bit fagged. Let's have a nightcap and turn in early for once.'

Chapter Four

Before leaving for Woodcombe on the following morning
Pollard called in at the Littlechester police station, and
found that some additional information on Leonard
Bolling and James Fordyce had come through from the
Yard. It did not, however, add much to the facts that
were already available. Leonard Bolling had sold the
premises of his bookselling business for a very considerable sum on his retirement. James Fordyce now had an
established reputation as a genealogist.

'So what?' Pollard enquired as he boarded the Rover
with Toye. 'It explains how Bolling has been able to buy
another house over at Wynford before the sale of Bridge
Cottage has got to the completion stage, and suggests that
he hasn't bothered to stand out for a top price. I can't
believe that there's much money in genealogy.'

'Sounds as though he's nuts, near as no matter,' Toye
said as they waited at traffic lights. 'Bolling, I mean.
Going to a Cash-and-Carry when he's got a pot of money.
What's he going to do with it, for heaven's sake?'

'Leave it to a noise abatement society, I should think.
Seriously, though, I'm getting cold feet over Bolling and
the longstone business. He's just on seventy and Deeds
says in his report that he's only about five foot. Would a
retired bookseller who fits that description be likely to
have the right sort of tools and the stamina for the job?'

'He may be a keen gardener,' Toye objected with his
usual caution.

'Deeds suggested something like a pickaxe for loosen-
ing the stones. Not a usual garden tool, I'd say.'

Toye conceded this point.

'But does it matter?' he pursued. 'I mean there's no proof that the longstone vandalism had anything to do with Tuke's death.'

'No proof. At present, that is. But I find it jolly hard to believe that two acts of deliberate vandalism committed within roughly twenty-four hours and five hundred yards of each other aren't somehow connected. And if Bolling didn't do the longstone job, who did? We've quite enough to investigate without having to start an enquiry into that, though.'

On arriving at Woodcombe they drove straight through the village and took the turning to Marycott, parking on the grass verge beyond Bridge Cottage, the use of which by the fishing syndicate had so incensed Leonard Bolling. They walked back and stood for a few moments on the bridge, looking down into the cottage garden. It was in a pathetically neglected state. Rampant forgetmenots, pansies and marigolds were fighting a losing battle against weeds, and the overgrown roses looked as though they had not been pruned for years.

'You win,' Toye said. 'He's no gardener.'

'Come on,' Pollard said. 'Into battle.'

They had only taken a couple of steps when he stopped dead with an exclamation and looked up and down the road.

'Notice anything?' he asked.

'Only that they've had the road up lately, and it hasn't been resurfaced yet.'

'This is it. Water main, Muggett said. I can't believe that the Manor hasn't been on main water for some time, so they could have been taking it to Marycott. The signpost says its four miles.'

Light suddenly dawned in Toye's eyes.

'Tools?' he queried.

'Just that. They could still be at it. Let's go and see. If Bolling "borrowed" a hefty spade and a pickaxe, it's possible that it was noticed. Chaps on a manual job can get quite possessive about the tools they're using.'

They followed the roughly filled-in trench for nearly three miles before arriving at work in progress. A mechanical excavator was in use, but some preliminary breaking-up of the surface was being done with pickaxes. In a small hut of corrugated iron a man was studying a blueprint. He looked up as Pollard and Toye came towards him.

'You can get through, gents,' he told them. 'There's no ditch this side.'

'We don't want to go any further,' Pollard told him. 'We've just come along to see if you can give us a bit of help.' He held out his official card, and the man's eyes widened.

'You're the foreman, I take it?'

'That's right. The engineer comes out from Littlechester Roads Department, but 'tis straightforward, and us carries on most times. Dave Wilson, I am.'

'Well, this is what we'd like to know, Mr Wilson.'

As Pollard talked, he sensed interest and response. The job had been started in mid-April. Woodcombe was on the mains already, and it was a case of taking the water over to Marycott where they'd been creating for it for years. They'd started the job just beyond Woodcombe Manor, which was as far as the mains went. Yes, they'd thought that some kids had been mucking about with the tools, one night right at the start. It was before they'd had the hut for locking up odds and ends. Some muddle at the blooming depot. One of the chaps had found his spade and pickaxe lying in the hedge. He'd call it to mind.

A stentorian bellow brought a burly figure with tightly-curling red hair out of the ditch. He regarded Pollard and Toye with extreme suspicion, but on hearing what was wanted became highly voluble. Yes, he remembered it well enough. He'd put his tools away proper, propped against the digger. Best he could do, seeing the hut hadn't come out. Come the morning, they'd been chucked into the hedge just past the Manor gates. Dratted boys from the village, sure enough.

'We're interested in this,' Pollard told the two men. 'I suppose you can't remember what day it was when you found the tools had been moved?'

'April twenty-third, it wur.'

'How can you be so sure after all this time?'

The red-haired man guffawed. April the twenty-second was his birthday and they'd kept it up a bit at home the night before. He'd come to work with a thick head, and finding his tools mucked about with had made him proper mad.

The interview ended on the best of terms with a clink of coins and references to the birthday party. A field gate was opened to facilitate turning the Rover, and work came to a general halt as its departure was watched with keen interest by the whole work force.

As they drove back to Woodcombe Toye expressed admiration.

'A real breakthrough,' he said. 'The penny'd never have dropped with me.'

'The pickaxe did it,' Pollard replied. 'It just didn't seem to match up with an undersized retired bookseller of seventy, and yet it was the obvious tool for the job. That water main being put in was a sheer stroke of luck. We can risk a frontal attack now, I think.'

In response to Toye's knock Leonard Bolling, a diminutive figure powerfully charged with hostility, flung open the front door of Bridge Cottage. He had surprisingly rosy cheeks like a boy's, untidy grey hair and a small ragged moustache, and surveyed them with sharp eyes from behind old-fashioned gold-rimmed spectacles.

'No need to waste time telling me who you are,' he said in a surprisingly loud voice before Pollard could introduce himself. 'I know. And I've nothing whatever to tell you about the drowned American. I never set eyes on the fellow.'

He made to shut the door, but Toye had unobtrusively manoeuvred a foot across the threshold.

'Mr Edward Tuke's death isn't the immediate reason for this call, Mr Bolling,' Pollard told him. 'We've come to see you about something else in the first instance. No doubt you know very well what it is. May we come in, or would you rather come with us to Littlechester police station and help us with our enquiries there?'

He thought he detected a flicker of malicious amusement, behind the spectacles.

'I detest visitors at all times, and particularly when I am moving house. However, at the moment it appears to be the less obnoxious option.'

Pollard gave Toye a swift wink as they entered the house, squeezing with difficulty past the tea chests of books in the tiny hall. They were led into what appeared to be the main sitting room. This, too, was full of tea chests into which an extensive library was being carefully packed. Any chairs were inaccessible, having been stacked in front of the windows.

'Empty cases over there if you want something to sit on,' Leonard Bolling said, manoeuvring himself into a space in front of the fireplace and remaining standing. 'Now then, get on with it. What do you want to know?'

'Certainly,' Pollard said. 'With apologies to Churchill, having acquired the tools for bringing down the longstone, why didn't you finish the job by putting them back where you found them? Or was chucking them down by the Manor gates meant to be an additional gesture of contempt to Mr Kenway-Potter? You must have realised that the chaps on the road works would notice that somebody had been mucking about with their gear.'

Leonard Bolling gave a short sarcastic laugh.

'Police College, I suppose? Possibly post-graduate entry? However, I'll concede that you've got eyes in your head, Mr Chief Superintendent Pollard, and some wits in it as well to have worked it out. I underestimated the job, as you call it, and ran out of time. People were beginning to get moving. I'd nearly made it back to the roadworks with that damned heavy spade and pickaxe when I heard a car coming from the Marycott direction, and only had time to chuck the things down and go to ground just inside the Manor gates. Since we're going in for quotations, I decided that the better part of valour was discretion, left 'em there, and came home by cutting through the trees down to the river path. Anyway, I was flat out. I'm seventy, and as you see, pint size.'

Pollard recognised a note of bitterness and frustration.

'You must be remarkably fit for your age. What was it that took you so much longer than you expected?'

'The bits of rock the longstone was bedded in were jammed so tight that it was the hell of a job to loosen 'em and get 'em out. The bloody pickaxe weighed about a ton, and I could hardly manage the thing. Then I ran it too fine. When I'd got the longstone down I ought to have called it a day, but I was hell bent on getting that bastard Kenway-Potter's Godalmighty notices down as well.'

There was a brief silence.

'Were you successful?' Pollard enquired.

Leonard Bolling gave a snort of frustrated rage.

'I was not. The blasted football louts who were rampaging in the village late on Tuesday night had beaten me to it. I came down by the steep path from the longstone to Upper Bridge, and they'd chucked the notices into the river and fouled the whole place with their nauseating litter.'

'Spoilt your fun, in fact, Mr Bolling. But they'd left you the other notice, hadn't they? The one at the end of the disused footbridge warning people that it was unsafe.'

Leonard Bolling stared at him blankly for a moment. Then his face expressed genuine outrage and anger.

'Trying to m-make out that I murdered that American chap now, are you?' he spluttered.

'The suggestion,' Pollard replied tranquilly, 'is yours. Mine is that you looked on the warning notice as another bit of Kenway-Potter property suitable for vandalising, and sent it to join the 'Private Fishing' ones in the river some time during Wednesday, April the twenty-third. If you can give a satisfactory account of how you spent that day, I'm ready to withdraw the suggestion. Incidentally it doesn't contain any implication that you removed the notice to bring about Mr Tuke's death.'

Still spluttering with rage Leonard Bolling eventually provided a timetable of his activities on April the twenty-third. After disposing of the pickaxe and spade and taking cover in the Manor garden he had returned to Bridge Cottage, pretty well all in. It had been ten minutes to six when he arrived. After making himself some tea he had rested on his bed for an hour, having set his alarm-clock for seven for fear of oversleeping and being late for the County Court hearing. He had then bathed and shaved, eaten a little breakfast and set off in his van for Littlechester. After the expected verdict he had slipped out and driven straight home to find a representative of Ford's, the estate agents entrusted with the sale of Bridge Cottage, erecting a 'For Sale' notice in the garden, and about to inspect the property to collect a few further particulars about it to be circularised to possible buyers. The man had been a decent chap and glad of a cup of coffee with his sandwiches. He had finally driven off at about twenty past one.'

'How is it you remember the time so clearly?' Pollard enquired, allowing a hint of scepticism to appear in his tone.

With a barely-controlled snarl Leonard Bolling replied that he himself had an appointment with his solicitors in Littlechester for two o'clock, and had left Bridge Cottage as soon as he had locked the place up when Ford's man had gone. Toye impassively took down the name, address and telephone number of the solicitor, and the name of

73

Ford's representative. Protesting that he didn't spend his life looking at his watch, Leonard Bolling thought that he had spent about half an hour with his solicitor and then gone on to Ford's to discuss the conditions of sale of Bridge Cottage. Accompanied by another of the firm's staff he then viewed two properties on the far side of Littlechester with a view to purchase, and finally drove home to Woodcombe, arriving just before six o'clock.

'What did you do then?' Pollard asked.

'Having had practically no sleep since the Monday night, I went to bed. And as I've nothing further to add to what I've told you, I'd like to know if I'm still suspected of murder.'

'You know perfectly well, Mr Bolling, that you are being interviewed about malicious damage, not intent to murder. Let's keep to the point. You admit digging out the longstone on Mr Kenway-Potter's property and causing it to fall. He may take legal proceedings against you, but that's no concern of ours. We shall check the statement you have made about your movements on April the twenty-third with the people involved. If they confirm what you have told us we shall accept that it would have been virtually impossible for you to have removed the warning notice.'

'Virtually impossible be damned!' Scarlet in the face with fury Leonard Bolling rose on his toes, ludicrously suggesting an enraged bantam cock. 'What the hell do you mean? When could I possibly have pulled up the bloody thing? I keep as clear of the village dolts as I can, but everybody knows Muggett saw it when he ran up the flag on the Wednesday morning. He's been telling the whole place.'

'Let's recap, shall we? Mr Tuke was due at the Manor at seven o'clock that evening. He went up through the woods to see the longstone and the view from the top, starting at roughly six-fifteen. Presumably he would have

74

come down again between six-thirty and six-forty five, intending to collect his car from the Green Man and arrive at the Manor on time. So if you got home here just before six o'clock, there's about twenty minutes unaccounted for. Barely time to have done the job, but just adequate starting from here. And your frankly regrettable motive was very strong: you've made no secret of your obsessive dislike of Mr Kenway-Potter... One more topic, and we'll leave you to get on with your packing-up. Obviously you're a great reader, Mr Bolling'—Pollard indicated the mass of books around them as he spoke. 'Is writing another of your hobbies? Letter-writing in particular?'

Leonard Bolling gave him a look of sheer venom.

'For Detective Chief Superintendent read "licensed bully". Because I'm half your size, you jump to the conclusion that I skulk behind anonymity instead of fighting people in the open who try to do me down, and get away with it under the law, what's more. I shall enjoy seeing you trying to scratch up proof that I wrote those letters. When I write a letter I put my name to it. Lord God Almighty Kenway-Potter will have had one from me this morning if the Post Office is still functioning, telling him I dug up his bloody longstone and if he likes to sue me for damages, he can. He won't, of course. Infra dig.' Leonard concluded with a sardonic chuckle. 'And now you can clear out. If you want me at the police station you can take me by force.'

'That won't be necessary, thank you, Mr Bolling,' Pollard replied equably. 'You've given us all the information we need at the moment. Good morning.'

'Proper little bastard if ever there was one,' Toye remarked uncharacteristically when the front door of Bridge Cottage closed behind them.

'You can't help being sorry for him, you know,' Pollard replied. 'It must be hell to have his obviously above-average intelligence and be next door to a dwarf. Think of people turning round to look at you in the street. Giggling girls in particular.'

'You don't seriously think he hoicked up that notice, do you?' Toye asked as he unlocked the Rover.

'No. On timing it's theoretically possible, but I simply can't believe that a chap of his size and age would have had the stamina when you think of how he'd spent the last eighteen hours or so. We'll check up on his statement, but write him off for the moment, anyway. . . . I can hear a car coming from behind us. Keep your head down in case the Kenway-Potters are coming out of their gate. I want to tackle Fordyce next . . . Good Lord, what's up, do you suppose?'

In the driving mirror they watched an ambulance emerge from the Manor drive. It was closely followed by a Chrysler driven by Rodney Kenway-Potter. He gave the Rover a fleeting glance as he passed but made no attempt to stop. There were no passengers in the car. Both vehicles crossed Lower Bridge and turned right through Woodcombe.

'Heading for Littlechester,' Pollard said. 'There's no point in following for the moment. We'll give them time to get clear of the village, and then drive up to the house and ask if K-P is in. There's almost bound to be a daily woman around at this hour, and we can find out what's happened.'

They let a reasonable interval elapse. Toye then turned the car and they went slowly up the drive towards the Manor, drawing up at the front entrance. As they did so an elderly woman in an overall came out, a key in her hand, and stood staring at them. As Pollard got out and went towards her he saw that she was crying.

'Good morning,' he said. 'I've called to see Mr Kenway-Potter . . . Is something wrong?'

'Oh, sir,' she answered with difficulty, choking back a sob, 'Mrs Kenway-Potter's tried to make away with herself. They've taken her to hospital in Littlechester.'

Back at Littlechester police station Pollard asked at once for enquiries to be made about where Mrs Kenway-Potter had been taken. The information was quickly forthcoming. To his relief she was not at the City's General Hospital, but in an expensive nursing home, St Kilda's, where, he hoped, there would be less red tape to contend with. He decided, however, that it would be self-defeating to try and make contact with Rodney Kenway-Potter at any rate until mid-afternoon.

'Look here,' he said to Toye, over an early snack of sandwiches and lager, 'we can't just sit on our bottoms for this next few hours, all the same. I want you to go around checking the wretched Bolling's various alibis for the afternoon of April the twenty-third, picking up anything useful that you can. The solicitor will be sticky, but you might get some uninhibited opinions on the chap's sanity from the estate agents. I'll stay put in case anything comes in, and do a bit of thinking. O.K.?'

Toye, always methodical, consulted a street map and came to the conclusion that in view of the traffic congestion in the city centre that he would cover the ground more quickly on foot. As he had three people to interview at Ford's, the estate agents, he decided to start there. Although the lunch hour had already started there was a reasonable chance of at any rate one of them being available. His luck was in. Mr Carter, who was handling the sale of Bridge Cottage, saw him almost immediately and proved expansive.

'Extraordinary little cove, Mr Bolling, isn't he?' he said chattily. 'I nearly fell flat the first time he was shown in here. My secretary never batted an eyelid, and I told her afterwards that she deserved a rise if only we'd got the money. What do you want me to tell you about him? Clients' affairs are confidential you know.'

'Merely a routine check, Mr Carter. We understand

that he came to see you on the afternoon of Wednesday, April the twenty-third. Have you a record of when he arrived and how long he stayed?'

The admirable secretary was summoned, and it was soon established that Mr Bolling had arrived at a quarter to three and stayed until about ten minutes past.

'Then Mr Franklin took him over to see a property at West Nethercott, and another at Hanford St John,' she added helpfully. 'He—Mr Franklin, I mean—is out at lunch, but he'll be back at one-thirty.'

'Wotta girl, isn't she? Thank you, m'dear,' Mr Carter commented breezily. 'See that he hangs on when he gets back. Inspector Toye wants to see him.'

Toye asked if it would be possible to have a word with whoever had gone out to Woodcombe on April the twenty-first to put up a 'For Sale' board at Bridge Cottage.'

'That'll have been young Green. See what he's up to, Pam, and tell him to stand by.'

By now Mr Carter had become uninhibitedly garrulous but his opinion of Leonard Bolling was entirely predictable and Toye learnt nothing new. Money was certainly no problem to him. He had paid a fancy price for Bridge Cottage and was dropping a packet on it without turning a hair. Buying a nice little place outside Wynford, too, and not even waiting for completion before clearing out of his Woodcombe house.

Mr Green turned out to be a junior member of the firm, rather overawed at being interviewed by a Scotland Yard Inspector. He stated that he had arrived at Bridge Cottage at about a quarter to twelve on April the twenty-third, and had hardly started getting the board up when the owner arrived. A suspicious little gent who had followed him from room to room while he was collecting particulars that Mr Carter wanted. Watched him through a window while he ate some sandwiches in the firm's car afterwards, too, but he had laid on a mug of coffee.

78

'Can you remember what time you left?' Toye asked.

'Quarter past one. I'd got two more jobs to fit in that afternoon, and was keeping an eye on my watch.'

Toye thanked him and made a note of the time. It fitted in with Leonard Bolling's appointment with his solicitor at two o'clock. If he was going to make it he would have had to start off by one-twenty or one twenty-five at latest, just allowing him time to lock up Bridge Cottage before starting.

Mr Franklin had returned punctually from his lunch and was available on the stroke of half-past one. He was intermediate in age and rank in the firm between Messrs Carter and Green, and struck Toye as more perceptive than either of them. He volunteered the information that Mr Bolling was recognised by Ford's as a bit of an oddity, and that he himself had not looked forward to escorting him to view properties. However the drive to West Nethercott had been an unexpected let-up. The old gentleman had got into the back of the car and dropped off to sleep.

'As a matter of fact, Inspector, I didn't think he looked too good,' Mr Franklin said. 'I hoped he wasn't going to have a heart attack or a stroke or something. Anyway we got to West Nethercott all right and he perked up. The vendor of the property had moved out, so we could give the place the once-over pretty thoroughly. Mr Bolling said the house would suit him well enough, but when he went round the garden and found it backed on to the garden of another house he turned the property down there and then. No privacy, he said. He must have got a thing about privacy judging by the report in the local paper about that fishing syndicate injunction business.'

The visit to Hanford St John had been a complete frost. The house they were due to inspect turned out to be immediately opposite another one. Mr Bolling had refused even to get out of the car.

'What time did you get back here?' Toye asked.

'Twenty to five. Mr Bolling had slept all the way again, and I was honestly rather rattled to think of him driving himself home to Woodcombe. I thought a cuppa might buck him up so I asked him if he'd care to come and have one. I was a bit surprised that he accepted, but he seemed glad of it. He'd got the palm of his right hand bandaged up, and I asked him if it made driving difficult, but he said no. He'd had a minor accident but it had almost healed.'

'What time did he leave?' Toye asked.

'Just gone five. I went down to our car park where he'd left his van and saw him off, not feeling too good about it with the rush hour traffic building up.'

Toye thanked Mr Franklin for his help and started off for the office of French, Halliday and Broughton, Leonard Bolling's solicitors. He reflected that the call on Ford's had at any rate produced some evidence that Bolling was pretty well all in by the end of the afternoon of Wednesday, April the twenty-third. Add to this the delays of the rush hour, and it seemed that he probably would not have got back to Bridge Cottage earlier than just before six o'clock, arriving home in no state to rush out and pull up the warning notice. Not conclusive evidence, but a step nearer to it.

After some delay at the solicitors' office Toye was admitted to the presence of Mr Halliday, the partner who dealt with Leonard Bolling's business. He was coolly received, but on his stating that he merely wanted to make a routine check on times the atmosphere became more relaxed. Asked about the time at which Leonard Bolling had arrived to keep an appointment on April the twenty-third, Mr Halliday consulted his engagement book. He clearly remembered, he said, that the last appointment of the morning had outrun its allotted time, and consequently he had been late in going out to lunch and a few minutes late in returning. Mr Bolling had already arrived and had been announced at about ten minutes past two. He had stayed for about twenty minutes. This was confirmed by Mr Halliday's secretary who had noted Mr Bolling's departure at two-thirty-five.

'Thank you, sir,' Toye said courteously, playing for time by making an entry in his notebook. He sensed that behind his professional decorum Mr Halliday had his full share of normal human curiosity. 'Is it in order to ask you if Mr Bolling seemed to be his usual self that afternoon?'

Mr Halliday toyed with a paperweight.

'Presumably you have met Mr Bolling, Inspector, so we can take it as read that his usual self, as you put it, would appear unusual to most people. The thing that struck me that afternoon was that he was much less aggressive than usual. Quite pleased with himself, in fact.'

'In spite of the fact that he had failed to get an injunction against Mr Kenway-Potter's fishing syndicate that morning, and been landed with costs into the bargain?' Toye commented.

'I needn't tell you that I had done my utmost to prevent him from applying for that injunction. He's not a fool by any means, and in the end came to realise that he hadn't a hope of getting it. But I couldn't persuade him to withdraw his application. He's as obstinate as a mule, and said he intended to go down with all his guns firing, and then clear out of the place. Money's no problem for him, I may add. No, reverting to his looking pleased with himself, I think it was probably relief at getting the whole business over.'

'I think I can add a further explanation, sir, speaking in confidence. Mr Bolling admitted to Chief Superintendent Pollard and myself this morning that he had brought about the collapse of the Woodcombe Manor longstone in the early hours of April the twenty-third. He also told us he'd written to tell Mr Kenway-Potter that he was responsible, what's more.'

'Good God! How on earth did a chap of his size possibly manage it?' Mr Halliday exclaimed. 'I wonder if Mr Kenway-Potter will institute proceedings for trespass and wilful damage? And,' he went on, viewing the situation from a personal angle, 'whether Mr Bolling will want us to go on acting for him when he has moved to Wynford ... I remember now that he had his right hand bandaged. It's a whacking great thing, that longstone. He was damn lucky that it didn't fall on top of him. No wonder he was feeling pleased with himself, and looked a bit tired, I noticed, too. Been up most of the night, I suppose'. . . .

Toye, sensing that a number of awkward questions were taking shape in Mr Halliday's mind, decided to extricate himself before they were put to him.

'Well, sir,' he said, 'I'm grateful for your help. I must get back now and report to Chief Superintendent Pollard.'

Outside on the pavement he paused briefly to consider his next move. Over years of working with Pollard he had learnt to recognise his Chief's need for spells of solitude in which to chew over the current case. Checking Leonard Bolling's alibis had not taken quite long enough, and there was a bit of time to fill in. Up to now the Woodcombe affair had been elusive and vaguely unsatisfactory. Possibly his presence would not be required later in the evening. He decided that it would be a good idea to find out what was on at Littlechester's cinemas. With any luck there might be a Western, his favourite brand of film.

*

In their small temporary office at the police station Pollard had flung up the window and installed himself on a chair as close to it as he could get, his feet up on another. For a few minutes he deliberately made his mind a blank. Then he allowed conscious thoughts to filter back into it and group themselves.

The basic question established itself in the foreground. Had Edward Tuke's death been deliberately engineered, or had it been the chance result of mindless vandalism on somebody's part?

Here at least, Pollard decided, some tangible progress had been made in a short time. The football fans were out of it, and so, he felt personally convinced, was Leonard Bolling. The check-up Toye was now carrying out was necessary for the record, but quite apart from considerations of timing and stamina, uprooting the warning notice on the bridge really didn't fit in very convincingly with the anti-Kenway-Potter motivation behind Bolling's activities at the time. The notice didn't assert Kenway-Potter's status and rights in the way that the prehistoric monument on his property, well-known in antiquarian circles, and his claim to private fishing in the Honey waters did. So all things considered, exit Bolling as a suspect. Unless, of course, some utterly unforeseen fact about him came to light. One could never entirely exclude such a possibility in an investigation.

Well, then, Pollard argued with himself, how about the notice having been pulled up and chucked into the river by some mindless vandal just for the hell of it? Or by someone apparently normal who was intermittently and unsuspectedly round the bend?

He sat staring out of the window and considering these possibilities at some length. Children were, of course, unpredictable. The very young were ruled out because of the physical strength required, and Inspector Deeds had made very detailed enquiries into the activities of the older Woodcombe children after they had come back from Littlechester on the school bus that afternoon. The result of his enquiries had been entirely negative. There was, too, the additional fact that practising for the sports to be held on the forthcoming Bank Holiday was the main preoccupation of the village young at the time. On balance Pollard felt that the children could be ruled out.

He also decided that the idea of a complete outsider with vandalistic leanings appearing in Woodcombe, pulling up the notice and vanishing again, all without trace must be discarded, too. Extraordinary things did happen, but this was really beyond the limits of credibility. There remained the possibility of undetected mental instability in a local resident. Having been born and brought up in a village himself, Pollard was well aware that personal idiosyncrasies rarely pass undetected in small communities. Moreover, Inspector Deeds had also considered this possibility, and made a number of judicious enquiries with no result whatever. Where he had failed, it seemed highly improbable that strangers from Scotland Yard would succeed.

Pollard shifted his position and faced the inescapable outcome of his reasoning up to date: Edward Tuke's death had been brought about deliberately.

His thoughts moved at once to the small group of people with whom the young American was definitely known to have made contact. The Fordyces, the Kenway-Potters, the Wonnacotts and Mrs Rawlings. There had been quite a lot of people in the bar of the Green Man towards the end of Wednesday morning, but no one had come forward and claimed to have been in conversation with Tuke. At first sight this seemed surprising, but no doubt general interest was focussed on the outcome of the County Court case about which he would have known nothing. Of course he had talked to Canon Hugh Allbright in Littlechester Cathedral during the afternoon, but to include this dignitary in a list of potential suspects would be utterly ludicrous on all counts. On the other hand Tuke might have met someone by appointment in Littlechester. An appeal by the local police for any such person to come forward had met with no response. A photograph of Tuke supplied by Integrated Oils had been published in the local newspaper, and it had produced a response from a few people who thought they remembered seeing him in the city on the afternoon of April the twenty-third. However, their evidence was too vague and inconclusive to warrant following up. In any case no one had reported seeing him with another person.

Pollard's mind went back to the incredibly small number of Edward Tuke's known contacts in Woodcombe during the few hours that he had spent there. What conceivable motive could any of them have had for virtually ensuring his fatal fall? At the word 'motive' he pulled himself up sharply. Wasn't it dinned into you from your first day in the C.I.D. that a criminal investigation didn't begin with an enquiry into motive, but with a detailed study of means and opportunity?

His mind went back to the visit to the longstone on his first afternoon in Woodcombe, and the possibility of deliberate misdirection of Tuke that he had suggested to Toye and Deeds. There seemed to be two feasible reconstructions of what could have happened. Somebody who knew that Tuke was going up to see the longstone removed the warning notice in advance, went up himself or herself, simulated surprise at meeting Tuke, managed to delay him until he was running it fine for his supper date with the Kenway-Potters, and finally advised the short cut over the disused bridge to save time. Alternatively, someone met him at the longstone by chance, and persuaded him to go and look at something else of interest while assuring him that the short cut would get him back to his car at the Green Man in ample time, apologised for not escorting him to this second objective on the grounds of a previous engagement, and then took the short cut in order to remove the warning notice and clear off before Tuke came down again.

In the hope of being on some firmer ground at last, Pollard allowed the subject which had been lurking on the threshold of his mind to come to the surface. Mrs Kenway-Potter's attempted suicide might very well have

85

no connection whatever with the case, but she was one of a very small group of possible suspects, and if she had survived, she would have to be interviewed as soon as this was practicable. So, too, would her husband. Except for James Fordyce, he appeared to have had more contact with Edward Tuke than any other member of the group, with possibly the exception of Mrs Rawlings. He turned to the case file again and looked through the notes on the various Tuke contacts. The information had been collected locally and supplemented by reference to the Yard. None of those concerned had a police record. Mrs Rawlings had originally trained as a librarian in a London borough, but soon left her post as an assistant and married, only to be widowed at an early age. She appeared to have small private means as well as a pension, and to have drifted from one temporary job to another until settling at Woodcombe, working part-time for the Littlechester Public Library and becoming a folklore addict with a modest local reputation of being quite knowledgeable.

Pollard pushed the file to one side, and after a brief pause reached for the telephone and asked the operator to put him through to St Kilda's Nursing Home. Three o'clock in the afternoon seemed a suitable time to ring. Medical establishments needed tactful handling...

'St Kilda's Nursing Home,' announced a competent but friendly voice. 'Can I help you?'

'Detective Chief Superintendent Pollard speaking. Would it be possible for me to have a word with Mr Kenway-Potter do you think?'

There was momentary hesitation.

'I think the best course would be for me to put you through to Matron, Chief Superintendent. Would you be kind enough to hold the line for a moment?'

A click was followed by silence. After a full minute's silence an equally pleasant but decidedly more authoritative voice came over the line.

'Good afternoon, Chief Superintendent Pollard. This is Matron speaking. I understand from our receptionist that you want to speak to Mr Kenway-Potter?'

'I should be very grateful if I could, Matron. As I expect you may have heard, I have been sent down by my superiors at Scotland Yard to carry out the reopened enquiry into the death of the late Mr Tuke. As it took place on Mr Kenway-Potter's property, I need his help. To save time, I know the reason for Mrs Kenway-Potter's being in St Kilda's. Is it in order to ask how she is?'

'She is no longer on the danger list, but in a weak state of course. Mr Kenway-Potter has been with her almost continuously. Under the circumstances I think the best thing would be for us to let him know that you are anxious to contact him, and to ask him to call you as soon as he can.'

'Thank you, Matron. That would be most helpful. If he could ring 731485 and ask for me, he will be put through to my temporary office. I shall be there for the next few hours, and in any case he could leave a message' ... 'Yes, quite,' he replied to a further comment, making a hideous grimace at Toye as the latter came quietly into the room, 'I quite understand. Again, many thanks, Matron. Goodbye.'

Pollard rang off and stretched himself.

'That, as you no doubt deduced, was the Queen Pin of St Kilda's Nursing Home,' he told Toye. 'Mrs Kenway-Potter is off the danger list but understandably still in a poorish way. Her husband is with her, but is being informed that we want to contact him. With any luck he'll ring before long and we'll know what the prospects of interviewing him are. Meanwhile, what have you been doing all this time, apart from tactfully leaving me to brood in solitude?'

Toye grinned and gave a resume of his various enquiries.

'I reckon we can scrub Bolling on common sense

grounds,' he concluded.

Pollard agreed.

'I've been thinking over every other possibility of someone removing that bloody notice without any criminal intent,' he said. 'Plain vandalism by local kids, or a mentally disturbed stranger or some unsuspectedly dotty local. I've come to the conclusion that we can scrub the lot of them out, too, unless some new evidence turns up out of the blue. This means working on the assumption that Tuke's death was deliberately engineered. So in the best tradition of C.I.D. investigators we concentrate first on opportunity, and resist the temptation of speculating about motive. And obviously we begin by concentrating on the Woodcombe people known to have been in contact with him. How's that for a programme?'

'Spot on,' Toye replied without hesitation.

'Right. Well, this is how I think it could have been done.'

As Pollard finished outlining the alternative methods of directing Edward Tuke to the broken footbridge that he had thought out, the desk telephone bleeped and he picked up the receiver.

'K-P', he mouthed to Toye as he waited for the incoming call to be put through.

There was no telephone extension in the room so Toye had to be content with piecing the conversation together in the light of Pollard's contributions. He waited patiently, as usual occupying himself with sorting and rearranging the papers scattered on the table.

'We're going over to Woodcombe Manor,' Pollard announced at last. 'As soon as we've had some grub. Kenway-Potter says he simply must go home and cope with the faithful retainer we left in tears. He offered to come back here again, but I felt that in common humanity I must make the offer. He's had one hell of a day. All right, I see you look disapproving. I know a suspect is in a stronger position if he's interviewed on his home ground,

88

but a show of humanity can be disarming... There's only one thing I thought was just a shade off-key. I thought the chap sounded—well, almost buoyant.'

Toye looked surprised.

'Wouldn't you feel on top of the world if Mrs Pollard had been snatched back from attempted suicide?'

Pollard's imagination struggled to conjure up a situation in which Jane had taken an overdose of sleeping tablets washed down with whisky.

'My God, yes ... I suppose years in this soul-destroying job make it difficult for me to accept decent human explanations of people's behaviour. Let's go and find something to eat.'

Before they had reached the door the telephone bleeped. Pollard swung round on his heel and grabbed the receiver to learn that he was wanted by the Coroner's Office.

'Inquest to be reopened,' he told Toye a couple of minutes later. 'Come on before anybody else rings us.'

Chapter Five

Rodney Kenway-Potter's study was at the back of Wood-combe Manor with a view across the garden to the Honey winding through the meadows below Lower Bridge. French windows stood wide open, letting in the soft warm air of the June evening and the scent of flowers. Pollard, also conscious of well-filled bookcases and some good pictures, felt briefly envious.

'Shall we sit over by the windows?' Rodney suggested, beginning to propel inviting leather armchairs with Toye's assistance. 'All the advantages of being out of doors without the midges. As you're on official business I won't press drinks on you, but don't think me inhospit-able.'

'Far from it,' Pollard assured him. 'One doesn't often find people accepting the drill as a matter of course ... I do like this view of yours.'

'Pleasant, isn't it? I do like some foreground as well as background. I shouldn't care to look straight out to sea, for instance.'

During a brief exchange of generalities Pollard was again conscious of a latent buoyancy in Rodney Kenway-Potter. He put out an exploratory feeler.

'We're grateful to you for seeing us tonight,' he said. 'You must have had a harrowing day. We'll be as brief as possible.'

'Don't apologise, Superintendent. You've got your job to do. And as far as I'm concerned it's a case of Jordan passed. The doctors assure me that there's no longer any immediate anxiety about my wife. The sheer relief has sent me over the moon. It's been a miracle, really. I went off to an important committee meeting in Littlechester at nine this morning. I'm up to the neck in local conservation projects, and we were due to meet a chap from the Department of the Environment. We'd hardly started arriving when a message came through that he'd had a car crash en route and was in hospital. The meeting was postponed, and I came home almost at once, just in time.'

Relaxed in his chair, with one arm hanging down and a hand fondling a golden cocker spaniel's ear, he gave Pollard a smile that could have been taken as encouraging. Pollard felt his hackles stir slightly.

'First and foremost, Mr Kenway-Potter,' he said in a more official tone, 'please understand that your wife's action this morning is no concern of ours unless it has a bearing on Edward Tuke's death. It's to establish whether it has or not that makes it necessary to ask you for some information, I'm afraid. But you can be assured that anything non-relevant that you tell us won't go any further.'

Rodney Kenway-Potter released the spaniel's ear and shifted his position.

'Unfortunately,' he said, 'it very definitely is involved with the poor chap's death. If you hadn't contacted me this afternoon I should have got on to you after what my wife told me at St Kilda's. Briefly she's had five of these bloody anonymous letters. She never let on, or I should have insisted on them being handed over to the Littlechester police, of course. I hate to tell you, but she's burnt the lot.'

'This is important.' Out of the corner of his eye Pollard registered Toye with his notebook on his knee. 'Was Mrs Kenway-Potter able to give you any details about them?'

'Yes. As far as I could gather, they—the actual letters—were identical in externals with the ones the police and the *Littlechester Evening News* had. Block capitals made with a stencil on ordinary greaseproof paper.

The envelopes were different in one respect. They were the ordinary business manila sort, but my wife's name and address were stuck on the outside, and had been cut off the postcards with printed headings that she uses for her official correspondence. I'll give you one from her desk'...

Alone for less than a minute, Pollard and Toye exchanged glances. Rodney Kenway-Potter returned with a couple of white postcards of standard size. Their heading read MRS R.J.W. KENWAY-POTTER WOODCOMBE MANOR WOODCOMBE LITTLE-CHESTER L132 3PZ. Telephone Littlechester 59432.

'Thank you,' Pollard said. 'We'll keep these, if we may.' He passed them over to Toye, who asked about postmarks.

'They were all posted in Littlechester and sent by second-class mail. The postmarks showed the dates, but not the times of posting. We only have one delivery of mail a day out here. It arrives about 9.30 a.m. Except for the first and last ones my wife is by now uncertain of when the others arrived.'

'Has Mrs Kenway-Potter much official correspondence?' Pollard asked.

'Yes, quite a bit. Here in the village she's the W.I. president and secretary of the P.C.C. Then she's involved in various things in Littlechester like the National Trust Centre and an Old People's Home and so on. I'm afraid there's the heck of a lot of these postcards around.'

'Can we go on to the content of these letters now? To put it crudely, were you satisfied that your wife was clear-headed enough this afternoon to tell you—well, accurately—about this?'

'A perfectly fair question, Superintendent. Yes, I was. I should have said before that she mercifully underestimated the lethal dose of the sleeping tablets she took. Also, the relief of telling me about the letters at long last had the effect of making her relax.'

'Quite. About the contents, then?'

Rodney Kenway-Potter crossed his legs, folded his arms and frowned slightly.

'Naturally I couldn't press her for the exact wording. The first three seemed to be variations on the theme that this house was an ideal base for going down unobserved and yanking up the warning notice on the old bridge. The fourth was more specific, and asked what she was doing at five past six in the evening of April the twenty-third, when the writer claimed to have rung this number and got no answer. This one rattled my wife badly. Apparently she had gone into the vegetable garden to get some fresh parsley and actually heard the telephone ringing just at this time. She hurried back, but whoever it was rang off just as she got to the house. The fifth letter, which came this morning soon after I had left for Littlechester, suggested that it would be better for me, and our children, if my wife made away with herself.'

Silence descended as Pollard mentally reviewed this information. One of the French windows swung inwards in a light breeze. Toye got up unobtrusively and fastened it back. A sudden outpouring of song came from a thrush perched on a rhododendron bush.

'Once again,' Pollard said, 'all this points to someone living in, or very near this village. Do you know of anyone who is hostile to your wife and almost certainly unbalanced into the bargain?'

'No,' Rodney Kenway-Potter replied, without hesitation. 'She is a charming and genuine person, as you will see for yourself, and does a lot for Woodcombe without the Lady Bountiful touch. It's fair to say that she's much liked. Loved in some cases. Of course we've got a few families with leftish views who are anti-gentry on principle, but I've never felt that they're personally hostile to me or my family. The idea of any member of them sending my wife those letters is just fantastic.'

'I'd like to ask you about Mrs Kenway-Potter's general

state of physical and mental health lately,' Pollard said, after a further pause. 'Has she been suffering from depression, for instance?'

'Until this Tuke business she seemed absolutely her normal self. Of course, time passes. She is fifty-one: at the so-called 'difficult age' for women, and has been apt to get tired more easily than she did ten years ago, but nothing more than that. The row over the fishing syndicate with the wretched Bolling didn't bother her unduly, although it has been a damned nuisance. But young Tuke's death upset her badly. You see, it was the second time there'd been a fatal accident on our property. Six years ago a young boy from the village fell out of a tree in the woods not far from the house. He fractured his skull and was dying when found. He was trespassing, poor little blighter, and the coroner emphasised that we were absolutely blameless, but naturally we were very distressed. So when the Tuke disaster happened, again on our property, you'll understand how we felt. Once more the coroner went to some length to say categorically that we had taken all proper precautions and were not at fault in any way, but you can imagine how upsetting it was. However, by the middle of May my wife had braced up and was carrying on with her various activities, and I had no qualms about going up to London for the inside of a week to deal with arrears of business. I should explain that the family owns Woodland Hotels. I went up on May the twelfth, leaving early by car, and the first anonymous letter arrived after I'd left. I rang my wife several times and thought she seemed a bit preoccupied, but assumed that she was catching up on things as I was myself. When I got home again on May the seventeenth I found her decidedly edgy and quite unlike herself. The obvious conclusion was that we both needed a good holiday, and I tried, not very successfully, to interest her in plans for going abroad in early June. Then, as you know, a letter went to the *Littlechester Evening News*, and by last weekend we were being subjected to a frankly outrageous invasion by newsmen and photographers. My wife took refuge indoors and I kept them at bay as best I could. By Wednesday evening most of them had gone off, and I persuaded her to come out in the car and have a drink in Littlechester for a change of scene. By this time it was common knowledge that the Yard had been asked to look into Tuke's death, and the prospect of the whole thing being reopened seemed to upset her. You'll remember we saw you in the bar of the Ring and Crozier, and she was unwilling for me to make contact with you as I felt I should do. She also had been reluctant for me to go to the committee this morning, in case the Press returned, but later yesterday evening she changed her mind and said I obviously ought to go... Look here, Superintendent, don't let's beat about the bush. It sticks out a mile that either my wife or I could have taken up that warning notice in the late afternoon or early evening of April the twenty-third, and whoever made that telephone call is trying to prove that she did. What the hell can we do to convince you that neither of us had ever set eyes on young Tuke until that brief encounter in the Green Man, that morning? I suppose you'll want to question her?'

'Not, of course, until we have her doctors' permission,' Pollard replied soothingly, 'and of course we shall try to cut down the interview to the minimum. You probably don't realise that enquiries made both here and in the States have failed to find any link between you and your wife on one hand, and Edward Tuke on the other. I know it's irritating to be asked to repeat oneself, but it would help us to get a clear picture of exactly what happened in the afternoon and evening of April the twenty-third if we could just run through the statement you made to Inspector Deeds. We've got a copy here.'

'Of course I'll go through it again if it would be helpful. Some point might strike a fresh mind coming to it, I suppose.'

Toye found the statement in the file, and at a nod from Pollard read it aloud. The Kenway-Potters had arrived home from luncheon with Rear-Admiral Slade and his wife in Marycott at about three-thirty. Mrs Kenway-Potter had gone up to her room and rested until about four-thirty, when she brought out a tea tray to her husband who had been sitting in the garden with the newspapers. At about five-thirty she had gone indoors to begin preparations for supper, and he had taken the dog for a walk on the Marycott road. A friend, John Scott, who lived in the next village beyond Marycott and commuted daily to Littlechester, had overtaken him and drawn up. They had chatted for about five minutes before he went on and Rodney Kenway-Potter retraced his steps. After going on to Lower Bridge for a look at the river, he returned home. His wife was having a bath and changing, and Mrs Boggis, their domestic helper, was functioning in the kitchen. He had gone upstairs himself to change into a clean shirt, and come down to assemble drinks. From then on they had waited, at first patiently and finally with some annoyance for Edward Tuke. When he had still not turned up at eight o'clock, Rodney had rung firstly the Green Man and then James Fordyce, before going out to check up on the paths leading to Old Grim. He had discovered Edward Tuke's body at about half-past eight, dragged it clear of the water and run to the Green Man for help.

As he finished reading, Toye looked up.

'Just one point, sir. When you went down to take a look at the river, did you see any sign of Mr Bolling?'

'Never set eyes on the old devil. That reminds me'. . . .

'May we come back to Bolling in a moment?' Pollard said. 'Is Mrs Boggis the lady we met outside the house this morning in such distress?'

'Yes, and thank you for being so decent to her. She's been with the family ever since she left school at fourteen.'

'Is she resident here?'

'Yes and no. She married one of the gardeners, and when he died and my father wanted the cottage for another man he made a small flat for her over the stables. She comes in every day from nine to twelve, except Fridays and Sundays, and helps out if we entertain in the evenings. She's back on an even keel now that I've convinced her that my wife is going to be all right. Will you want to see her?'

'I think we'd better have a word with her for the record. Would tomorrow morning be possible?'

'No problem. She'll be doing her usual stint in the house here between nine and twelve. I'll tell her to expect you. I shan't be around myself. Our daughter is coming down from London on an early train, and I'm meeting her at the station and taking her straight to St Kilda's'...

'You were going to say something about Mr Bolling, I think?' Pollard said.

'What I feel like saying would turn the air blue,' Rodney Kenway-Potter replied, getting up and going to his desk. 'Just read this. It came by the first post today, after I'd gone to Littlechester. I've only just got round to opening my mail.'

Pollard read the letter of which Leonard Bolling had given him an accurate summary early in the day.

'Will you bring an action against him for malicious damage?' he asked.

'No. I'm not giving him the satisfaction of getting me into court again. To be honest, the longstone doesn't mean a thing to me. It's rather a bind to have to let the public go up and look at it, but one can't be very well refuse, and outrage the archaeologists. With all the vandalism that goes on these days the fewer people who wander about one's property, the better.'

'You've had it re-erected, I see,' Pollard commented.

'I felt I had to. Quite apart from the archaeologist

97

johnnies, it's a sort of status symbol to the village. If Bolling's got any sense at all he'll clear out before it gets round that he dug the thing up. He's disliked enough as it is.'

'Harking back for a moment to the information you gave Littlechester about your conversation with Tuke in the pub, did he strike you as an obsessional sightseer, as one can fairly say some Americans are when they come over here?'

'He certainly seemed to have enjoyed seeing the stock sights and going around, but I should have thought him too intelligent to rush about covering as much ground as possible.'

'Did it surprise you to learn that he'd gone up to see the longstone?'

Rodney Kenway-Potter suddenly grinned.

'Now you put it to me, yes. You haven't met Mrs Rawlings, yet, have you? She's quite knowledgeable on local history, but once she starts on folklore she's apt to hand out the most awful twaddle as solid fact. I felt a bit conscious-stricken at letting her loose on Tuke, but my wife and I had to hurry off to lunch with the Slades. I thought he might be amused by her yarn about Old Grim and a boss in the church. I wish to God I'd never done it, or asked the poor chap up to supper that night. To answer your question, I shouldn't have expected him to want to see the longstone after listening to her tripe about it.'

'Well, thank you for being so co-operative, Mr Kenway-Potter,' Pollard said, getting to his feet. 'We'll now take ourselves off. All things considered, I imagine you'll welcome your change of neighbours at Bridge Cottage in the near future.'

He thought, but was not sure, that there was an almost imperceptible pause before Rodney Kenway-Potter agreed heartily, adding that James Fordyce was a most awfully good chap.

*

Clearly Woodcombe kept early hours. The Rover passed along the deserted village streets where only a few lights showed in upper windows and the Green Man presented a blank dark facade. As Toye halted at the road junction the church clock striking eleven was distantly audible. He turned right for Littlechester and the car swept effortlessly up the long hill through the woods. Pollard watched the flat theatrically scenic effect of an endless succession of tree trunks and hedgerows caught in the glare of the headlights, while allowing his thoughts to assemble and reassemble without conscious direction.

'Let's pull in for a bit,' he said suddenly as they came out of the woods on to the crest of the rise.

Toye drew up by the gate where, six weeks earlier, Edward Tuke had leant, drinking in the landscape and planning his future. Pollard let down the window and breathed in the soft air redolent with warm moist earth and young bracken. There was still a faint luminosity in the midsummer sky, and on the far horizon a harsher light indicated the city of Littlechester. It was a still night and the enfolding silence absolute.

'Well, one thing's a dead cert,' he said after an interval, 'Edward Tuke wasn't a premarital indiscretion of Mrs Kenway-Potter's. That possibility's ruled out by the official statement of his parentage and date of birth that came through from the States by way of the F.B.I. and the Yard. He was born over there in '52, and the K-Ps were married in '50. Whatever made her try to kill herself it wasn't the prospect of her having had an illegitimate kid coming out.'

Toye agreed.

'And no motive you can see for her husband to team up with her over getting rid of Tuke, was there?'

'It's occurred to me that there is another possibility, you know,' Pollard said meditatively. 'Suppose Mrs K-P

99

had an illegitimate child by Tuke Senior before he emigrated in '48. She's fifty-one now, her husband says, so
she'd have been about eighteen when he went. Did he
slope off and leave her in the lurch? Her people could
have hushed it up and had the child adopted, and then
thankfully married her off to her cousin in '50. Of course
young Tuke wouldn't have identified her under her
married name, but his name could have given her a nasty
jolt And there might have been a resemblance to his
father, too.'

'You'd hardly think old Tuke would have told his son
about a woman he'd seduced, right down to her name,'
Toye objected.

'In theory Edward Tuke could have got on to it in some
other way. He was his aunt's sole legatee, and must have
gone through her personal papers and belongings after
she died. He might have come across some reference to an
older illegitimate nephew.'

Toye remained dubious.

'The way people carry on these days,' he said, 'you'd
hardly expect a woman in the Kenway-Potter class to
commit murder or suicide because she'd slipped up over
thirty years ago.'

'The moral climate's changed quite a lot since 1950,
but she'd probably feel that the story would disgrace the
K-P set-up if it got out. And Edward Tuke's reason for
coming to the U.K. was to research into his parents'
history. It could have come out. If there was a child the
birth would have been registered. And who'...

Pollard's voice trailed off suddenly. There was such a
lengthy pause that Toye shifted his position.

'I think it's unlikely,' Pollard said at last, 'that if Mrs
K-P had an illegitimate child before marrying K-P she
would have told him about it. From her local commitments she seems to have a sense of status, and he certainly
has. He mightn't have been prepared to marry her if he'd
known about a previous lapse. Has he found out through

getting interested in his family history? And if so, doesn't it seem possible that Fordyce knows about it too? He's been teaching Kenway-Potter the ropes over making searches. They're buddies: wouldn't they have decided to keep quiet? And then, out of the blue, young Edward Tuke turns up' . . .

'Do you mean,' Toye asked, after digesting this idea, 'that they might both have been in on his death?'

'An unholy alliance between them would have made the whole business much more workable, wouldn't it? Fordyce could have persuaded Tuke to go up to the longstone. Said it really was a chance to see an outstanding prehistoric monument. We know he showed him the way up. But instead of coming straight home he could have nipped along the river bank and removed the notice. Meanwhile Kenway-Potter leaves the Marycott road, cuts through the woods, meets Tuke at the longstone, chats, advises him to go on up to the top to see the view and shows him the short cut down to the bridge. Then he heads for the Manor, arriving in time to spruce up for Tuke's arrival at seven, possibly going down the road to Lower Bridge first, as he said.'

The two sat in silence, contemplating the new possibility.

'We must get a much firmer grasp of facts before taking any action on this,' Pollard said. 'Timing's tight, for one thing. K-P's alleged meeting with his commuter pal must be checked. There's a lot of work ahead, but I think we'll stick to the plan of seeing the Boggis woman first tomorrow.'

'Before we tackle Fordyce?' Toye asked in surprise.

'Yea. For one thing we don't want to alert K-P. We said we'd be going along to see Mrs Boggis tomorrow morning so we'd better stick to it. For another we may get some quite unexpected gen from her. She's been with the family man and boy and I bet there's precious little she doesn't know about them. We'll get her talking—that

101

probably won't be difficult—and try to steer the conversation towards useful topics. Whether Rodney K-P and James Fordyce see a lot of each other, for instance. But you know it's a depressing thought that quite apart from finding out who directed Edward Tuke to that bridge with criminal intent, there's the problem of who's behind these anonymous letters. Who wrote the ruddy things? If Kenway-Potter and/or Fordyce engineered Tuke's death, who has it in for Mrs K-P quite independently? Is there some other local person who had a link with Tuke, and if so, who the hell is it? The incontrovertible evidence that he was born in the States and never left there until he came over here last March is damned inconvenient, isn't it?'

Toye agreed. They relapsed into silence again. An owl suddenly hooted from the woods behind them. Pollard leant out of the window of the car, cupped his hands and replied with such a faithful imitation that the usually impassive Toye exclaimed in astonishment. After a couple of moments the owl replied on a note of suspicion and annoyance.

'Exactly how I'm feeling myself,' Pollard commented. 'I learnt that trick from an old chap in the village when I was a kid. Come on, we'd better head for base and get some sleep. I'm pinning my hopes on Boggis being garrulous tomorrow. Better still, indiscreet.'

Chapter Six

When Pollard woke the next morning his thoughts quickly reverted to James Fordyce and the conversation with Toye the night before. Curious, he reflected, that one wasn't struck more forcibly by the obvious. After all, Fordyce was the one person in Woodcombe who was known to have previous contacts with Edward Tuke. After the Boggis interview, he decided, they would go on to his bungalow. Anything that came up about the chap's relations with Kenway-Potter must be taken further, if possible. And they would go over Fordyce's statement on his dealings with Tuke in detail. Picking up his watch from the bedside table Pollard saw that it was already a quarter past eight; a perfectly reasonable time at which to ring someone about an important appointment. A local telephone directory was provided and he sat on the side of the bed and dialled the Fordyce number. A woman's voice, of the type which he classified as 'bright', answered.

'May I speak to Mr James Fordyce, please?' he asked. 'This is Chief Superintendent Pollard.'

A little gasp at the other end of the line was followed by a fluttering assurance that the speaker would get him at once. There was an agitated cry of 'James', the sound of running footsteps and distant conversation. Then a purposeful tread and a man's voice.

'Fordyce here,' it said briefly.

'I'd be glad of some help from you, Mr Fordyce. As I'm sure you know, the coroner has reopened the inquest into the death of the late Mr Edward Tuke, and I have been instructed by my superiors to conduct an enquiry into the circumstances. My apologies for calling you so early but I have a lot to fit into today. Would it be convenient if I called at about ten this morning?'

There was a moment's hesitation.

'As a matter of fact I'd planned to come into Littlechester this morning to work in the reference library. How about my coming along to the police station? Any time would suit me if you'd just give the librarian a ring and ask him to contact me. It's only a few minutes' walk.'

Once again Pollard heard a small gasp.

'That's a very helpful suggestion, Mr Fordyce,' he replied. 'Thank you. I'll do just that. It will be some time in the later part of the morning.'

He jotted down the telephone number he was given and rang off. As he dressed he remembered that the Chief Constable had said that Fordyce had married a woman much younger than himself.

'It sounded to me as though he might have fallen for a dolly with a pretty face and precious little behind it,' he told Toye over breakfast. 'It certainly stood out a mile that he'd no intention of being interviewed by us with her in the offing. Given to listening at doors, perhaps? I'll swear he'd no idea of coming in to the library this morning before I called... You know, if Boggis doesn't take more than about half an hour it might be possible to fit in Mrs Rawlings too, if she's around.'

Toye agreed that this made sense, and half an hour later they were once more on the road to Woodcombe. They turned into the Manor drive just before half-past nine. As they rounded a curve in the drive they saw that the front door was standing open, and a moment later the grey-haired woman they had met on the previous day appeared on the steps.

'This might take quite a bit of time,' Pollard told Toye as they drew up. 'You can't hustle a Faithful Retainer.'

It transpired that Rodney Kenway-Potter had told Mrs

Boggis to take them to his study. The armchairs had been returned to their usual position, and it was with difficulty that Pollard persuaded her to occupy one of them. She perched on the edge of the seat and looked anxiously at the callers. A period piece, Pollard thought, registering her servicable overall, thick stockings and flat-heeled shoes.

'I'm afraid you had a dreadful shock yesterday, Mrs Boggis,' he began sympathetically. 'We feel very bad at bothering you so soon, but it's the people who were on the spot who can help us so much when something goes wrong. Did you go into Mrs Kenway-Potter's room and find her unconscious?'

'Oh, no, sir,' Mrs Boggis twisted her work-worn hands together. 'I wasn't over here. That was the dreadful thing. And I can't help feeling that was why Mrs Kenway-Potter chose yesterday to do what—what she did. That, and Master Rodney being over to Littlechester for a meeting. But the Good Lord was watching over us'. . . .

With a few questions Pollard and Toye managed to get the record straight. Friday was Mrs Boggis's day off. She didn't come in on a Friday, not unless something very particular was on, and then Mrs Kenway-Potter would make her take another day that week. No, the first she'd known of anything wrong was the telephone ringing over in her flat. They'd had it put in to save the running backwards and forwards, and in case she was scared in the night, being on her own, or was took bad. Master Rodney told her to come at once and she'd run all the way over. He'd rung for the ambulance and told her to get hot bottles quick.

None of this information was particularly valuable although it filled a gap in the record, and Pollard took the conversation back to another traumatic occasion: the evening of April the twenty-third . . . She had come over a bit early, knowing what a tiring day they'd had going to court, and all because of that wicked old man down at Bridge Cottage telling lies about the fishing and the cars making a noise. The gentlemen as came over to fish parked nearer to her than to him, and she'd never been bothered by them. And the wickedness of him knocking down Old Grim and writing to say he'd done it, bold as brass. Why, when it was found out that the football hooligans hadn't pulled up the notice at the end of the bridge, people couldn't understand why the old wretch wasn't taken up by the police for doing it. Just up his street, it was.

Pollard assured her that the police had gone into absolutely everything Mr Bolling had done after coming out of court on April the twenty-third, and were satisfied that he would not have been able to commit this particular anti-social act. A mulish expression came into her face, and he hastily introduced the topic of her long association with the Kenway-Potter family. The diversion was almost too successful. Now highly voluble, Mrs Boggis poured out a stream of reminiscences covering an association of fifty-four years and the regimes of Master Rodney's grandfather and father, working up to his own marriage in 1950 and inheritance of the estate in 1962. At intervals she got up to fetch photographs, and Toye used the opportunity to jot down dates. Pollard commented with sincerity on Mrs Kenway-Potter's good looks to Mrs Boggis's pleasure.

'She was the loviest bride I ever saw, and she's passed it on to her daughter, Miss Amanda ... this is Miss Amanda, taken last year.... They're quite a good-looking family, no doubt about it. Master Rodney and his lady are cousins, although she came from a different branch of the family. A Miss Hartley, she was, from a village called Lockwood near Worcester. Very interested in family history, Master Rodney's become since Mr Fordyce came to live in Woodcombe, and they got to know each other. Mr Fordyce finds out about people's

106

families for a living you see, and he's shown Master Rodney how to do it. They've been up to London together to places where they keep old papers, and Master Rodney's working on his wife's side of the family now'....

★

'Pull up outside the gates for a minute until we recover,' Pollard said, as the Rover moved decorously down the drive.

'Fell into our laps like a ripe plum, didn't it?' Toye remarked with an uncharacteristically vivid turn of phrase. 'I could have done with that coffee she offered us, though.'

'Take courage. The folklore woman we'll call on next: she may offer us some made of ground acorns, I expect. We simply couldn't afford to spend any more time with Boggis, once we got what we hoped for. Let's face it. We've found out something we wanted to know, but all it amounts to is that Fordyce has got K-P keen on his family history and shown him the ropes. It's possible that they hit on something involving Tuke and Mrs K-P which added up to a motive for getting him out of the way before he learnt about it himself. But all this is pure conjecture at present. The next step is to get on to Fordyce, but there's time to take Mrs Rawlings en route. The thing we must try to get out of her is whether Tuke said anything to her in the Green Man about going up to see the longstone, or if she recommended him to go herself. Push these unworthy thoughts of elevenses out of your mind and we'll press on. She lives at the far end of the village, next door to the Fordyces apparently.'

'Her place is called "Yesterday",' Toye contributed sardonically, switching on the engine. 'I saw it on the gate.'

A couple of minutes later they drew up outside. It was a

cottage of the traditional Woodcombe type, built in grey stone and thatched. The small front garden was well-kept. Their arrival had been observed, and as they walked up the short gravelled path the door opened. Pollard was struck by the contrast between the attractive cottage and the woman on the threshold, clumsily built with a slightly but perceptibly deformed left shoulder and a large flat face. She wore a shapeless grey dress and plimsolls.

'Good morning,' he said politely. 'You are Mrs Rawlings, I think. I'm Detective-Chief Superintendent Pollard of Scotland Yard, and this is my colleague, Detective-Inspector Toye.'

He saw small sharp eyes taking them both in.

'You needn't trouble to tell me what you've come about,' she replied, ignoring his greeting. 'The whole village knows what you're here for. Come inside if you want to, but I've nothing to add to what I told the policeman from Littlechester, and put my name to when he'd had it typed out . . . My living room's upstairs.'

They followed her up a short steep flight of stairs into the front room on the first floor. From the window there was a view across the valley of the Honey to the Manor Woods and the clearing and the rock pile at the top of the hill. The room was more like an office than a place to live and relax in, Pollard thought. The walls were hung with photographs and mediocre watercolours of antiquities, and in a hasty glance he identified Stonehenge, the White Horse of Uffington, and old Grim in pride of place. In one of the bookcases he caught sight of the monumental unabridged edition of Sir James Frazer's *Golden Bough*. On the kneeholed desk in the window were box files and folders, a pile of typescripts, a portable typewriter and an expensive-looking pair of binoculars. Mrs Rawlings sat down in the revolving chair drawn up to the desk, twirled it round to face the room and pointed to two upright chairs. Toye deftly placed one for Pollard in a position which gave him a good view of her face. If she was aware of the manoeuvre she gave no sign of it.

'Well, now,' Pollard opened pleasantly, 'we've read the very clear statement you made to Inspector Deeds. There's no need to go over it in detail. The main thing we want to know is your impression of the late Mr Edward Tuke.'

He registered faint surprise and a suggestion of relief in the impassive face.

'It's wiser not to speak ill of the dead,' she replied, 'but since this is a police matter I suppose I've no choice. My impression of him? I could see he was one of these modern young men who think in their ignorance that they know everything there is to know.'

'That's a rather different impression from the one he made on Mr Kenway-Potter.'

'I can't help that.' Her tone was contemptuous. 'Some people can't see further than the end of their noses. And I didn't thank Mr Kenway-Potter for dragging me into a conversation with young Tuke. He came across to me in the Green Man and said there was a young American interested in Woodcombe folklore, and I ought to have a chat with him. The truth was that the Kenway-Potters wanted to get away and push him on to somebody else. I found that Tuke didn't know a thing about folklore, and didn't want to, either. He'd simply asked just out of idle curiosity why the pub hadn't got one of those painted signs hanging outside.'

'Well, what did you talk about when you found he knew nothing about your special interest?' Pollard enquired.

'He'd asked me a question and I answered it, although I knew it was a waste of time. There's a Woodcombe Green Man: a boss in the nave roof of the church. I had a photo of it on me and I showed it to him to explain why local people didn't want it on their pub sign. Perhaps you'd like to see it yourself if we've got to go into all this detail?'

'Certainly I should,' Pollard replied, ignoring her sarcasm.

The photograph was produced. He found the face singularly repellent, partly because of its savagely dynamic quality. He handed it back, managing to by-pass Toye.

'Striking,' he said. 'Unique, I should imagine, judging from examples I've seen up to now.'

Mrs Rawlings looked at him in astonishment and leant a little forward.

'You're interested,' she said, making the statement sound interrogative.

'A policeman needs wide interests. In the course of his work he comes into contact with a wide range of people.'

'You're right about the Woodcombe Green Man being unique,' she said after a short pause. 'A seventeenth-century manuscript says that the boss was carved by a local stonemason in the fifteen hundreds. He swore it was a copy of a face he'd once seen on Old Grim, the longstone up there in the woods. Old Grim's the Saxon name for the Devil. The stonemason was driven out of the village with his family.'

'Did you tell Mr Tuke this story?'

'I did. He was too opinionated to take any interest and tried to make fun of it—and me.'

'The young are often irreverent these days, aren't they?' Pollard replied, 'and American ideas of humour seem a bit brash to us at times. I don't suppose he intended anything personal.'

As he spoke he glanced up and saw a secretive smile on her face, and abruptly changed the subject.

'Did you advise Mr Tuke to go up to see the longstone, Mrs Rawlings?'

'No. Why should it be wasted on somebody like that? But he went. Made a fool of Mr Fordyce by asking to be shown the way up. Of course he'd been up already, as soon as I'd gone off on my job, and started digging around Old Grim.'

Could this statement conceivably be true, Pollard wondered.

'What is your job, Mrs Rawlings?' he asked, to conceal any show of interest.

'I work part-time for the Littlechester City Library, taking the Mobile Library van round to the villages three days a week. Wednesday's the day for the ones in this area. When I've done I have a snack at the Green Man before I drive the van back and do the paperwork. Then I come home in my own car.'

'What time did you get home on April the twenty-third?'

'Not till nearly four. There'd been a lot of requests handed in that day.'

'I see in your statement to Inspector Deeds that you spent the rest of the day at home. Is that correct?'

'Yes, it is. I was glad of a cuppa and a bit of a rest before I got down to an evening's gardening. I'm a vegetarian and grow most of my food out at the back.' She broke off and gave Pollard a hostile stare. 'Of course it was Tuke who got old Grim down. I'd like to know why the police are trying on this cover-up.'

Pollard patiently explained that a Canon of Littlechester had had a lengthy conversation with Edward Tuke in the course of the afternoon.

'That fact, and the time spent on the road and the fact that tools would have been needed completely rules out Mr Tuke. He arrived on time for his five o'clock appointment with Mr Fordyce, remember.'

'Tools,' she said contemptuously. 'Easy enough to come by round here.'

'Who do you suggest it was that removed the warning notice from the old bridge,' he asked with a swift change of subject.

She shrugged.

'That wouldn't have been anything to do with Tuke going up to Old Grim. Why, it was old Bolling did it, of course, to get a bit of his own back after losing out in court that morning. Mrs Trotman at the post office saw him coming back in his van just on six o'clock when she was shutting up shop. Plenty of time for the old bastard to nip along the bank and pull the notice up before Tuke came down.'

Pollard decided not to comment on this reconstruction.

'How did you hear of Mr Tuke's accident?' he asked.

'Why, from Mrs Fordyce next door. I was washing up my supper things when I heard their front door slam and Mr Fordyce go running down the road for all he was worth. It seemed a bit funny. Time went on and he didn't come back, so I thought I'd better just look in on Mrs Fordyce and see if she was all right. They don't usually lock their back door till they go to bed, so I went round the bungalow and called to her. She came running down the stairs and told me about Mr Kenway-Potter's phone call. It's a semi-bungalow with a room upstairs, and she'd been looking out of the window upstairs to see if she could find out what was happening down at the river, but said it was too dark. Then we heard the ambulance coming. She was so upset that I asked her if she'd like to come in with me until her husband got back, and we had a cuppa together.'

'Well, Mrs Rawlings,' Pollard said, 'thank you. That's all quite clear, and we now know your views about what's happened here recently. We must be getting along. You must be glad that the longstone has been put up again so quickly.'

'Put up again!' she almost spat at him. 'Dragged up and stuck into the hole as if it was a clothes prop. And it isn't reorientated properly. Where the face would come ought to be looking to Midsummer Day sunrise. They couldn't care less... You needn't trouble to go in next door if

112

that's what you've got in mind. They both went off early in the car.'

*

On the way back to Littlechester Pollard found himself thinking more about the Fordyces than the clearly eccentric Mrs Rawlings. By now he felt quite certain that James Fordyce had had no previous plan to go into Littlechester that day. He had simply seized on a pretext to avoid being interviewed at home. Did this mean not only that he was aware of his wife's curiosity but also that he had something highly confidential to say about Edward Tuke? Then there was that odd little gasp of astonishment she had given on hearing of his intentions. Was it just surprise, or could it have been dismay at the prospect of the police coming to the house yet again? It was difficult to see how she herself could in any way be involved in Tuke's death, but she might be anxious on her husband's account. Or was she just a silly little ass who over-reacted emotionally to everything that happened? Sooner or later she would have to be interviewed herself as Tuke had actually come to the house and met her, however briefly, on two separate occasions. But after James Fordyce, the vital person on the list was, of course, Mrs Kenway-Potter, and how long were they going to be held up for the medicos to give the all clear?

'I suppose there couldn't be anything in that old bag's rigmarole,' Toye said suddenly. 'About Tuke and the longstone, and Bolling and the notice.'

'Not possibly, you know, as far as Tuke goes because of the timing. After Mrs Rawlings cleared off he went to see the room he was having that night. Then he drove into Littlechester—say a good half-hour as he didn't know the road. He probably had a stroll round before going into the Cathedral, and then that quite lengthy chat with Canon Allbright before starting for Woodcombe again. He was back at the Green Man at a quarter to five, Tom

113

Wonnacott's statement says. So any excavating up at the longstone before he saw Fordyce is out. And I refuse to believe that he tackled it and got the stone down afterwards, still allowing enough time to get to the Manor at seven, presumably having cleaned up first. And we agree that the state Bolling was in when he got back rules him out, although I admit we've no absolute proof that he didn't somehow get along to the notice and pull it up... Curious type, Mrs Rawlings. I can see her as a sort of rabble-rouser, making impossible things sound quite plausible.'

'Do you think she believes that old yarn about the stone having a face?'

'Could be. Wasn't it the White Queen in *Alice Through The Looking Glass* who believed six impossible things before breakfast?.... We'll be in in five minutes, and we'll damn well have some elevenses before we ring the place where Fordyce is working—or says he is.'

This programme was satisfactorily carried out, and half an hour later James Fordyce was announced by a constable.

During the exchange of polite preliminaries and the introduction of Toye, Pollard experienced a succession of reactions. This man was intelligent, and keyed up to a high degree of vigilance beneath a quiet academic manner. All his trained professional perception was alerted.

'We're a bit cramped in here, I'm afraid, Mr Fordyce,' he said, 'and the chairs are hideously hard. Our apologies. We'll try not to detain you for long. We've been through the statements you made to the Littlechester C.I.D. at the time of Edward Tuke's death, and it's just a matter of asking you to fill in a bit here and there. The main thing we want to ask you is what was your impression of Tuke as a person? Do smoke, if you'd like to.'

'Thanks, but I don't,' James Fordyce settled himself on his unaccommodating upright chair and crossed one foot over the other. Looking up he met Pollard's enquiring gaze. 'I thought him an interesting and unusual young man, highly likeable.'

'Unusual in what way?'

'Chiefly in his sensitivity, I think. You know, no doubt, from the information about him sent over from the States, that he was orphaned as a baby and brought up by a maiden aunt, his mother's elder sister. From what he told me he had realised from an early age that his father had been *persona non grata* to his mother's family. All his enquiries about him had been stonewalled, and his U.S. citizenship drummed into him. For some reason the process hadn't worked: race memory activating itself, perhaps. At all events he looked on himself as British, and made up his mind to come over here as soon as he could, and find out about the possibilities of taking British nationality. His first—and sadly his only visit was through his employers, Integrated Oils. As you know, this is a multinational company, and he was sent over to the London office early in March. Through a friend in the States who had been a client of mine he got in touch with me with a view to tracing his English forebears, and arranged to come down to Woodcombe to see me.'

'You go up to London quite often, I imagine, in connection with searches that you are carrying out, Mr Fordyce. I should have expected Edward Tuke to meet you there. Was this visit entirely his own suggestion?'

'Entirely,' James Fordyce replied without hesitation. 'He wanted to visit this part of the country because the friend who recommended me to him had ancestors who emigrated to the States from this city. I have been able to trace the family tree back to the sixteenth century. Edward Tuke had undertaken to buy some books on Littlechester and do some photography for this friend.'

'I see,' Pollard said. 'You didn't gather that any personal contact perhaps connected with this friend brought him down here?'

'He didn't mention anything of the kind. I think that he was indirectly encouraged to come by the enormous pleasure he was getting by travelling around in Britain, and getting to know as much as possible about what he felt was really his own country.'

'Can we go on now to his meeting with you at Woodcombe? Presumably you discussed the searches he wanted you to make. We have the previous correspondence between you in the file of the case. Had he taken any steps on his own to track down his mother's people?'

'I don't think so. At any rate, if he had I feel sure that he would have told me. As it was he asked me to take on the whole job.'

'And were you prepared to?'

'Yes. I warned him that it would take time, and cost quite a bit, too, but he said that was no problem. He had a well-paid job with Integrated Oils, and the aunt who had brought him up had left him her money. A useful amount, I gathered.'

'I suppose the main difficulty you expected to run into was tracing his father's family, since he had so little information to give you?'

'Yes.' James Fordyce hesitated. 'You'll understand, I'm sure, that a self-respecting genealogist treats anything he unearths about a client's ancestry as confidential, anyway in the first instance. It goes against the grain, but in the present situation I feel I ought to pass on some remarks that Edward Tuke made to me about his father. He made it clear that what he said was simply speculation on his part, but here it is for what it's worth. He suspected that his father had left the U.K. in 1948 because he had got himself into trouble of some kind. He made the point that at that particular moment it wouldn't have been too difficult to get hold of a passport in another name, and rather reluctantly admitted wondering whether his father had deserted from the armed forces towards the end of the last war, and that 'Tuke' was an assumed name.'

Pollard's mind reverted to his conversation with Canon Hugh Allbright and the latter's mention of Edward Tuke's comments on the War Memorial Chapel in Littlechester Cathedral.

'Thank you for telling us this,' he said. 'In a complicated case like this one any scrap of information could unexpectedly turn out to be a pointer. But if Edward Tuke's hunch about his father having changed his surname is right, surely it would make any attempt to trace the family virtually impossible?'

'Extremely difficult, certainly, and very time-consuming. For that reason I don't regret the job having fizzled out, although it would have been interesting to have a go.'

'We mustn't be sidetracked, fascinating though the prospect of this sort of detection is,' Pollard said, 'but just where would you have started?'

'There's a mass of recorded and classified material about individuals. One might follow up young Tuke's desertion idea and consult the military and naval records at Hayes and the P.R.O. branch now at Kew.'

'And isn't there a place in Kingsway where all births, marriages and deaths are classified on a regional basis over the last century or so? I expect you often use it.'

'Yes. St Catherine's House. . . . One would just go on making shots in the dark in the hopes of finding a lead.'

'Well,' Pollard said, 'we mustn't keep you from whatever you're on the trail of at the moment. Was that all we wanted to ask Mr Fordyce, Toye?'

Toye, taking his cue, looked up from the case file.

'There's just the small point of his visit to Bridge Cottage on the afternoon of April the twenty-third, sir.'

'Oh, yes. We have to check up meticulously on timing in a homicide investigation, of course. In your statement, Mr Fordyce, you said that you left the Woodcombe post office at three, discovered that Mr Bolling was out, and

117

took the opportunity of examining as much of Bridge Cottage as you could from the outside, and then walked home along the north bank of the river. Mr Bill Morris, Mr Kenway-Potter's forester, says that you stopped for a chat with him at Upper Bridge at about ten to four. It seems rather a long time for so short a walk.'

As he spoke Pollard watched James Fordyce looking embarrassed. Not guilty, he thought, puzzled by the reaction.

'To tell you the truth, I sat down in the sun for a few minutes after leaving Bridge Cottage to think over the pros and cons of buying it—my wife was very keen, I knew—and I must have dropped off. I'd had a tiring drive down from London during the morning. The traffic on the roads seems to get worse every year. When I came to I looked at my watch, and was surprised to find that it was nearly a quarter to four.'

'Entirely understandable,' Pollard commented. 'It must have been very pleasant. Reverting for a moment to genealogists' treatment of information about their clients' family histories as confidential, you work from your own home at Woodcombe, I take it? So you presumably have a certain amount of material of this sort under your own roof?'

'Certainly I do. Each client for whom I'm carrying out a search—or have done recently—has a folder, and these are stored in a filing cabinet in my study which I keep locked, more on principle than because I can think of anyone—my wife or our visitors, for instance—taking the remotest interest in its contents.'

'And you have never, to your knowledge, had a client shown into your study to wait for an interview with you while this filing cabinet was unlocked?'

'Never. And in any case I really don't see that this has any relevance to Edward Tuke's death, since I had not started the searches he wanted done,' James Fordyce replied, with an unmistakable edge to his voice.

'Quite,' Pollard replied. 'It's just that in our line of business we have to think round every conceivable possibility in an investigation. I don't think we need bother you any further, Mr Fordyce. Thank you for the help you've given, and particularly for being so frank over Edward Tuke's conversation with you.'

★

When Toye returned from seeing James Fordyce out, Pollard was sitting with his elbows on the table with his chin cupped in his hands.

'A fundamentally decent chap, that,' he said. 'It's difficult to see him as a killer, either singlehanded or in partnership with Kenway-Potter.'

Toye guardedly admitted that it didn't look likely on the face of it, but that first impressions were often misleading.

'O.K. I'll grant you that. And in my opinion he took evasive action on three points.'

Toye, engaged in polishing his hornrims, looked across the table with interest, and said he had made it two.

'First of all,' Pollard said, doodling on the cover of the telephone directory, 'he didn't seem keen to discuss St Catherine's House. That's the place in Kingsway where they keep the National Indexes of births, marriages and deaths. There are four quarterly indexes for each year, going back to about 1840. Tuke *père* gave a date of birth when he took out nationalisation papers in the U.S. in 1951: that was one of the bits of information the Yard got from the F.B.I. when Edward Tuke's background was being looked into. It may not have been the actual date, but obviously the chap wouldn't have given one wildly wide of the mark. If the registration of his birth isn't recorded at St Catherine's House he must have emigrated on a faked passport or somebody else's called Tuke. I should have thought getting this cleared up might be a

119

starting point, and I'm wondering if Fordyce actually did get that far, and hit on something he doesn't want us to know about young Tuke or his father. If he did, we'll get on to it in the end with the help of some of the Yard ferrets . . . Your turn.'

'I think there was more to how he filled in that hour on the Wednesday afternoon than having a bit of kip in the sun.'

'I'm with you. The Kenway-Potters got back from their lunch party at half-past three. Did Fordyce hang around after peering in at the windows of Bridge Cottage in order to contact Rodney and pass on whatever it was he had unearthed? If you remember, Mrs K-P is alleged to have gone upstairs for a rest on her bed and would have been out of the way? I didn't think Fordyce looked guilty at this point, just rather uncomfortable, as if he'd being doing a bit of petty pilfering or something like that.'

'Perhaps he had,' Toye said, taking the suggestion literally. 'He's a scholar. Perhaps he'd got into the cottage through an open window and nicked one of Bolling's books.'

'It's theoretically possible,' Pollard replied, secretly amused. 'Are we together over Fordyce's third bit of evasion? Always keeping the filing cabinet in his study locked?'

Toye nodded.

'Got a bit rattled over that, didn't he? Stiffened up.'

'To me, you know,' Pollard said, resuming his doodling, 'there's another possible pointer there to Kenway-Potter. If Fordyce was teaching him how to research into his family tree it seems quite possible that he let him come over and consult reference books and whatever when he himself wasn't there.'

'Mrs Fordyce being on the spot would give her plenty of chances to have a look inside the cabinet if it ever was left unlocked.'

'From what she sounded like over the phone this

120

morning, I shouldn't think she'd be able to make much of the stuff he keeps inside it. However, that's a quite unwarranted deduction as I've never seen her. My first idea while we were talking to him about the filing cabinet was to ask if she had gone home and would be available if we went over later. But I decided against it. I'm convinced she wanted to keep out of my way this morning. It might just have been nerves, of course, but if she's been up to any funny business we're much more likely to get on to it if we turn up out of the blue. Anyway, if there was information relating to Edward Tuke in the filing cabinet, how did it get there? Fordyce stated categorically just now that he hadn't started on the search. Was he lying? I think our next move is to try to find out if he has recently been working at St Catherine's House. He must be known to the staff there, and it's possible that there could be some record of the particular indexes he consulted. It's a long shot, but worth trying, I think.'

'Back to London?' Toye asked.

'Yes, I think so. But there are one or two things to do first. We need the best photographs of Kenway-Potter and Fordyce that the people here can rustle up, for one thing.'

On enquiry there was no difficulty in getting a copy of a good photograph of Rodney Kenway-Potter on account of his involvement in local affairs which were frequently reported in the *Littlechester Evening News*. James Fordyce was more of a problem until Inspector Deeds remembered that on the occasion of his retirement from the Inland Revenue Office there had been a gathering of his colleagues at which a presentation had been made to him. After some delay, research into the files of the *Evening News* located an excellent photograph of him in the act of being handed a book and an envelope which doubtless contained a cheque. After further delay a copy of the photograph was produced.

In the meantime Pollard had contacted Mrs Kenway-

Potter's doctor and learnt that if she continued to make satisfactory progress he should be able to see her by the middle of the following week. As things were going at the moment he could assume that an interview on Wednesday was possible.

'Let's make for the Yard and home,' he said to Toye. 'There's nothing more we can do here at the moment. Perhaps this tangled-up affair will look better from a distance.'

Chapter Seven

In spite of the satisfaction of spending an undisturbed Sunday at home, Pollard, as always, found marking time in the middle of an investigation frustrating. At intervals the complex situation at Woodcombe irrupted tiresomely into the enjoyment of Wimbledon Common, helping the nine-year-old twins with their current enthusiasms and lazing in the garden. After supper his wife asked him what was biting him particularly about the case.

'Undercurrents,' he told her. 'Interlocking ones. Do undercurrents interlock, or am I mixing my metaphors?'

'You must mean cross-currents,' she suggested.

He threw a cushion at her and felt better.

On the following morning he asked for an appointment with his Assistant Commissioner on arriving at the Yard, and proceeded to give him a competent and rather humourless summary of the ground covered up to date.

'What the hell's the matter with you today?' the A.C. demanded when it came to an end. 'Hipped already because you haven't made an arrest? You haven't been on the job a week yet. You've brought off too many eye-catching coups over the years—that's your trouble.'

Pollard grinned a shade sheepishly.

'It's not just that, sir, I swear it isn't, though I admit to anyway average human vanity. It's the conviction I've got that the case is lousy with motives of one sort or another, and they're so bloody difficult to get at. With means and opportunity and all that, there's at least something concrete to work on.'

'You ought to be grateful for the chance of investigating something a bit out of the usual run instead of belly-aching about it,' the A.C. commented robustly. 'What do you propose to do next?'

'Work on the hypothesis that Edward Tuke's death was engineered because of something somebody at Woodcombe knew about him, sir.'

Pollard went on to explain why, in his opinion, James Fordyce and Rodney Kenway-Potter were the most probable people to have made such a discovery, whatever it was.

'I want to get one of the chaps we call on for tracking down information in records of various sorts to find out if either Fordyce or Kenway-Potter have recently consulted the National Indexes of births, marriages and deaths, for a start. I've got good photographs of both of them. I don't know if a note is kept of the volumes of the Indexes people ask for, but I think it's a line worth working on. And if Mrs Kenway-Potter had a child by Edward Tuke's father before she married her present husband in 1950, there must be a registration of the birth.'

'You better get that rum chap Hildebrand Robinson on to the job. There's nothing he likes better than ploughing through acres of the printed word to isolate a fact. In the meantime you'll see Mrs Kenway-Potter, I suppose? Even if Edward Tuke can't have been her bastard son she may fit into the picture somewhere. Your suggestion of a child by Tuke before he emigrated sounds feasible.'

'As soon as her medico gives the all-clear, she's the top priority, sir. Meanwhile I thought I might as well stay up here and try to clear my backlog.'

'If you find yourself with time on your hands that can easily be remedied,' the A.C. assured him, buzzing for his secretary as an indication that the interview was at an end. 'Press on, and keep motivated yourself,' he added.

Pollard returned to his own room and took steps to contact Hildebrand Robinson by telephone. In due course he was located at his home in Blackheath and undertook to come up to the Yard in the afternoon and be briefed on the search required. This having been arranged, Pollard plunged into arrears of work connected with his recent cases.

Hildebrand Robinson was announced in the course of the afternoon. He was a tall man of sixty-five and broad to match, with a large sagging face suggestive of a bloodhound. Only his eyes, bright blue and intent, indicated his mental alertness and pertinacity. He had been a distinguished classics master at a public school, where his policy of completely ignoring any boy unwilling to work to capacity had invested membership of his classes with a recognised cachet. On learning that the admission of girls to the sixth form was being seriously considered by the school governors he had promptly resigned in his late fifties. He had already carried out some searches into records of various types for Scotland Yard, and was now considered to be on call. In the intervals he composed, for a learned monthly, crossword puzzles of such difficulty that the number of successful solutions received was regularly given, and seldom went into double figures. Pollard, who had worked with him on several occasions, had genuine respect for his ability and also liked him.

'Well,' the expert said, after a brief exchange of cordialities, 'what's on offer this time? Something to bite on, I hope.'

'We're interested,' Pollard told him, 'in a chap who went over to Canada in 1948 to a job, moved on into the U.S.A. in 1950, took U.S. nationality in 1951, and was accidentally killed in 1953. He had applied for a U.S. passport and been given one in the name of John Frederick Tuke, born in Longshire, England, in 1919. There is some reason to suppose that he may have got into Canada on a forged passport, and that his legal name wasn't Tuke.'

'Helpful, if true,' Hildebrand Robinson commented, taking rapid notes. 'Narrows the field. I'll begin on the birth registrations for Longshire over the years from 1917 to 1924. If he acquired a forged passport or somebody else's, the date of birth probably isn't accurate. And if there's no trace of his birth? It's this case you're on down at Littlechester, I take it?'

'Yes. Edward Tuke, the chap who appears to have been manœuvred on to a broken bridge by somebody who had previously yanked up a warning notice, was J.F. Tuke's son, born in the U.S.A. in 1952. He worked for Integrated Oils and had been sent over to the London office in March on some assignment. He had an introduction to a Mr James Fordyce, a genealogist who lives in Wood-combe, a village in the Littlechester area, and went down to see him on April the twenty-third to talk to him about having his family history traced. Both his parents had died in the 1953 car crash. In the course of conversation he told Fordyce that his mother's people, who had brought him up, were always very cagey about his father, and that he had wondered when he was older if his old man had had to clear out of the U.K. for some reason, and if, perhaps, he had been a deserter from the armed forces in World War Two.'

'Quite a promising little job,' Hildebrand Robinson said ironically, 'especially if there is no record of the bloke ever having been born. However, there are the Ser-vices' records if there's anything in this deserter idea. Don't expect an answer by return of post, though, will you? Any idea who eliminated young Tuke?'

'Various ideas but no proof so far. That's why we've called you in.'

Hildebrand Robinson grinned.

'Flattery will get you nowhere. Is this all you want?'

'No. In 1950 a young woman called Amaryllis Hartley was married to Rodney Kenway-Potter, probably in the summer. I don't know for certain where the actual cere-mony took place, but she lived in a place called Great Lockwood, near Worcester. See if she produced an infant before, or shortly after J.F. Tuke headed for Canada in 1948.'

Hildebrand Robinson raised an eyebrow.

'To sport with Amaryllis in the shade' ... he murmured as he wrote.

'One more thing. I suppose you often inspect the records at St Catherine's House. Have you ever noticed either of these chaps working there?'

He passed over the photographs of James Fordyce and Rodney Kenway-Potter.

'Definitely not the country gent type,' Hildebrand replied after a careful scrutiny. 'I'm not sure about the other one. Can't be definite, though. Shall I try them out on some of the staff?'

'Yes, do. It might be useful if anybody remembers what area they were looking up.'

'Not a hope, I should say. Genealogy's one of the in things, and people come and go all the time. However, I'll have to go.'

'Thanks awfully. And for coming along and taking on the job. I'll hope to hear from you.'

Alone again Pollard found it difficult to concentrate on his backlog of paperwork. After a time he gave up the attempt and let his thoughts wander freely. He had a visual mind and a clear picture of Woodcombe took shape in it. The little River Honey made its way with tranquil persistence from Upper Bridge and the Littlechester road to Lower Bridge, beyond which it took a meandering course through meadows, east of the steeply rising slope of Manor Woods. Small though the Honey was, its course was attractively varied. Tranquil pools alternated with tiny rapids where it flowed over outcrops of hard rock, on one of which Edward Tuke had crashed to his death that April evening ...

Like all woods the Manor Woods had a secretive quality, he thought, as he visualised them. A quality of hinting at hidden surprises, not always pleasant. The

Manor itself was an agreeable one, an unassuming monument to eighteenth-century taste in its rose-red brick and perfect proportions. Deeper in the woods was that sinister survival of an earlier and less urbane civilisation: Old Grim. And somewhere in the sea of green was the tree from which a small boy living a life of secret fantasies had also fallen to his death. . . .

In imagination Pollard left the woods by way of the path along the north bank of the river and paused at Bridge Cottage. In spite of all the convincing arguments against it he still felt occasional qualms about Leonard Bolling's possible removal of the warning notice. Brushing aside the temptation to go over the evidence yet again, he moved on mentally across Lower Bridge to the village street and worked his way long it. Past the church, glancing up at the tower where the big breakthrough of eliminating the fans from the case had been so promising at the start. Past the Green Man and the down-to-earth Wonnacotts. Past the attractive period cottage, Yesterday, and its extraordinary owner who managed to combine a responsible job in the County Library Service and a positive obsession with the remote past. And next door, the last dwelling in the village: the rather discordant modern bungalow of the Fordyces, where a call would have to be made on returning to Woodcombe to conclude the series of interviews with all Edward Tuke's known contacts. . . .

That would be on Wednesday, Pollard thought, frowning. Uneasiness at the delay in getting on with the job once more made him feel restive. His hand began to move in the direction of the switch which would link him with one of the Yard's telephone operators. Why not check the Wednesday appointment with Mrs Kenway-Potter by ringing St Kilda's Nursing Home? He hesitated, and finally decided against the step. He had fixed things with her doctor before leaving Littlechester. If badgered, the medical profession was inclined to dig its toes in. And it wouldn't be expedient to appear to be unduly interested in Mrs K-P at this stage.

With an all-out effort of will-power he brought himself back to the actual job in hand, and was genuinely immersed when Toye appeared after half an hour to compare notes on progress.

★

It was almost twenty-four hours later when, with a certain inner satisfaction at his own self-control, Pollard put his signature to the last of an interminable run of documents, and asked to be put through to St Kilda's Nursing Home, Littlechester.

In less than a minute the receptionist came on the line. He gave his name and asked if Matron could take a call. There was a short interval of silence interspersed with small clicks. He sat gently drumming with his fingers on the top of his desk.

'Matron speaking, Superintendent Pollard.'

'Good afternoon, Matron,' he answered, with just the right nuance in his voice of one pillar of the establishment in communication with another. 'I hope this isn't an inconvenient time for you. I'm speaking from London, and just wanted to check with you that Mrs Kenway-Potter's doctor is willing for me to see her tomorrow.'

There was a fractional silence, but long enough to convey surprise and for Pollard to sense that his previous uneasiness was returning in an acute form.

'But Mrs Kenway-Potter isn't with us any longer, Superintendent.' The tone conveyed astonishment that he had not been informed. 'She was so much better that Dr Hastings agreed that she could go home on Sunday evening as she was so keen to. I think it was her daughter's visit on Saturday that speeded up her recovery. We were delighted, of course, although sorry to lose her.'

Years in the C.I.D. had made the judicious response

almost automatic.

'That's excellent news, Matron,' Pollard agreed. 'It doesn't matter in the least that somehow it didn't get through to me. I'm coming down tomorrow in any case, and I'll ring Mr Kenway-Potter at Woodcombe, and fix a time. So sorry to have bothered you unnecessarily.'

After a further exchange of courtesies he rang off. Simultaneously Toye, who had been following the conversation on an extension, came across the room with a list of telephone numbers taken from the file on the case. Their eyes met.

'Skipped,' Pollard said briefly, buzzing the Yard's switchboard once again. 'Get me Littlechester 59432. Top priority. And keep at it: it's a big place with grounds.'

During the seemingly interminable wait that followed his thoughts rearranged themselves. 'No,' he said, 'The Kenway-Potter type doesn't skip. Too much to lose. But there's something fishy going on. I swear'....

The receiver crackled.

'Keep at it for another thirty seconds,' he told the operator.

Toye nodded, signifying agreement on both counts....

'All right, pack it in,' Pollard said abruptly. 'Now then, this is still top priority. A Mrs Boggis lives in a building that's part of the Woodcombe Manor set-up which has the number you've been trying to get. She is on the phone and almost certainly has a separate number. Try to get her, will you?'

A longer silence followed.

'I may have overreacted,' Pollard admitted, 'but I've been in a state of suppressed tiz about this damn case for the past forty-eight hours.'

Toye remarked that it had been getting under his own skin a bit, too.

At long last Pollard was told that he was through. An

elderly voice painstakingly repeated a number and informed him that Mrs Boggis was speaking.

'Good evening, Mrs Boggis,' Pollard responded, with a relaxed normality which surprised himself. 'This is Chief Superintendent Pollard. You remember my coming to see you last week, don't you?'

'Oh yes, sir. I remember.'

'I want a word with Mr Kenway-Potter, but there's no answer from the Manor—just the ringing tone. I wonder if you can tell me when he's likely to be in?'

'Oh, but he's not there, sir. He went up to London Sunday evening on business. Something to do with the hotels the family owns.'

'Did Mrs Kenway-Potter go with him?' Pollard asked.

'Not with him, she didn't. Miss Amanda drove her up yesterday afternoon. She only came out of the nursing home on Sunday, you see. She's wonderfully better, but they felt she ought to have a night's rest before the drive.'

'Yes, of course,' Pollard agreed, restraining his impatience with a Herculean effort. 'I expect you know where she and Mr Kenway-Potter are staying? I could contact him there.'

'Yes, sir. If you'd kindly hold the line a minute I can give you the telephone number. They always leave it with me in case of an emergency, you see. They're staying at one of the hotels. Not right in London, but outside, to be a bit more restful-like for Mrs Kenway-Potter. She felt a little change would do her good after her upset'. . . .

'Quite,' Pollard said. Against a faint background of papers being turned over he ran his fingers through his hair and gave Toye a despairing glance.

'This is the number, sir,' Mrs Boggis came in at last, and dictated it slowly and carefully. He repeated it, thanked her, and was about to ring off when she spoke again.

'If the matter isn't urgent, sir, they'll be back again on Wednesday.'

131

He thanked her again and hastily put down the receiver.

'Could be in order,' Toye propounded.

'I know. But I'm not taking even a minimal chance. I'll get on to K-P now, and have the hotel put under observation if they really are there. It's essential not to put the wind up him. Do I sound just suitably efficient?'

'I'd know something was up, but anybody not used to working with you day in and day out wouldn't rumble it,' Toye replied without hesitation.

Rodney Kenway-Potter was located without difficulty at a Surrey hotel.

'Superintendent Pollard?' There was slight surprise in his voice. 'I hope you haven't had any difficulty in running me to earth? My wife was well enough to leave the nursing home on Sunday afternoon, so as I had to come up on business she thought she'd like to come too for a short break.'

'No, no problem, thanks,' Pollard told him. I got on to your Mrs Boggis. I just wanted to check that it would be in order for me to see Mrs Kenway-Potter briefly tomorrow. Dr Hastings mentioned Wednesday when I contacted him last Saturday.'

'Perfectly in order. We're driving home tomorrow morning. Would the afternoon do you? Say three o'clock?'

'That fits in very well with my schedule. I'll come along to Woodcombe Manor about three.'

'Right. We'll see you then. Goodbye.'

They rang off. Pollard sat frowning for a few moments.

'I still think this trip was damned odd,' he said. 'I wonder if she insisted on discharging herself from St Kilda's, and if so, why? Shall I try to get Dr Hastings? No, on the whole I think not. But I'm not taking any chances. We'll have the hotel watched all night, and somebody tailing them tomorrow morning.'

These arrangements having been put in hand, and an

early departure for Woodcombe on the next day fixed, there seemed no obstacle to going home for a domestic evening. Pollard headed for Wimbledon with a feeling that his recent apprehensions about the Kenway-Potters had probably been misplaced, but that it was a relief to know that they were now in no position to give him the slip. The evening was dominated by the exciting news that his twin daughter Rose, aged nine, had won first prize in her age group in a national poster competition. Later, when the children had gone to bed, Pollard and Jane agreed that they had succeeded quite well in boosting Andrew's self-esteem through a few subtle moves.

'I don't think he felt too outclassed,' Jane said. 'She's really good, you know. He'll have to learn to live with it.'

'He's more of an all-rounder,' Pollard pointed out. 'We'll build on that. To use the ghastly jargon, he's got to find and accept his identity'. . . .

'No inferiority complex, for heaven's sake.'

'Amen,' Pollard agreed. 'An I.C. can do the hell of a lot of damage, and not just to the chap who's got it. . . . I take it that there's some beer in the fridge?'

★

At a few minutes past six on the following morning the bedside telephone suddenly clamoured stridently. In an instant reaction Pollard had seized the receiver and silenced the din before Jane was fully conscious.

'Pollard here,' he said, possibilities already shaping in his mind as he spoke.

'Detective-Constable Hatherleigh speaking, sir. An urgent call has come through for you from Superintendent Newman of Littlechester.'

'Go ahead.' This was not what he had expected to hear in the moment of his waking. . . .

'At approximately 01.30 hours this morning a resident of Woodcombe saw flames emerging from a ground floor

133

window of Bridge Cottage. About five minutes after a 999 call was put through to the Fire Service an explosion took place. All attempts to rescue the occupier, Mr Leonard Bolling, failed. Fire-fighting appliances from Wynford and Littlechester finally got the fire under control by 03.30 hours. The house was burnt out, and Mr Bolling's body is believed to be in the wreckage which will be searched as soon as conditions permit. A preliminary police investigation suggests that the cause of the fire was arson. End of message.'

As he listened Pollard's mind worked at two levels. An upper level registered the message while a second level assessed it and made decisions.

'Right,' he said. 'Contact Inspector Toye at his home. Pass on the message, and tell him we'll leave from the Yard as near 7.30 a.m. as possible. Then get through to Littlechester, and tell them we should turn up at about ten. Got that?'

The gist of these orders having been repeated he put down the receiver, aware that Jane was already up. Her head came round the door as he flung back the bed-clothes.

'Breakfast's ready as soon as you can make it,' she said, and vanished again.

Over the years there had been not infrequent early morning calls and he had brought the technique of a light-ning shave and shower and presentable dressing to a fine art. At this stage he never allowed himself to be slowed down by speculation but concentrated on going into action in the shortest possible time. Jane had perfected her own procedure. As he knotted his tie and ran down-stairs he was greeted by the aroma of coffee and freshly-made toast. He slipped into a chair beside her at the kitchen table.

'Someone,' he told her as he munched, 'has blown up Bolling the bookseller. Sounds like Happy Families, doesn't it? Poor old blighter, but anyway I don't suppose he knew a thing about it . . . Yes, love. I damn well will have another cup'. . . .

A quarter of an hour later he had snatched up his overnight bag and unlocked the garage. As he drove out with a parting wave to Jane, he reflected that he was at least well ahead of the rush hour. Another encouraging thought came: if it was arson, presumably with intent to kill, at least the two Kenway-Potters were in the clear. Was there after all a homicidal maniac at large in Woodcombe, masquerading as a perfectly normal member of the village community? Of all possibilities this was the most daunting from a detective's point of view. As long as you could see the logic of criminal behaviour, however deplorable the motives impelling it, there was a decipherable pattern to unravel. In the case of the really mentally deranged there was no demonstrable relationship between thought and action.

Pollard reminded himself that he had already given this possibility serious thought and rejected it in the light of his personal experience of life in a village community. There was no point in reconsidering it at this stage unless some entirely new evidence had emerged. Superintendent Newman's early call seemed to suggest that he felt the fire and Bolling's death in it had some connection with Edward Tuke's.

On arrival at the Yard he found that Toye had contrived to get there before him, and that the Rover was at the ready. A report had come in at six o'clock from the watcher on duty outside the Kenway-Potter's hotel, stating that they had made no attempt to leave during the night. The man's relief was due at eight and would ring in on taking over from a nearby callbox. Pollard arranged with his own office to make a telephone contact at half-hourly intervals on his drive down to Littlechester, and shortly afterwards left with Toye. The latter was reacting to the new development with his habitual caution.

'Sounds to me as if Littlechester have got the wind up,'

he said. 'Not that you can blame them. But from what Mr Kenway-Potter said, he thought there'd be a lot of feeling against Bolling once it got round that he was responsible for bringing that stone down, and it didn't sound as though he meant to keep the matter to himself. Kenway-Potter, I mean.'

'If it was arson as a revenge for Bolling's vandalism, don't you think the explosion takes a bit of explaining? A deliberate attempt to kill Bolling seems to be going a bit far. I should have thought ducking him in the river or something along those lines would have been more likely.'

'I reckon the explosion could have been an accident, unintentional, I mean. Suppose the idea was to scare Bolling by starting a small fire well away from the stairs—say in the kitchen, and the old chap had got a can of paraffin near a window where inflammable stuff was dropped in and set alight?'

'You may have got something there,' Pollard said thoughtfully. 'Or could it have been a cylinder of bottled gas? Anyway, in the first instance the whole business is Littlechester's pigeon. Our job is to find out who's responsible for Edward Tuke's death. Unless they've got some conclusive link between the two, or apply to the Yard for us to take it on, we'll go ahead with questioning Mrs Fordyce and hopefully Mrs K-P ... Stop at the next callbox you see, and we'll ring back to see if anything's come in about the K-Ps.'

They were informed progressively that a couple of suitcases had been loaded into the boot of the Kenway-Potter's Chrysler, and that the couple had left the hotel at half-past nine, heading westward with the observation car following at a discreet distance.

'With any luck, we shan't hear any more until they get to Woodcombe,' Pollard commented. 'I left a message for the chap to ring us at the Littlechester station when he's seen them safely home. The village'll be swarming with newsmen and photographers, so he won't be obvious.'

They had made good time and arrived at Littlechester shortly before ten. A harassed Superintendent Martin was obviously relieved at their arrival.

'Decent of you to come down at the drop of a hat,' he said over cups of coffee in his office. 'That bloody village is getting in my hair. I suppose this latest development is on our plate at the moment, but I can't help feeling that it must tie up with the Tuke business somehow, and ought to be on yours. Since I contacted you our forensic chaps have rung to say that it looks like arson. They can't get in yet to make a proper examination. I've told them to keep their mouths shut, of course. This is how they think it was done. . . .

As Superintendent Martin talked, Pollard found that he could visualise the layout at Bridge Cottage perfectly clearly. From the road a gate wide enough to admit a car opened on to a gravelled space. From this the path which he and Toye had followed branched off on the left and led round to the front door. A short drive followed the east side of the house to a yard at the back containing several outbuildings, one of which was presumably used by Bolling as a garage. The whole property was enclosed by a stone wall about four feet high, except on the river side where there was a boundary hedge.

'Just the four walls standing,' the Super was saying, 'but the back door's still there although it's partly burnt. There's one of those cat flap affairs at the bottom of it. Our chaps say there's a distinct smell of paraffin just there. They think whoever started the fire pushed newspaper or shavings or whatever soaked in paraffin through the cat flap and put a match to it. This would have set the lino alight, and the heat seems to have made a cylinder of bottled gas explode and the whole place went up in a matter of minutes. By that time anyone could have got over the wall at the back and disappeared into Manor Woods.'

137

Toye asked who had first seen the fire and raised the alarm. It had been a woman living next door to the post office, close to the south end of Lower Bridge. She had been up in the night with a sick child, and, chancing to look out, had seen a flickering glow in one of the downstairs windows of Bridge Cottage. There was a telephone kiosk outside the house and she had run down and put through a 999 for the fire brigade, and then started rousing neighbours.

'How long was it before the explosion happened?' Pollard enquired.

'Say about five minutes,' Superintendent Martin replied. 'Some of the men had rushed over with a ladder and put it up to Bolling's bedroom window, and were hit with bits of brick and tiles. He slept at the far end from the kitchen but they were driven back by the smoke and heat. The fire people are hoping they'll be able to get the body out by the end of the morning, but there's no chance of going through the debris until it's cooled down. They think there's a risk of part of the back wall caving in, too.'

'I suppose there's no doubt that Bolling actually was in residence?'

'Meaning that he might have fired the place himself for the insurance money? Doesn't seem likely as he'd sold the place, although I hear the contracts haven't been exchanged, luckily for Mr Fordyce. No, I think there is no doubt that he was there all right. The woman at the post office says she saw a light in his bedroom window at about eleven last night. Anyway, we'll soon know for sure. I've got a couple of chaps seeing if they can find any traces of somebody getting away along the river bank, and over the wall at the back into the Manor woods, but it doesn't seem very hopeful. It's only in detective novels that criminals are obliging enough to leave bits of their jackets hanging on bushes ... Come in.'

'Telephone message for Chief Superintendent Pollard, sir.'

Pollard was handed a folded paper and read the few lines of information it contained.

'Thanks,' he said to the constable who had brought it. 'No answer.' As the door closed he turned to Superintendent Martin. 'Well, one thing's definite. Whoever did the job, always assuming that it was arson, it wasn't the Kenway-Potters. They spent the night in a Surrey hotel with one of our people parked in a car outside, and are only just back at the Manor.'

There was an astonished silence.

'I thought she was in St Kilda's Nursing Home, officially with a threatened appendix.'

Pollard grinned.

'So did we until yesterday evening. Interesting, isn't it? We're seeing her this afternoon. Not that I'm expecting much to come of it, but we've one or two other irons in the fire. I'd like to know what the forensic chaps find when they can get into Bridge Cottage.'

'Sure. Look in on me about six this evening if you're around. We may be a bit further on by then, and I'd be glad of your opinion. I suppose I'll see my home again some day' ...

*

'Well, that's that,' Pollard remarked a few minutes later as they went out into the car park. 'Arson at Bridge Cottage a strong possibility. Obviously Martin can't wait to push it on to us, but I'm not playing until a definite link with young Tuke's death emerges. We've quite enough on hand. Mrs Fordyce next. I'm not expecting much from her, although I suppose Tuke may have had a lengthy chat with her when he went along on the morning of April the twenty-third to fix up his appointment with her husband. Something else has occurred to me. What do you think would have been a reasonable time for Fordyce to take for escorting Tuke to Upper Bridge and showing him up the path to the longstone? According to him he came straight home. We'll check with her.'

Toye considered.

'Ten minutes at the outside. It's no distance, and they'd have said all they wanted to say by then, barring goodbye.'

'I'd put it at that myself. Just on chance we'll bring the conversation round to it.'

When they drew up at the gate of the Fordyces' bungalow the front door was half open.

'You never know who's listening, do you?' Pollard remarked *sotto voce*. Avoiding the path which bisected a small rectangle of lawn they approached silently by walking on the grass. A heated argument became audible.'

'You've told me a dozen times already that the sale hadn't gone through because the contracts hadn't been exchanged. Fair enough, but why don't you DO something. Ring Ford's and say we'll buy the site and rebuild. Somebody else may get the idea. Get up and go, for Heaven's sake.'

The feminine voice was shrill and indignant.

'I've also told you several times,' James Fordyce replied, his voice suggesting nearness to the limit of control, 'that the site is now part of Bolling's estate. He may or may not have left a will and appointed executors. In any case there is bound to be considerable delay in settling his affairs. To start with there'll be an inquest.'

'I want to GET IN FIRST. Why can't you ring our own solicitor and tell him to contact Bolling's, then?'

With a quick glance at Toye, Pollard took a few heavy steps on the path and proceeded to ring the doorbell loudly. Dead silence descended within, followed by the sound of someone coming from the rear of the bungalow, and the door was flung open by James Fordyce who gave Pollard a quick dismayed look.

'Good morning, Mr Fordyce. I hope this isn't an inconvenient time for your wife, but we'd be glad of a few minutes with her, as we understand that Edward Tuke called here before you yourself got back on April the twenty-third.'

Pollard's tone was business-like but pleasant. James Fordyce relaxed perceptibly.

'Good morning,' he said. 'Do come in. I'm afraid we're rather at sixes and sevens this morning and you'll find her a bit upset. You know what happened here in Wood-combe today, of course?'

'Yes, we do. A spectacular disaster almost on your doorstep is enough to upset anyone. We won't keep her long.'

They were propelled into a fair-sized sitting room with a dining alcove from which a serving hatch led into the kitchen, James Fordyce remarking that he would tell his wife that they were there. Pollard glanced round and diagnosed a studied effect produced by someone with social ambitions. An indifferent portrait of a young woman in mid-nineteenth century garb hung over the fireplace. One or two good pieces of furniture were care-fully sited to catch the eye. Easy chairs and a settee were over-supplied with opulent cushions. A few coffee-table books and copies of *Country Life* were in evidence. Quick footsteps coming downstairs suggested that Mrs Fordyce had been carrying out hasty repairs to her make-up. The next moment she came into the room, shutting the door behind her, and addressed herself to Pollard a shade breathlessly.

'I'm so sorry to keep you waiting: we hardly know where we are after this dreadful disaster. . . . Do, please, sit down, won't you?'

Pollard was sympathetic, introduced Toye, and took a chair facing Eileen Fordyce with its back to the light. She was more attractive than he had expected, and it was easy to visualise her appeal in her early twenties. At the moment there were signs of tension in her face and small

141

red blotches in the region of her cheekbones. He decided to encourage her to talk about the fire in order to get her more relaxed.

'I suppose the first you knew about the fire was the explosion?' he asked. 'It must have been terrifying in a quiet place like this.'

She shuddered slightly.

'It was terrible. The whole bungalow shook and the windows rattled so violently that I can't think why the glass didn't crack. We scrambled out of bed half asleep and went to look out, and could see the glow of the fire at the other end of the village—this is a semi-bungalow with a room upstairs. I thought it must be the I.R.A. I think I screamed ... James was dragging on some clothes and saying he must go and see if he could help get people out. I didn't want to be left alone so I began to grab some clothes, but he wouldn't wait. Just told me to go in next door and see if Mrs Rawlings was all right.

'Was she?' Pollard asked, to keep the narrative flowing.

'I saw that her light was on, so I didn't stop. I ran on and a fire engine overtook me. I couldn't find James in the crowd. Everybody was running about and shouting. As soon as I saw it was Bridge Cottage that was burning I started calling at cottages where old people are living on their own. Keeping tabs on them is Mrs Kenway-Potter's and my special thing, you know, the poor old dears. I felt I simply must get round to them all, as she's been ill and wouldn't have been able to come down.'

Pollard found this implication of intimacy with Woodcombe Manor surprising, and put out a feeler.

'Yes, of course,' he agreed, 'even if she had been at home. As you know, no doubt, she's been away for a short break with her husband, and they only got back this morning.'

The incredulity and anger in Eileen Fordyce's eyes were unmistakeable. Obviously she had known nothing about the trip to Surrey.

'Yes,' she replied unconvincingly.

'What I really came to ask you about, Mrs Fordyce,' Pollard went on, 'is the contacts you had with Mr Edward Tuke. We are interviewing everybody known to have met him, you see, just on the chance that some fact might come to light that might explain the puzzling circumstances of his death on April the twenty-third.'

Watching her expressive eyes closely he thought he saw signs of wariness.

'I can't add anything to what I've already told Inspector Deeds,' she said. 'You see, I hardly met him. He called here about half-past eleven that morning to fix a time to see my husband, and we just said good evening to each other when he came for his appointment at five and I let him in. I heard him leave with my husband soon after six, but I was talking to Mrs Rawlings next door, over the garden hedge out at the back, and didn't come in.'

'He didn't actually come into the house when he called in the morning, then?'

'No. Naturally I asked him in and offered him coffee. We try to be friendly to visitors in this village. But he said he wanted to look round and go over to Littlechester.'

'It was your husband who took him up to see the longstone, then?'

'Oh, no, my husband didn't go up with him: just showed him where the path starts and came straight back. We had a lot to discuss. Bridge Cottage had just been put up for sale and we were considering making an offer. And now'—she gave a little shrug and lifted her hands expressively.

'It must have been a great shock to hear of Edward Tuke's death so soon after he had left here.'

Eileen Fordyce swept her hand across her brow.

'It was simply *terrible*. I shall never, never forget it.'

By professing a show of interest Pollard elicited the sequence of events from Rodney Kenway-Potter's first telephone call to James Fordyce's precipitate departure.

'I wanted to go too, of course. I thought I might be some help to Amaryllis, but James said I'd better keep out of the way. I went upstairs to see if I could follow what was happening from the window, but it was too dark ... It was a relief to hear our neighbour, Mrs Rawlings, calling up from the kitchen door. Then we heard the ambulance go past. She isn't exactly a *friend* of ours, of course, but when she asked if I'd like to go in and have a cup of tea I was quite glad to. It was nearly ten before James came back. He'd been up at the Manor.'

Husband acceptable, wife not, Pollard thought, discerning a note of resentment.

'Well, Mrs Fordyce, we needn't take up any more of your time, and thank you for your help. We'll just drop in on your husband for a moment, if we may, if you'll show us which is his study.'

James Fordyce was sitting at a desk covered with a variety of papers and reference books. He glanced up, looking tired, strained and defensive.

'I'm sorry to have to bother you again,' Pollard told him, 'on top of what happened during last night, but you'll understand we have to push on with the Tuke enquiry come hell and high water.'

'Come in and sit down,' James Fordyce replied briefly. 'Sorry there's so little room. What do you want to know?'

The study was a narrow strip at the back of the bungalow with a single window overlooking the back garden. Bookcases, a large desk and a freestanding filing cabinet made it uncomfortably congested. Pollard and Toye manoeuvred themselves on to a couple of upright wooden chairs.

'You've lived in Woodcombe for about five years haven't you?' Pollard asked. 'So you must know the inhabitants quite well, at any rate by sight. And you must have had an excellent opportunity of studying Edward Tuke's face, since you were talking together in here for an

144

hour or so that Wednesday evening. Did any resemblance between him and any local resident occur to you?'

To his surprise James Fordyce suddenly smiled.

'I'm flattered to see that my mind's been working on the same lines as a Yard Ace's,' he said. 'The answer's a categorical no. As you say, I had an excellent opportunity of studying him at close quarters, and no suggestion of any such a resemblance struck me at the time or since.'

Thanks very much,' Pollard said, 'and that really is all . . . I'm sorry about Bridge Cottage from your personal point of view. You were on the point of buying it, weren't you?'

'Yes, I was. Fortunately the contracts hadn't been exchanged. I must say that I was looking forward to a bigger study, but of course this bungalow has its points. It's quite well built and easy to run, and handy for the bus stop at the road junction for my wife when I'm away with the car on a search. I've tried to teach her to drive but she's hopeless with anything mechanical, so hasn't a car of her own. . . . Perhaps if you'll extricate yourself first, Inspector?'

Pollard squeezed his way out, followed by Toye and James Fordyce himself. Eileen emerged from the kitchen opposite, and the callers were escorted to the front door with formal politeness barely concealing relief.

'Let's go and have a snack in a Wynford pub,' Pollard said as they drove off. 'No point in going all the way back to Littlechester as we're due at the Kenway-Potters' at three.'

'What was in your mind when you asked whether Tuke looked like anybody living in Woodcombe?' Toye asked when they were out on the main road. 'We know he can't have been Mrs Kenway-Potter's illegit?'

'Nothing about Tuke at all, actually. I had to think up something to get us into Fordyce's study. I wanted to see his filing cabinet and the general lie of the land. Did you notice that the kitchen and study doors were bang oppos-

145

ite? If Fordyce ever did go out leaving papers on his desk or the cabinet unlocked, Mrs F was pretty well bound to notice it—the papers anyway.'

Toye agreed, admitting that he had missed out on that particular point.

'She's by no means the fluffy nitwit I expected,' Pollard said. 'It shows how misleading it is to form an impression of somebody on the strength of about ten seconds on the blower. Let's find a large bar in Wynford where we shan't be noticed, and compare notes in a quiet corner.'

Half an hour later, comfortably settled and disposing of a satisfactory snack, they pooled their impressions of Eileen Fordyce, agreeing that the conversation they had overheard on arrival was illuminating. Behind the outward immaturity and emotionalism, both probably cultivated to some extent as a useful technique, there was toughness and possibly ruthlessness, the driving force being social ambition.

'Her husband fits in O.K. with the nobs up at the Manor and she doesn't,' Toye summed up. 'That's the length and breadth of it, and why she's tearing mad about that cottage going up in smoke.'

'Yes,' Pollard said thoughtfully. 'Living on the Kenway-Potters' doorstep in a classy little place like that would have been a status symbol. And she was very put out at not having known about the Surrey trip after parading her matey relationship with Mrs K-P... Hell hath no fury, etc. You know, I'm beginning to wonder'...

'If she wrote the anonymous letters?'

'Yea. Let's apply the time-honoured formula. Motive, to start with. We've seen what a driving force acute frustration can be in some of our other cases, haven't we? She's got enough intelligence to realise that she isn't in the same street as her husband intellectually, and she's been unfortunate enough to land up in a small place where it stands out a mile that she isn't his equal socially, either. Added to this she's a strong character with an apparently one-track mind . . . Are we together so far?'

'Yes,' Toye said slowly, 'I'll go along with all that.'

'It seems to me,' Pollard pursued, absently gathering crumbs together with a spare fork, 'that in this particular situation means and opportunity have to be considered together. There would be no difficulty in actually producing the letters. Did you notice some embroidery and a workbox in that sitting room? I've seen Jane stencil a pattern on to material. Posting them would be the main problem. She would have to post them herself because the block capitals and bits stuck on the envelopes would attract attention if she asked someone else to do it.'

Toye pointed out the convenient nearness of the bungalow to the bus stop.

'Yes, I know, but there were eight letters altogether and she doesn't drive a car. Fordyce doesn't strike me as the sort of chap who'd be taking his wife into Little-chester for shopping several times a week. And he'd think it odd if she kept on going in on her own by bus. If he was away I'm sure other people would have noticed it, and a few judicious questions might be worthwhile. But none of this really gets to the root of the matter, does it? What sparked her off? If she wrote those letters she must have got on to something connected with Tuke which was a link with Mrs K-P. I simply can't believe that Mrs K-P would have made her ineffective attempt at suicide unless she knew for sure that the writer had information which she simply couldn't face coming out. That hypothetical baby by old Tuke seems to be getting more of a possibility, doesn't it?

'So we're back to Fordyce's study and his filing cabinet, then?' Toye asked.

'This is it. And to papers left lying about on the desk when he dashed off in a hurry the night Tuke was killed.' Pollard made an abrupt movement, pushing away fork and crumbs. 'Look here, Kenway-Potter rang Fordyce at eight, didn't he, to ask if Tuke was still with him? It's in the statements that both the Fordyces made to Deeds. Mrs Fordyce answered the phone and her husband took over from her. This looks as though he was working in his study when the call came through, and he'd probably have gone back there to carry on. Kenway-Potter's second call to say that he'd found Tuke's body in the river was at about 8.40 p.m. He took it himself, and according to his wife rushed out of the house to go and see if he could do anything to help. This is confirmed by Mrs Rawlings who told us that she heard the bungalow door slam and Fordyce running down the road as she was washing up her supper things. She went on to say—and I think this could be important—that she thought it a bit odd when he didn't come back as time went on, and went out of her cottage and round to the Fordyces' back door. She called to ask Mrs Fordyce if she was all right, and she—Mrs F—came downstairs from looking out of the top window. Agreed so far?'

'That's what she said all right. What we don't know is how much time had gone on since Mr Fordyce went off.'

'Exactly. Would it have been enough for his wife to have a look at any papers he'd left on his desk? Or possibly to spot that he'd left the key of the filing cabinet in the lock and decide to investigate the Tuke folder? You know, it's a bit difficult to imagine even the most meticulous bloke stopping to put everything away in a sudden crisis like Tuke's death. And I think it's reasonable to suggest that if he had been working when Kenway-Potter rang him the second time, that he'd have been thinking over the data Tuke had given him.'

'Of course,' Toye pointed out, 'Fordyce was pretty strong about never leaving information about his clients lying about, and he definitely stated that he hadn't started on the search Tuke wanted done.'

'A bit over-strong, I thought, about professional ethics re confidential information. I remember making some

148

remark about it when he'd gone. As to whether he'd already started on the search as the result of Tuke's letters, well, I'm hoping that Hildebrand Robinson may be able to dig up something there.'

They sat on in silence for several moments. Finally Toye, always cautious, admitted that they could be on the right track.

'But what was the idea of his clamming up—if he did?' he asked. 'Had he tumbled to it that his wife had snooped and started up the anonymous letters on the strength of something she'd found out about Mrs Kenway-Potter, and he was trying to do a cover-up?'

'Who for?'

'Why, for his wife.'

'Do you know, I'm not a hundred per cent sure about that. Could it have been for Mrs K-P? Has one result of his unfortunate marriage been that he has fallen for her? Nourishes a profoundly secret passion for her, in fact, as he's undoubtedly a buddy of her husbands.'

Toye sat staring at him.

'Come on,' Pollard said, suddenly realising that the bar was almost empty. 'We shall be chucked out in a minute. Anyway, we're due at Woodcombe Manor in half an hour.'

In the car Toye made no attempt to start up the engine.

'There's one point it would clear up. If Mr Fordyce is in love with Mrs Kenway-Potter, I mean. The Wednesday afternoon, when he took all that time to get along the river bank. They came back from their lunch with friends at half-past three, didn't they? He might have waited in the trees just to get a glimpse of her.'

'You just aren't true, old man,' Pollard told him. 'Is that the sort of thing you got up to when you were courting Mrs Toye?'

'I won't say I didn't make a detour past the house now and again,' Toye admitted a little coyly as he inserted the ignition key.

Chapter Eight

Twenty-four hours after the fire at Bridge Cottage Wood-combe was still showing signs of disorganisation. As Pollard and Toye approached the turning from the direction of Wynford a police car emerged and drove off towards Littlechester. Groups of people were standing about in the village street, and the acrid stench of burning hung in the air. Some obvious newsmen and press photographers were gathered at the gate of the blackened ruin of the cottage, and inside the garden some firemen were conferring with a small group in plain clothes.

'The forensic blokes?' Pollard queries as they drove past. 'Insurance people?'

They were aware of curious eyes following the progress of the Rover as it went past and continued on up the hill towards Woodcombe Manor. As they drove up to the house the golden cocker ran out barking, and Rodney Kenway-Potter appeared at the front door, a hand raised in greeting ... curtain goes up on Scene One, Pollard thought: landed proprietor greets expected visitors. He's as buoyant as before, if not more so ...

'My wife's all the better for the change of scene,' Rodney Kenway-Potter was saying, escorting them across the hall. 'She's in here.'

He led the way into what appeared to be the main reception room of the house, spacious and with fine windows and some good period furniture, but a lived-in room, not a period piece, Pollard thought. He stepped forward to take the hand extended by Amaryllis.

He was at once struck by her undeniable good looks.

Tall and elegant in build, her head was beautifully poised on her shoulders. While her features were not classical in the strict sense they were well-cut, and her hazel eyes full of vitality. It's a face full of character, Pollard thought, and she's gained rather than lost by maturity: time's mellowed her. He saw that she had made no attempt to camouflage the touches of grey in her auburn hair which she wore short and piled high. She looked tired and rather pale, but at the same time seemed relaxed.

'Do, please, sit down,' she said to him and to Toye when her husband had introduced them.

'Shall I stay?' he asked.

'No, darling,' Amaryllis cut in decisively before Pollard could answer. 'If three's a crowd, four would be a public meeting, don't you think? I'll call you if I don't know the answers to Superintendent Pollard's questions.'

'Right,' he replied. 'I'll be in the study.'

When the door had closed behind him Amaryllis looked at Pollard.

'I'd like to start this conversation, Superintendent, by apologising for having given you a lot of unnecessary trouble,' she said, dropping the note of light banter in her previous remarks and dispensing with any preamble. 'I know that I've behaved very foolishly, to say the least of it.'

He decided to respond with equal directness.

'What made you decide to try to kill yourself, Mrs Kenway-Potter?'

'I suppose,' she replied, clasping her hands in her lap, and continuing to meet his gaze, 'it was the build-up of the anonymous letters on top of the tragedy itself—poor young Edward Tuke's death. It was so shattering that it happened on our property, and as a direct result of my husband's invitation to him to come up here for supper that night. I know it was irrational to feel responsible for what happened, but the thought kept coming back that if only the invitation hadn't been given the boy would still

151

be alive. Do you know that there was a previous fatal accident in the woods six years ago, when a child fell out of a tree and broke his neck?'

'Robin Westbridge? Yes, we know about him. It's understandable that the second fatality brought back your feelings about the first. May we go on to the anonymous letters now? Had you ever received any before?'

'Never,' she replied spontaneously. 'Until all this happened I thought of them—if at all—as the sort of thing that happened to other people.'

'There were five altogether, weren't there, Mrs Kenway-Potter? What was your reaction to the first one?'

'For the first moment or two I took it for a practical joke in very bad taste, and wondered who would possibly have sent it to me. Then when I'd read it over several times I felt upset and rather frightened. As you know, I burnt all the letters, but I remember the wording perfectly well. It was "Easy for you to slip down and pull up that warning notice, wasn't it?" It seemed so personally vindictive. And although I'd never before felt nervous about sleeping alone in this house when my husband was away I barricaded myself into my room that night. He had gone up to London for a few days. And I went on doing it until he came back. I'd had a second letter by then, saying that I needn't hope for a cover-up.'

'What I simply can't understand,' Pollard said after a pause, 'is why you didn't tell your husband about these letters.'

Amaryllis Kenway-Potter unclasped her hands and sat looking down at her fingers.

'As I said, the first two came while he was away,' she replied without raising her eyes, 'so I had plenty of time to think. It stood out a mile that I *could* have gone down and pulled up the notice without being seen. Between half-past three and half-past four on the day Edward Tuke died, when my husband thought I was resting upstairs, and a bit later, for about three-quarters of an hour

152

from half-past five when he had taken the dog for a walk. That was the time when the writer of the letters thought I did it. The fourth letter said that he—or she—had rung this number just after six and got no answer. It was quite true that somebody rang then. I'd gone out to the garden to get some parsley and heard the telephone ringing, but it had stopped by the time I got back to the house. I began to feel trapped... The fifth letter came on the day we heard that Scotland Yard had taken over the enquiry.... I was with my husband in the Ring and Crozier that evening, and you were there ... I'd been thinking all day that I was bound to be suspected. Whoever was writing the letters would contact you, and I'd be asked to "help the police with their enquiries" as it's called. That sort of thing soon gets round, especially in a place like this, and the mud would stick. It would be so appalling for my husband and children. Much the simplest thing for them seemed to be for me to fade out. I suppose I had been coming round to this idea almost from the time the first letter came. That's why I never told my husband about the letters. I felt I must think things out for myself,' she concluded, raising her head and looking straight at Pollard.

Long experience of interviewing persons in connection with serious crime had developed in him a sixth sense where truth and deception were concerned. He knew beyond doubt that the statement he had just been listening to incorporated both. What Amaryllis Kenway-Potter had said about her motive for attempting suicide rang true with him. On the other hand the reasoning behind it was not only unconvincing, but impossible to reconcile with her intelligence and the general experience of life of a woman in her position.

'We'll start with a straight question,' he said. 'Did you in fact go down to the footbridge and remove the notice?'

'No,' she replied this time meeting his eyes directly.

'We'll go on to the matter of opportunity to do so, then.

After you and your husband came home from lunching with your friends, you were both alone for periods of time, and either of you could have removed the notice. Why has somebody picked on you rather than on him?'

'I've absolutely no idea,' Amaryllis replied.

'Please try to think carefully, Mrs Kenway-Potter,' he said. 'It sounds melodramatic to ask if you have any enemy in Woodcombe but peaceful-looking villages can harbour the most surprising hostilities.'

'I can only say that I know of nobody who dislikes me so much that they'd try to get me accused of murder. In fact, I don't know of anybody who really dislikes me. I've never found it difficult to work in with people over village affairs, or felt that they thought I was patronising or anything like that if I tried to help anyone in trouble, for instance.'

Pollard let a few moments pass and switched over to a different approach.

'There wouldn't have been much point in pulling up the notice unless you knew for sure that Edward Tuke would try to get back to the Green Man by way of the footbridge, would there? Don't you think that the police could hardly have failed to realise this?'

Her answer came so readily that he felt sure that she had foreseen that a need for it would arise.

'There were plenty of witnesses to my having talked to Edward Tuke in the Green Man that morning. I knew Mrs Rawlings would tell him about the longstone and I could have advised him to go up and see it, and told him that there was a short cut back to his car if he was pressed for time after seeing Mr Fordyce.'

Pollard glanced at Toye who was composedly taking notes and wondered how he was reacting.

'Have you any views on who was responsible for Edward Tuke's death. Mrs Kenway-Potter?' he asked abruptly.

'Why, yes,' she replied, once again with the spontaneity that he had previously found convincing. 'Now that he's dead I don't mind saying that it seems obvious to me that Leonard Bolling was—unintentionally. He'd already vandalised the longstone, and would see the notice just as another bit of my husband's property he could smash up. I can only suppose that the police know something that absolutely clears him of doing it, just as the football fans were cleared. The fact that they didn't take any action against him was one of the things that made me so worried about my own position.'

Pollard let a couple of moments elapse and then abruptly shot his final question at her.

'Just exactly what was the link between the late Edward Tuke and yourself, Mrs Kenway-Potter?'

'I am ready to state on oath, Superintendent that I didn't even know of his existence until we met that morning in the Green Man,' she replied composedly.

He knew that she had anticipated the question and had her answer in readiness.

'I only wish,' he said, getting to his feet, 'that you had been completely frank with me. I must add that I am not prepared to leave the matter as it stands.'

As he went out of the room followed by Toye, Rodney Kenway-Potter emerged from his study with an enquiring glance.

'Want to see me as well?' he asked.

'Not this time, thanks,' Pollard replied.

'Have you got this ghastly affair at Bridge Cottage on your plate as well?'

'Not at present, I'm glad to say. It's on Littlechester's at the moment.'

'Well, I hope to God they get it cleared up quickly. There seems to be an absolute hoodoo on this village.'

'Have you any personal views on what happened?' Pollard asked as they made their way to the front door.

'I feel pretty sure that things weren't meant to go as far as they did,' Rodney Kenway-Potter said, 'and that the explosion was simply an accident. I don't believe that whoever fired the place knew that there was paraffin or bottled gas just inside the kitchen. I suspect the idea was to give Bolling a damn good fright and see he got out all right. He was highly unpopular in the village as you know, and people were furious about his digging up Old Grim when the story got round. I didn't—perhaps wrongly, with hindsight—keep it to myself. There are one or two chaps who'd be quite capable of taking drastic action when roused. No doubt Littlechester will get on to it in due course.'

'At the moment the forensic experts are waiting to be allowed in to sift the wreckage,' Pollard told him. 'I think we'll stop off and show a spot of interest.'

'It's a ghastly mess, and the house is beyond repair. I've no idea what the legal position will be, but I've decided to try and buy the whole property back. It was part of the estate until quite recently. Turn it into woodland again, probably. We can do without a momento of the last couple of years,' Rodney Kenway-Potter added, escorting Pollard and Toye to their car.

A few minutes later they drew up at the roofless blackened ruin that was all that remained of the former attractive little early-nineteenth-century house. The back wall had partly collapsed and was being shored up to make it safer for the forensic experts. The roof and most of the upper storey had collapsed into the ground-floor rooms, forming a tangled mass of debris. The fire officer in charge was pessimistic. It would have to cool off overnight, he said, before anybody could start shifting it. Runnels of dirty water were still trickling from the open and badly scorched front door, turning the path into a mass of trampled mud. The garden was littered with broken tiles and bricks and masses of blackened paper, the remains of Leonard Bolling's library. At intervals gusts of wind blew charred fragments into the river to be carried away under Lower Bridge by the current.

Looking through a rectangular opening that had once held a ground floor window, Pollard and Toye identified the twisted metal skeleton of an armchair. Some bookshelves hung at drunken angles from a wall.

'There was nothing we could do by the time we got here except keep the blaze from spreading to the woods,' the fire officer said who had come up behind them. 'We hadn't wasted any time getting off and had a record run on a clear road. We slowed down for about ten seconds when we'd turned into the village road. The call was to Bridge Cottage, and we weren't sure which bridge was meant. But there wasn't any sign of life at the bungalow or the cottage on the right as you go in, and we spotted a glow further on and stepped on it. Nearly ran down a fool of a woman running like mad to see the fun. But we beat Littlechester to it, anyway.'

'You're the Wynford Brigade?' Pollard asked.

'That's right. Littlechester turned up quarter of an hour later. They've a more powerful engine, but it's ten miles further. Not that it made much difference. The local chaps had managed to get a ladder up to the old gent's window but the smoke and heat drove them back. We managed to get the body out about midday. The ambulance men said fumes and the shock of the blast would've put paid to him, and it was very unlikely he'd have known a bloody thing about it.'

Pollard and Toye went round to the back of the premises and found a police car parked in the yard. They learnt that the burnt-out house was being kept under observation overnight at the request of the forensic experts.

'And local people might come pokin' around an' get hurt,' the Sergeant added. 'We're not sayin' anythin' official about arson yet, but it stands out a mile to my mind.'

'Well,' Pollard said, 'I suppose we we may as well push on. Hardly a cheerful scene, and what a foul stink a fire makes. Hope you'll soon be relieved, Sergeant.'

He received a respectful salute and returned to the Rover with Toye.

'I could do with a cuppa, couldn't you?' he said. 'Several, in fact. Let's head for Littlechester.'

After they had been driving for several miles Toye asked him if he believed it was possible that Mrs Kenway-Potter hadn't known that Mrs Fordyce had it in for her.

'I've been thinking about that myself,' Pollard said. 'At first it seems incredible, but I've come to the conclusion that it's quite possible that it's never got through to her. While she—Mrs K-P—isn't at all the sort of caricature of a snob you'd see on the stage, she's very conscious of being the Lady of Woodcombe Manor for all that. From what her husband said she seems pretty well to run the place. Didn't you pick up her remarks about working in with people over village affairs, and not being thought patronising when she tried to help anybody who was in trouble? All a variation on the Them and Us theme, you know. I don't suppose it's ever dawned on her that anybody as obviously Them as Mrs Fordyce could think herself on an equal footing with Us at the Manor.'

Toye, while asserting that the finer points of class distinctions were a bit beyond him, agreed that there could be something in all this.

'As I told the A.C.,' Pollard said discontentedly after several further silent miles, 'what makes this bloody case such hard going is all the different motives that seem to be mixed up in it. Mrs K-P may have been afraid of something in her past coming out through Tuke which would jeopardise her family relationships and local status. Anyway, she felt strongly enough about the risk to attempt suicide. Mrs Fordyce, because of frustrated social ambitions, quite probably wrote the anonymous letters which drove Mrs K-P to try to kill herself. She's limited enough to believe that if Mrs K-P were out of the way she'd automatically become the Queen Pin of Woodcombe herself. James Fordyce may have decided to eliminate Tuke so that the commission to investigate his family history would lapse, and something Mrs K-P would want kept dark need never come out. It could be that Rodney K-P had also acquired this knowledge, and that he and Fordyce were in it together with a common motive. Fordyce may have wanted to protect Mrs K-P because he adores her silently from afar. Also, because he's the sort of bloke who would take marriage vows seriously and remembers taking on his wife for better and for worse. If he suspects her of writing the anonymous letters he realises that worse could be pretty bad for her. And he may have another motive for clamming up on us: plain, professional pride. If he went off leaving highly confidential information about Tuke, a client, lying about, I'm sure he'd hate to admit it.'

'And then there's Bolling,' Toye contributed, 'maybe getting mixed up in Tuke's death by accident because he was dead set on getting even with Kenway-Potter over losing the case. Not to mention village thugs with the motive of paying out Bolling for digging up that stone affair and being antisocial generally.'

Pollard consigned everyone mentioned to perdition.

'Too much to hope that anything will have come through from Hildebrand, I suppose,' he added gloomily.

On arriving at the Littlechester police station this prediction turned out to be depressingly correct. No message from any source awaited them. Toye collected a tray of tea from the canteen.

'Well,' Pollard said, pouring himself out a cup and pushing the teapot across to Toye, 'we've interviewed every single person known to have been connected with this enquiry. We've waded through reams of gen. Now I'm simply pinning my hopes on old Hildebrand's unearthing something about Tuke's forebears that'll link up with Mrs K-P. I'm convinced that's where the root of the matter is. And I'm not sure that we aren't making a

159

mistake in concentrating so much on the Tuke side and not nearly enough on hers.'

The words were hardly out of his mouth when the telephone bleeped. He picked up the receiver. Toye, watching with interest, saw him suddenly alerted.

'Put him through, please.' He looked at Toye, and eyebrow raised. 'Hildebrand,' he mouthed. 'Hallo! Pollard here. Anything for us?'

'Not what you asked for,' came the reply, 'but something I thought you might feel was worth following up. I decided to work on the Longshire births from 1917 to 1924 to cover the 1919 date you gave me. I unearthed something rather unexpected. On May the twelfth, 1923, Paul George Tuke, stationer, of 81 High Street, Waldenhurst, and Emily Jane, née Simpson, his wife, produced a son. He was registered as George Thomas Tuke on May the fourteenth. Any good?'

'It's a lead. Possibly a valuable one. Stout work on your part.'

'Elementary, my dear Watson. Want me to carry on to see if your John Frederick Tuke's birth turns up? Perhaps I'd better go forward and back a bit prior to '23.'

'Yes, do keep at it a bit longer. Anyway until we've been down to Waldenhurst and done a spot of fieldwork. If we have any luck I'll contact you at once, and then you can tackle the Amaryllis Hartley job. Did you get on to anything about those two chaps we're interested in?'

'Not much. The donnish type is quite well-known and called Fordyce, as you doubtless know already. He seems to have been working on a number of searches in the last six months, so I gave up at this point, thinking that you'd rather I got on with the Tuke business. Nothing definite about the country gent. He can't go in much, from the sound of it.'

They exchanged a few pleasantries and rang off. Toye, on being given the gist of the conversation, remarked temperately that it could be a breakthrough.

'At any rate it's given us something to do,' Pollard said, beginning to stuff papers into his brief case. 'You go along to the hotel and tell them we don't want a room for tonight after all. Pick up our bags and I'll meet you at the car when I've let the people here know what we're doing.'

Superintendent Martin admitted to feeling envious.

'At any rate you're on to something that may lead somewhere,' he said. 'Deeds is out at Woodcombe trying to keep the Press at bay on the arson issue, and making phoney enquiries about whether everything possible was done to get Bolling out as a means of checking on who was around. It's pretty hopeless, he says. Practically the whole village was milling about in the street and on the Marycott road in a matter of minutes.'

Pollard was sympathetic.

'Keep going,' he said. 'If you should come across anything that links up with our job you know where to find us.'

Chapter Nine

'Quite right to go down to Waldenhurst yourself,' the A.C. said on the following morning after listening to Pollard's report. 'This Paul George Tuke the bookseller could quite well still be alive if he married young, and only too pleased to natter to somebody about another son called John Frederick who emigrated after World War Two and just faded out. Anyway, George Thomas, born 1923, should still be around or traceable. Waldenhurst has grown a lot but older residents have long memories, and names over shop windows impress themselves unconsciously on people's minds, don't you think? Once you've established that John Frederick Tuke really existed and wasn't just a name on a faked passport, there's a reasonable prospect of finding a link with somebody in Woodcombe... What do you make of this fire-cum-fatality down there? I've been expecting a formal application from Robert Gregg for you to take it over.'

'I was half afraid it would have come in already, sir,' Pollard replied. 'It would have if the decision had been up to Superintendent Martin. I gathered from what he just didn't say that it was Mr Gregg who wanted Littlechester to handle the job. I think he—Mr Gregg—has felt a bit sore that they missed out on clearing the football fans over the warning notice being taken down.'

'I expect you've seen this morning that the Press has gone to town on the fire, with broad hints about arson thrown in? The fishing rights row has been resurrected, but they've been careful to make the point that the Kenway-Potters weren't in residence that night... Who do you think was responsible—if it really was arson?'

'Speaking without any detailed knowledge of local feeling, sir, I think there's something to be said for the theory that outraged village patriotism was behind it, and that it got out of hand. Cumulative outrage at the way Bolling had behaved since he came to live in Woodcombe finally exploding over the fishing rights business and the vandalising of the longstone.'

'H'm,' commented the A.C. 'Rum places, villages. Well, you'll want to push off to Waldenhurst. Hope you strike lucky and arrive at last at the motive to end all motives.'

'Thank you, sir,' Pollard replied gravely.

*

Meanwhile Toye had been doing some homework on Waldenhurst. As they drove down, he told Pollard that it looked like being quite a hopeful place for picking up some gen about a family that had owned a bookshop there in the nineteen-twenties. The present day population was only just over twelve thousand, and it must have been a good bit smaller in those days. Small enough to be a community, in fact. Not on a motorway or main trunk road at all. More like the market town and shopping centre for quite a big rural area.

Pollard agreed that all this seemed promising and asked about the police situation.

'There's a station,' Toye told him, 'down as not being continuously manned. They're in the Rockwater area. I rang there when there was no answer from Waldenhurst and they were very helpful. There's a sergeant and a couple of constables in police houses at Waldenhurst, but they provide routine cover for quite a wide area. Rockwater are sending an Inspector Forth over to meet us. I said we ought to make it by two o'clock.'

Pollard gave an affirmative grunt and relapsed into

silence. On the face of it the day was off to a good start. It was a perfect June morning. A recent rainy spell had freshened trees and hedges, and once clear of London's tentacles you could catch intermittent whiffs of new mown hay and roses as the Rover swept past fields and gardens. Back at the Yard the A.C. had been in a good mood, and Toye's researches gave ground for hope that the beginning of the end might be located in Waldenhurst. Pollard shifted his position at this point in his thinking. It was the prospect of what the end could turn out to be that was taking the edge off things. Perhaps the discovery of a link between Amaryllis Kenway-Potter and Edward Tuke's family startling enough to give her a really strong motive to put an end to his search for his forebears and surviving connections. It was undeniable that she could have slipped out of the Manor during the later afternoon of April the twenty-third and removed the warning notice on the old footbridge. And this was equally true of her husband. . . . As Pollard visualised them both their context suddenly changed into one of a squalid sequence of arrest, trial and prison sentences. Not for the first time he was seized with a violent distaste for his job. . . . He pulled himself up sharply. Edward Tuke had a right to live, hadn't he? Toye was saying something. . . .

'. . . Waldenhurst once we get to the top of this hill.'

'Fine,' Pollard replied, a shade heartily. 'We've made good time.'

Toye, an experienced map-reader, was quickly proved right. As they came over the crest they saw a small town not much more than a mile ahead. It nestled cosily at the southern foot of the next ridge of downland, dominated by a fine church tower gleaming in the strong sunlight. The oldest part of Waldenhurst was clustered round it, indicated by close-packed roofs. Down the centuries the town had grown to east and west with larger houses and more open spaces. The expansion of the second half of the twentieth century was shown by terminal planned housing estates and a few larger buildings which could house light industries, Pollard reflected. They drove in through this recent development at the eastern end, and were directed to a street flanked by pleasant eighteenth-century houses. One of these had been adapted to serve as a police station. As Toye drove into a reserved parking space outside a tall burly man in uniform appeared in the doorway and came up to the car.

'Detective-Chief Superintendent Pollard, sir?' he asked. 'I'm Inspector Forth, over from Rockwater, and very glad to have this chance of meeting you.'

Not for the first time Pollard reflected on how much more pleasant the atmosphere was when one came to ask for help from a local force. None of the stickiness of the occasions when one was called in to take over an enquiry.

'I hope you'll feel the same when you discover that we've come about some tedious digging up of the past,' he replied as they shook hands and Toye was introduced.

As Inspector Forth escorted them into the building he asked if the visit was connected with the Woodcombe case.

'I've been following it all through,' he said, 'and so has the wife. She's a real crime fan.... There's a cup of coffee on the go, sir, if you'd both care for one.'

'Yes, it's Woodcombe all right,' Pollard told him when they were settled. 'Since you're genned up on the job I'll come to the point straight away. We're trying to trace a family called Tuke who had a stationer's business here in the nineteen-twenties. The owner was a Paul George Tuke. He and his wife produced a son in 1923 who was registered as George Thomas Tuke. We think it's remotely possible that this son was the father of Edward Tuke who was killed at Woodcombe last April. I suppose it's too much to hope that any of them are still around?'

Inspector Forth looked regretful.

'The name doesn't mean a thing to me, sir, I'm afraid.

As far as local back history goes, I wasn't born till 1930, and my family didn't move to these parts till after the war. But with any luck Sergeant Withers may know something. He had a spell here as a young constable, and he's been in charge locally since 1975. I asked him to come along to see you. That's his car outside now from the sound of it.'

Sergeant Withers was an older man with a stolid face but a pair of shrewd blue eyes. At Inspector Forth's invitation he joined the coffee party and was introduced to Pollard and Toye.

'You're Chief Superintendent Pollard's best bet, I reckon Sarge,' the Inspector went on. 'Perhaps you'd just put him in the picture, sir.'

Pollard once again outlined the sequence of events that had brought him to Waldenhurst. Sergeant Withers listened attentively and sat for a few moments in unhurried reflection.

'Well, sir,' he said, 'one thing I'm quite certain of is that there was no stationer's business whatever in the High Street when I came here as a young copper in 1948. The town was quite a bit smaller then, and I'd remember it if there'd been one.'

'That's cleared up one thing, then,' Pollard said as Toye made a note. 'Paul George Tuke had either moved elsewhere or died by 1948. If he'd died we shall soon get on to it. Now, Sergeant, can you tell us if there are any Tukes who are living here now who might be descendants of his?'

This time Sergeant Withers reflected at greater length.

'Got it!' he said triumphantly at last. 'There's an old Mrs Tuke living in the Staddon Almshouses.'

'Thought you'd come up with something,' Inspector Forth remarked with obvious satisfaction at this display of competence by a colleague.

It transpired that the Staddon Almshouses were a seventeenth-century foundation for the elderly poor of

Waldenhurst. There was a warden to keep an eye on the inmates, and Sergeant Withers suggested giving her a ring.

'I've only seen old Mrs Tuke once,' he said, 'back in 1977 when a chap was going round trying to con people into giving orders for parcels of tea and paying in advance. She seemed on the spot all right then, but I can't say what she's like now.'

Urged to go ahead by Inspector Forth he put through the call. A fairly lengthy conversation followed during which Pollard and the Inspector exchanged rather disjointed remarks *sotto voce* on current police problems. Finally Sergeant Withers replaced the receiver and reported that Mrs Tuke was not senile, according to the warden, not by a long chalk, but inclined to get a bit muddled over anything unexpected. She—the warden—would tell the old lady that somebody interested in her family was coming round to see her. She thought it would be better if Chief Superintendent Pollard would come alone if that was convenient. And she was quite sure that Mrs Tuke's husband who had died a long time back had owned a shop in the town, although whether it was a stationer's she didn't know.

'It looks as though this could be it,' Pollard said. 'Jolly smart work on your part, Sergeant: we're most grateful. Are these almshouses far from here?'

On hearing that they were a bare five minutes' walk from the police station, he said that he would walk round and leave Inspector Toye to do a bit of sightseeing, but perhaps it would be as well to wait for ten minutes or so to give the warden time to get Mrs Tuke tuned in. Both the local men were obviously keen to hear some further details of the Woodcombe case, and he accordingly obliged. Finally the gathering broke up on the best of terms, and with his undertaking to let them know the outcome of his interview with Mrs Tuke.

He located Staddon's Almshouses without difficulty,

and stood for a few moments admiring the little cloister which formed their frontage on one of the streets in the older part of the town. Its roof was supported by elegant stone pillars, and benches of dark oak flanked the inner wall where the inmates could sit and watch the passers-by. Entrance to the cloister was through a gate under an engraved tablet of stone. This bore an inscription stating that John Staddon and his wife Margaret had founded the almshouses in the year 1677 'for ye care and comfort of ye aged poor of this town'. He pushed open the gate and went into the cloister, receiving a greeting from two old men seated on the bench who informed him that if it was the warden he wanted, her door was first on the right. He thanked them and passed under an archway opposite the gate into a cobbled courtyard round which were about twenty attractive little stone houses. A well head with an ancient bucket and chain formed the centrepiece of the pleasing lay-out. He turned right and saw that the first house had a small noticeboard over its door with the legend WARDEN in block capitals.

A grey-haired woman in a plain navy blue frock with white collar and cuffs answered his knock and eyed him rather warily.

'You be the gentleman from Scotland Yard that Sergeant Withers rang me about?' she said. 'I'm Mrs Foster, the warden in charge here. Will you please to step inside before I take you over to Mrs Tuke?'

Pollard sensed that his visit was something outside her experience, and that she was anxious to conceal the fact by emphasising her status.

'Thank you, Mrs Foster,' he said. 'I'd be very glad of a word with you first and to have your advice. Perhaps I could just tell you why I've come to Waldenhurst.'

Mrs Foster led the way into an impeccably neat little sitting room and indicated the larger of two modest arm-chairs, seating herself opposite to him.

'Well,' Pollard said, 'I don't suppose that a busy person

168

like you with all your responsibilities has much time for reading crime news in the papers, so you won't know that I'm investigating the murder of a young man called Edward Tuke at a place called Woodcombe in Buryshire. He was an American citizen, the son of an emigrant called John Frederick Tuke. We are anxious to trace any members of the family who are still living in England, and find that a man called Paul George Tuke had a stationer's business here. A son was born to him and his wife in 1923 and registered as George Thomas Tuke. We felt that it was worth finding out if the couple had another son, our John Frederick Tuke and the father of Edward who was murdered.'

A regretful look, similar to Inspector Forth's on being unable to supply the required information, passed over Mrs Foster's face.

'I don't think he could be,' she said. 'Mrs Tuke here is the stationer's widow all right. He died about the end of the war, and for a while she lived with a sister who came to join her, and when the sister died she was given one of our almshouses, being such an old Waldenhurst resident. It was before I came, so I don't know the exact dates. But I've always understood that there were two sons, and both were killed in the war. But it's only what she's told me from time to time, and I wouldn't like to swear to it.'

Pollard asked if being questioned about dates would be likely to fluster Mrs Tuke.

'Not the way you'll put them, I shouldn't think,' Mrs Foster replied. 'You see, you're used to asking people questions and finding out what you want to know. But I wouldn't go on too long, if I may be plain. She gets tired, and I've even known her drop off while a visitor's still with her.'

'That's very helpful advice, Mrs Foster,' Pollard told her. 'Thank you. Perhaps you'd take me along, then?'

As they crossed the courtyard Pollard admired the almshouses and commented on how beautifully kept

the place was. He learnt that part of the Staddon endow-
ment had been in land, and that the trustees had sold
some of it ten years earlier and used the proceeds to re-
store and modernise the whole property, putting in
electricity and water heaters and even a shower in every
almshouse.

'Properly in clover, they are,' Mrs Foster told him,
'what with being so comfortable and not a penny of rent
or rates to pay out. Mind you, there's always some that'll
grumble. Not that Mrs Tuke's one of those.'

Mrs Tuke was tiny, with snow white hair cut short and
a little wrinkled face, but her eyes were as bright as a
bird's. It was a warm June afternoon but she was wearing
a cherry-coloured cardigan and had a rug over her knees.
Every available inch of her sitting room was crammed
with ornaments and faded photographs, and a motley assortment of pictures covered the walls. To Pollard's relief
she showed no surprise that he was interested in her
family history. The shop in the High Street, he gathered
had been a first-rate little business, but that dreadful war
had killed it. Her husband had been called up and she
couldn't get enough stock, and so it had gone right down.
When he came back he was so poorly with some nasty
germ he'd picked up in Burma that they hadn't been able
to get it going again. Anyway it hadn't seemed worth it
with both the boys gone through that cruel wicked
war. . . .

Pollard seized this opening to head her off the shop and
bring the conversation round to her children.

'Were both your sons killed in the war, Mrs Tuke?' he
asked sympathetically.

'Our Tommy was, our youngest. He was sent over to
France when they started up the Second Front, and was
killed in the fighting there. Only twenty-one, he was.
Johnny was wounded so bad in Italy they invalided him
out. His stomach it was. They couldn't get him right
again. Gave him a pension, but he didn't live for long

after the war. Left a young widow, too. A nice good girl. Always kept in touch with me, she has, even though she married again. . . . She said it seemed disloyal to Johnny, but I told her, no . . . No, I said . . . it's what Johnny would want . . . you . . . to . . . do.'

The little bright eyes closed and the head drooped. Pollard glanced at Mrs Foster who nodded affirmatively. They got up quietly and left the room. When the door had closed behind them she turned to Pollard.

'If it would be any help I can give you Mrs Tuke's daughter-in-law's address. Not that she's really her daughter-in-law seeing that she's married again, but she acts like next-of-kin, and Mrs Tuke's left her all she's got.'

'Thank you,' Pollard said. 'It doesn't look very hopeful from our point of view, but it might possibly lead to some other branch of the family. Did Mrs Tuke ever have any daughters, do you know?'

'No, she didn't. That's something I'm sure of, for she's often said she wished she'd had one.'

Ten minutes later Pollard arrived back at the police station and found Toye waiting at the wheel of the Rover.

'No go,' he said, getting into the passenger seat, 'but another possible lead: Marsden. We'll go back to Town for tonight, though. For one thing I can put Hildebrand Robinson on a more useful track. There were two sons, but one was killed in action and the other was invalided out, and according to old Mrs Tuke died soon after the end of the war. We'll get this verified, but we can rule out either of these lads being Edward Tuke's father. It just isn't on. Let's go. I'll fill you in a bit more on the way.'

*

There was a frequent, fast train service between London and Marsden, an industrial town in the West Midlands, and to Toye's disappointment Pollard decided

171

to make use of it in order to save time. Mrs Nelson, formerly Mrs John Frederick Tuke, was on the telephone and he made a call to the house at nine o'clock on the following morning. She answered herself, and he got the impression that her second marriage had translated her to a higher social level. After brief initial surprise when he introduced himself and told her the purpose of his proposed visit, she reacted with interest rather than agitation. She had followed the Woodcombe case, having noticed that the murdered man was called Tuke, and assured Pollard that she would be glad to give him any information she could about her first husband's family. It was arranged that he would visit her in the early afternoon.

Once settled in the train Toye was meditative, and finally asked Pollard what he hoped to get from Mrs Nelson.

'Probably nothing that we haven't got already, barring a few dates to tidy things up for the record,' Pollard replied. 'Possibly a line on other branches of the Tuke family. Just possibly a break that we've never even thought of.'

Toye blinked behind his horn rims.

'Meaning you've got one of your hunches?'

'Don't bully me. It's alleged to be a free country, isn't it? Read that rag you've bought and give me a chance to think.'

Toye grinned and settled himself comfortably in his corner. Pollard sat opposite to him watching the landscape flash past. Just what were the chances, he wondered, of eventually running a Tuke to earth who had fathered a child of Amaryllis Kenway-Potter's? And even if one did, would it ever be possible to bring a viable murder charge against her and for her husband on grounds of opportunity as well as of motive? He admitted to himself that this was frankly unlikely, and that the case looked depressingly like being shelved. Unless, of course, some unexpected evidence turned up involving the late Leonard Bolling or James Fordyce. His hopes that something might emerge from the investigation into the fire at Bridge Cottage were beginning to wane: no message had come through from Littlechester. Presently he gave up retreading all-too-familiar and well-worn ground and attacked a crossword puzzle.

The train ran into Marsden station on time. An inspector of the city's C.I.D. was waiting on the platform and they were driven to impressive modern police headquarters. Here they received V.I.P. treatment. Pollard found this tedious, especially the interest shown in the Woodcombe case. He felt himself fretting to get on with the job in hand, and by implying that he had an appointment with Mrs Nelson at two o'clock managed to get away soon after one-thirty. Another police car conveyed Toye and himself to a modern housing estate of modest type on the outskirts of the city. The constable driver drew up as directed at a gate with a name place inscribed 'INNISFREE'. He leapt out and opened the rear door. Pollard extricated himself with a wink at Toye, and told the constable that he did not expect to be paying a lengthy call. The young man saluted smartly.

'About time you pulled up your socks when you're driving me around,' Pollard muttered out of the side of his mouth to Toye as they walked up a few yards of concrete path to the front door. Toye raised one eyebrow and pressed a bell push, setting off melodious chimes.

A middle-aged woman with a sensible kindly face, and wearing a neat two-piece in dark green and white and a modicum of costume jewellery, opened the door. She greeted Pollard pleasantly and without fuss and led the way into a sitting room overlooking a small garden. Pollard noted a bookcase filled with an assortment of titles suggesting membership of book clubs and some reproductions of flower paintings on the walls. When they were all seated, Mrs Nelson came straight to the

173

point.

'It's my first husband you've come to see me about isn't it?' she said, reaching for a folder on an occasional table. 'This is our wedding group, and there's a good one of him besides taken just before he went off to the war.'

Pollard thanked her and studied both photographs carefully before passing them on to Toye. At Littlechester he had scrutinised the much enlarged photograph from Edward Tuke's passport, but could not find here the least trace of a family likeness.

'Mrs Tuke has a wonderful collection of family photographs, hasn't she?' he said, steering the conversation in the direction of the old lady and past history.

Mrs Nelson was warm in her remarks about her former mother-in-law.

'She's always so brave and cheerful,' she said, 'although she's had so much trouble in her life. I expect she told you that her youngest son was killed almost as soon as he was drafted over to France in 1944. Then my Johnny was very badly wounded in the landing in Italy and after a while he was invalided out. He never picked up, and died at Christmas time in 1947. Then his father went a couple of months later ... They'd given up the shop and were living over it, but Mrs Tuke joined up with her sister who came to live with her in Waldenhurst'. . . .

All this information came out easily, but Pollard had a feeling that in some curious way Mrs Nelson's mind was not wholly on what she was saying. He introduced another topic.

'It's a tragic story for you all,' he said. 'What did you do when you were left a widow?'

'Well, there was a pension, of course, but I'm not one to sit about doing nothing. So I went back to my old job ... I'd been a shorthand typist ... Then after a bit I chanced to meet Dick. We got married in 1951 ... He's been a good husband to me, and a good father to our boy and girl' ...

Her voice trailed off. Pollard decided to plunge.

'Mrs Nelson,' he said, 'I think you've got something on your mind, haven't you? Something that this visit of ours has stirred up. I hope you're going to feel you can tell me about it.'

She sat with her head bent, twisting a handkerchief between her fingers.

'It's my Johnny,' she said. 'I know he oughtn't to have done what he did, but I couldn't bear him to be disgraced now. He was always a bit too kindhearted, that was the trouble.'

'If you know, as I think you do, that something he did probably ties up with this case we're investigating,' Pollard said, 'it could be very important indeed. You see, innocent people may be under suspicion.'

'I can see you're right,' Mrs Nelson said after a pause. She raised her head and looked directly at Pollard. 'Only don't let his memory be shamed. Not if you can help it, will you? And if you'll excuse me, I'll just fetch something you ought to see.'

Toye got up quickly and opened the door for her. He stood by it, exchanging a long interrogative look with Pollard. There were footsteps overhead, and the sound of a cupboard opening. A pause followed. Finally footsteps came down the stairs and Mrs Nelson rejoined them. She handed Pollard an envelope without speaking. He took out a familiar dark blue British passport and opened it.

'I see this passport was issued in 1938 to Henry Benchley,' he said, making the statement sound interrogative.

'That's right,' she replied. 'When I got round to sorting out Johnny's things after he'd gone, I found it with his birth certificate and other papers. But his own passport wasn't there: only Harry Benchley's.'

'Your first husband had a civilian passport then?' Pollard asked.

'Yes, he did. I'd been on holiday to France before I met him, and he took one out so we could have a week's honeymoon in Switzerland. In April 1939, that was. It was Mr and Mrs Tuke's wedding present.'

'I rather think,' Pollard said gently, 'that you are going to tell me that your first husband exchanged passports with Henry Benchley, for some reason?'

She nodded without speaking.

'Was this Henry Benchley in some trouble which made him anxious to get out of the country before the police caught up on him?'

'That's right.'

Bit by bit the story came out. John Frederick Tuke and Henry Benchley were first cousins, born within days of each other. Benchley had been wild from the start: always in trouble at school, and then over girls and betting. A good-looker with a way with him. He'd joined up when war broke out and deserted after a couple of years. The family gave out that he was missing. Then in the autumn of 1947 he'd suddenly turned up at the Thomas Tukes' home, told them that he'd married a girl with money coming to her, but wanted to be able to fade out if the police ever tracked him down as a deserter. A passport in somebody else's name would be just the ticket.

'Johnny knew he was dying,' Mrs Nelson said, staring past Pollard out of the window. 'He'd always had a soft spot for Harry, and so they changed over passports. There was quite a likeness, you see. . . . I didn't know it was done until Johnny'd gone.'

'I don't think,' Pollard reassured her, 'that you need worry at all about this information coming out. It will have to go into my report, but that will be a confidential document. But I want you to let me have this passport of Henry Benchley for a time. Inspector Toye will give you a receipt for it, and it will be returned to you later on.'

'I don't want it back,' she said vehemently. 'It mustn't ever come to the house. I've never told anybody about it up to now—not even Dick, dearly though I love him.'

'All right, Mrs Nelson. Inspector Toye will make out a

176

brief statement for you to sign . . . Did you ever hear any more of Henry Benchley?'

'Never. I remember Johnny saying he thought he'd get over to America and just disappear. It's a great big country, isn't it? I often wonder what happened to the poor girl he married. If there was such a person, of course. I never believed half he said. But when I read that Edward Tuke was the son of a man who'd emigrated to America in 1948 and married an American girl, that passport business kept coming back to my mind.'

★

On returning to the police headquarters at Marsden Pollard called his office at the Yard briefly but urgently. He then succeeded after some delay in contacting Hildebrand Robinson at St Catherine's house.

'Robinson,' came the familiar dry voice. 'What's up?'

'You can scrub the pursuit of another Tuke in the early nineteen-twenty birth registrations,' Pollard told him. 'I've beaten you to it. In fairness I'll admit you put me on the right track by unearthing Paul George Tuke of Waldenhurst. Details when we meet.'

'Do I transfer my efforts to Amaryllis Hartley and her alleged lapse from virtue?'

'Never mind about that. Just try to find out if she married a Henry Benchley between—say, early 1946 and late 1947.'

'There seems to have been a variety of options open to the lady. Any idea where they might have got spliced.'

'No evidence at the moment. London seems the most probable venue, I think. A London registry office.'

'Well, let me know if you beat me to this one, too. Where are you speaking from?'

'Marsden. We shall be going down to Littlechester tomorrow. You can always get on to me through the Yard. Good hunting.'

Hildebrand Robinson reciprocated and rang off.

After a further exchange of courtesies and after expressing renewed thanks to his Marsden hosts, Pollard boarded another police car with Toye en route for the railway station. They arrived at the Yard soon after seven. Pollard's secretary handed him a message. A call at the Faculty Office in Westminster had produced the information that on the previous Monday a Special Marriage Licence had been issued to Rodney Silvester Kenway-Potter, bachelor, of Woodcombe Manor, Woodcombe, Littlechester, and Amaryllis Eleanor Tuke, widow, of the same address. Further enquiries had established that the couple had been married at a central London registry office on the following day.

'Bigamy,' Toye said disapprovingly after reading this information. 'I'll admit I never thought of that one.'

'Cheer up,' Pollard replied. 'I didn't either. But at least we've managed to get the info before all these places close down for the weekend.'

Chapter Ten

Toye was still in a state of outraged astonishment as they drove down to Littlechester on the following morning.

'I'd never have believed it of her,' he said, referring to Amaryllis Kenway-Potter. 'Not somebody of her sort.'

'You've got to think back, old man,' Pollard reminded him. 'She's fifty-one. Born in 1929. Eighteen years old in 1947, and a damn goodlooking girl. Too young to have been in the women's services and browned off by a dreary wartime adolescence, probably. I can remember a good deal of kicking over the traces by her age group, jobs and flats in London and whatever.'

'It didn't usually end in marriage,' Toye observed.

'True. But according to Mrs Nelson, Benchley was the attractive adventurer type and thought he was on to a good thing financially ... I suppose you realise that we're not much nearer to being able to charge either or both of the K-Ps?'

'Bigamy's a much stronger motive than a bastard kid.'

'That's beyond dispute. And so's the fact that either of them could have chucked that ruddy notice into the river. But I doubt if we can ever produce satisfactory proof of their knowing that young Tuke would come down that way and try to cut across the footbridge.'

After they had driven for some time in silent meditation Toye asked what the programme was.

'We confront the K-Ps this afternoon and see if we can startle anything out of them. I doubt it. And there's always the possibility that after all there's nothing to startle. If we draw a blank we beaver away at finding someone who saw either of them acting suspiciously between 3.30 and 6.30 pm on April the twenty-third, or alternatively, can clear them. As a last resort we go back to the Fordyces, the Wonnacotts, Mrs Rawlings and Bolling, keeping a weather eye open for A.N. Other whom we've overlooked altogether. Take heart, though. We'll fortify ourselves with a good lunch first.'

Toye declined to rise to this proffered crumb of comfort.

'You're spot on about the chance of startling the K-Ps into giving themselves away,' he said, 'now that they've been sharp enough to get themselves legally married. They'll know that nothing that either of 'em says can be used in evidence to incriminate the other. Nice work, but why didn't they do it before, for heaven's sake? Anything might have gone wrong, having to rush it like that. It's nearly two months since Edward Tuke's death.'

'I'll hazard a guess that Mrs K-P came clean in the nursing home, in the emotive atmosphere of the failed suicide. One can see that they're still in love, and he's an astute cool-headed chap who knows the ropes, and he put his mind to getting things fixed quickly in case we got wise to the situation and started putting an oar in. After all, they had other reasons for wanting to legalise the situation: legitimising their children, for one. And there's a lot of property to be disposed of ultimately.'

'What'll happen to her?' Toye asked. 'Over the bigamy, I mean?'

'My guess is, nothing, unless she's found guilty of murder or of being an accessory. It will be referred to the highest levels, of course, but Henry Benchley's been dead for nearly thirty years and I can't visualise her being prosecuted after all this time, other things being equal.'

'You don't believe they did the job, do you?' Toye said suddenly some minutes later, his tone faintly accusatory.

'I suppose I'd better admit to a hunch that they didn't, damn your eyes,' Pollard replied rather reluctantly. 'But for God's sake don't ask me who did.'

An hour later, when they arrived at Littlechester police station, they found that the investigation into the fire at Bridge Cottage and Leonard Bolling's death seemed to be heading for stalemate. The forensic experts had confirmed their original theory of how the fire had been started and then spread with horrifying rapidity after the explosion of the cylinder of bottled gas. Every man, woman and child over eight years of age in Woodcombe had been questioned about his or her movements during the fire. The general confusion had been such, however, that people had little or no clear recollection of whom they had seen about or at what stage.

'The one single bit of information we got that might lead to something came from one of our Littlechester firemen,' Inspector Deeds said. 'Our engine didn't get to Woodcombe until about quarter of an hour after Wynford's. As it came down the hill to Upper Bridge one of the chaps says he thought he got a glimpse of somebody crouching down behind the wall on the north side of the stream, just by the stile where you get on to the path along the bank. Couldn't see if it was a man or a woman, only that it looked like a human being caught in the headlights for a split second. We went out there and it would have been perfectly possible to see over the wall: a fire engine's crew are mounted quite high. We've been over the spot with a toothcomb but there wasn't a single recognisable trace of anybody having hidden there. The paraffin used must've been brought in a container of sorts but it hasn't turned up. We've alerted the refuse collectors and the water bailiffs downstream, but no luck so far.'

'If the fireman actually did see somebody at the bridge the timing's worth considering, don't you feel?' Pollard said. 'Think yourself into the arsonist's shoes. You get everything lined up and then stand clear to make sure it's all going according to plan. Then quite suddenly there's a noise like an atom bomb exploding and obviously the whole village will be around in minutes. What would be your best escape route?'

'Close to the hedge on the Marycott road, and in at the Manor gates and sharp left into the woods. Keep under cover in the trees and head for the stile at Upper Bridge,' Inspector Deeds replied without hesitation.

'That's what I'd have done,' Pollard agreed, 'with the long term aim of unobtrusively joining the crowd in the village street from behind, so to speak. But I'd know that the Wynford fire engine would be along, followed by the Littlechester one, and police cars and ambulances and whatever, so I'd go to ground as near the main road as I dared. All the same, I think I'd have made a dash for it sooner than X did. You can hear a car coming a long way off at that hour... Care to hear what we've been unearthing?'

After an initially stunned reaction to Pollard's narrative Superintendent Newman and Inspector Deeds became increasingly pessimistic. In their view the Kenway-Potters hasty marriage by special licence could only mean one thing: an attempt to make it more difficult for the police to make a convincing case against them of having engineered Edward Tuke's death.

'Not that it was ever plain sailing,' Superintendent Newman observed. 'You'd have to establish beyond reasonable doubt that they knew Tuke was going up to see the blasted stone when he did.'

'Well,' Pollard said, 'under the circumstances one can't rule out the possibility that they're both completely innocent. All I can say is if you get any further with the fireman's alleged human shape lurking at Upper Bridge on the night of the fire, you can't let us in on it too quickly. Without any real evidence to go on I can't help feeling convinced that there's a link between the two deaths.... Come on, Toye. We'd better head for Woodcombe Manor and confront the Kenway-Potters.'

They drove through the village at half-past two getting

a few curious stares from children enjoying their Saturday holiday, but otherwise the place was drowsing after the midday meal. Notices had been erected warning the public to keep out of the ruins of Bridge Cottage, and some demolition had been carried out in the interests of safety. Pollard wondered briefly if Rodney Kenway-Potter would succeed in buying back the little property and obliterating all traces of Leonard Bolling's occupancy. The Rover turned in at the Manor gates and finally drew up at the front door. This was standing open, and a burst of barking came from inside the house. As Pollard and Toye reached the threshold Rodney Kenway-Potter came out of his study, shielding his eyes from the bright light at the door with his hand.

'Ah,' he said. 'Scotland Yard. Come in... All right, Drogo boy. Down.'

As on their first visit to the Manor the French windows of the study were wide open. An armchair was drawn up to them, and a copy of *The Times* had been thrown down on the floor. Once again Toye helped to bring two more chairs forward.

'I haven't seen you around just lately,' Rodney Kenway-Potter remarked conversationally when they were all three seated.

Pollard very seldom decided in advance on an opening gambit when about to interview a potential suspect. He seized the opportunity now offered to him.

'No,' he said. 'We've been making enquiries in various places up and down the country and in London ... Mr Kenway-Potter, when did you first know that you and Mrs Kenway-Potter weren't legally married?'

'Last March. About a month before young Tuke turned up.'

The reply was so unexpected that Pollard was taken aback and had to make a swift effort to retain control of the conversation.

'How did you come to know about it?'

'By becoming interested in my family history through my friendship with Mr Fordyce, who is, as you know, a professional genealogist. He told me about sources of information, and how to collect and record facts and so on. We were a Lancashire family originally, mill owners who did pretty well out of American cotton. My great-grandfather seems to have felt it was time to move up a bit in the social scale, sold out his interests and bought this estate, where we've been ever since. I've collected all the gen back to my great-great-grandfather who laid the foundations of the family fortunes, so to speak, and found that one of his daughters had married a man called Hartley, and taken off for the south and higher things a generation ahead of our branch. My wife's maiden name was Hartley, so I thought I would work back and see if she was a distant cousin, which she turned out to be. The Hartleys seem to have been a prolific lot, and it was when I was searching in the marriage registrations of a London district I caught sight of my wife's unusual Christian name.' At this point Rodney Kenway-Potter paused in what had been a relaxed and measured statement.

'Go on, please,' Pollard told him.

'The name led me to the registration of her marriage in December 1947 to John Frederick Tuke.'

'I'm sorry to have to press you on this subject,' Pollard said, 'but what further steps did you take?'

'I made a search in the records of divorces which had taken place between January 1948 and July 1950, the latter being the date of my own marriage with Amaryllis.'

'And had a divorce taken place between her and George Thomas Tuke?'

'No.'

'Did you then tell Mrs Kenway-Potter, as she now legally is, that you knew of her first marriage?'

'Not then.'

'But the subject must have been discussed between you both, since you were married by special licence on

Tuesday of this week?'

'Quite.' Rodney Kenway-Potter folded his arms and looked Pollard straight in the face. 'You see, she told me about it herself. In the nursing home last week, after she had tried to kill herself. And I then told her that I already knew about her first marriage... Look here, Chief Superintendent, you strike me as a human being as well as a C.I.D. ace. Surely you see that the only way we could weather the situation was by convincing each other of our mutual love and trust? After the trauma of Edward Tuke's appearance and proposed investigation into his family history, and still more after his death, I felt certain from her state of tension that she was going to tell me about her first marriage. The mistake I made—if it was a mistake as things turned out—was letting things drift on to danger point.'

'Yes, I do see,' Pollard said after a few moments of silence, wondering at the same time if Toye would be utterly appalled at this somewhat unprofessional reaction. 'But I also have my professional duty to consider.'

'Of course you have. And we both realise that now my wife's first marriage has come out we can be seen to have had a strong motive for getting rid of young Tuke. We'—

Rodney Kenway-Potter broke off at the sound of footsteps on the stairs. The door opened and Amaryllis came into the room.

'Good afternoon,' she said, as the three men rose formally to their feet. 'I saw your car outside, Chief Superintendent, and felt I ought to be in on this meeting with my husband... Thank you,' she added as Toye brought up another chair. As she sat down Pollard was aware that she was far more relaxed than when he had interviewed her before.'

'Chief Superintendent Pollard knows about our marriage on Tuesday, darling,' Rodney said. 'And all the back history.'

She gave Pollard a long clear look.

185

'Of course it can be said now that we had an outsize motive to—to eliminate that poor boy, can't it?'

'It can,' he replied. 'But charges aren't brought on grounds of motive alone.'

'Where do we go from here?' Rodney asked.

'We shall, of course, see if there is any reliable evidence that either of you knew what Edward Tuke's movements were going to be on the evening of his death. We shall go on making enquiries about your movements between your return from your lunch party and the discovery of his body. And also about the possible involvement of anyone else in his death ... Mrs Kenway-Potter, we shall have to ask you for a statement on your first marriage at some point. Would you be prepared to make one this afternoon?'

'Yes, I'm quite prepared to here and now,' she replied calmly. 'I've nothing to tell you that my husband doesn't know already, so I'd like him to be here, if that's in order.'

'Quite in order. Inspector Toye will take notes, and we'll have what you say typed out for you to read over, and to sign if you agree it's an accurate version.'

Amaryllis Kenway-Potter sat for a few moments as if assembling her thoughts, her hands clasped loosely in her lap. Normally, Pollard thought as he observed her, she's so good to look at that you stop there and miss out on the strength of character and latent drive ...

'On my twentieth birthday in 1947,' she began without circumlocution, 'I came into an income of three hundred a year. Quite a bit in those days. My home life with rather elderly parents had been very orthodox and conventional, and I kicked over the traces, and went to live in London on my own, and got a job in Harridges. I enjoyed my independence and my untidy bedsitter and the absence of routine immensely. And the—well, classlessness, after years of social segregation. I felt that I was really living for the first time ... Is this the sort of information you

186

want?'

'Yes,' Pollard told her. 'Please carry on, Mrs Kenway-Potter.'

'I met John Tuke and we fell for each other. He was different from any boy friends I'd had at home, which was part of his appeal, of course. I stood out for marriage because I was green enough to believe that it would make my new lifestyle permanent. We married in a London registry office in December 1947 without telling anybody. In March 1948 I came in rather late one evening and found a note. It said that he had to get out of the country at once as the police were catching up on him as a deserter during the war. He had fixed a passport and was leaving for Canada that afternoon. As rational moderns he was sure that I would agree with him that we must wash out our marriage and make fresh starts. I could absolutely rely on never hearing from him again.'

Silence descended. . . . End of story as far as her personal reactions went, Pollard thought.

'And did you,' he asked, 'ever hear from him again?'

'No, never.'

'And do you know that Henry Benchley—for that was his real name, not John Tuke—was killed in a motor accident in U.S.A. in 1953?'

'Yes, I heard it from James Fordyce when he was telling us about young Edward Tuke's—Benchley's—visit to him. . . . May I ask you a question?'

'Certainly. I'll answer it if I can.'

'Shall I now have to face a charge of having made a bigamous marriage in 1950?'

'Your past history must, of course, be included in my report to my superiors. Other things being equal,' he went on, speaking with deliberation, 'I think it is possible that no action will be taken in the matter owing to the lapse of time since Henry Benchley's death . . . One more question from me, now. What made you so certain that young Edward Tuke was your first husband's son? Was there a marked resemblance?'

'Not marked, but it was his smile ... the name had given me a jolt, and then there was the American accent. And what James Fordyce told us filled in the picture.'

'Which, incidentally, was not until the day after young Tuke's death,' Rodney Kenway-Potter remarked. 'You can ask him.'

*

'Quite an afternoon for a chap as hooked on romance as you are,' Pollard remarked as soon as the departing Rover was out of earshot of Rodney Kenway-Potter on the front steps of Woodcombe Manor.

Toye, who appeared abstracted, conceded that he'd never come up with a story to equal what they'd just heard, not in his whole time in the Force. Romance and moral principle were obviously contending for mastery in his mind. He asked if the next stop was the Fordyce's bungalow.

'Not on your life,' Pollard replied. 'I'm not interviewing James Fordyce with his wife outside the door of that box of a study with her ears flapping. I'll ring him from Littlechester and ask him to come over. The Kenway-Potters may be priming him at this moment about when he told them about Edward Tuke's disclosures, but we'll have to risk that, anyway.'

On arrival at the Littlechester police station, however, he found to his surprise that James Fordyce had tried to contact him. A message was handed to him stating that Mr Fordyce had called in person at 15.50 hours hoping to see him, and would be returning at 16.45 hours.

'So what?' Pollard passed the message to Toye. 'At least it's a change to have somebody else taking the initiative. We've just about time for a cuppa.'

James Fordyce was announced punctually at a quarter to five, greeted politely and offered the spare chair in the

188

crowded little room.

'Thanks,' he said abruptly, and sat down. 'I've come to say that I want to amend one item of the statement I made to you recently. I'—

'Just one moment,' Pollard said. 'Let's have out the file copy of Mr Fordyce's statement, Inspector... Right. Please go ahead, Mr Fordyce.'

'You commented that I had taken a long time to inspect the outside of Bridge Cottage and cover the short distance to Upper Bridge where I met Bill Morris. I said that on leaving the cottage I sat down by the stream to think over the pros and cons of making an offer for it, and dropped off to sleep. Only the first part of this is true. I did not drop off to sleep.'

These remarks were delivered in a somewhat disjointed fashion which puzzled Pollard... It's as though the chap's mind is on something else, he thought.

'What did you do, then, Mr Fordyce?' he asked.

'There's a low stone wall backed by a hedge between the river bank and Manor Woods. When I heard the Kenway-Potters' car returning to the Manor I got up and watched their arrival through a gap in the hedge.'

'Both Mr and Mrs Kenway-Potter have stated that they returned home on the afternoon of April the twenty-third at approximately half-past three. How long did you stay at your observation post, as we'll call it?'

'I suppose until about a quarter to four.'

'Do you want to make a statement about what you observed during this time?'

'Yes, I do.' James Fordyce sat looking at the table in front of him, his long face tired and drawn. 'Mr Kenway-Potter helped his wife out of the car, unlocked the front door and then drove the car round in the direction of the garage. He came back, spoke to her in the hall for a few moments, and finally came out with some newspapers and settled in a deck chair on the terrace. Mrs Kenway-Potter apparently went upstairs to the room over the drawing room which is on the left of the front door, and which is probably her bedroom. She appeared briefly at the window, having taken off the green and white frock she was wearing. I did not see her again.'

'When you left at about a quarter to four was Mr Kenway-Potter still in the deck chair on the terrace?'

'Yes. He appeared to be asleep.'

'Why have you come to amend your original statement in this way?' Pollard asked after a short pause.

'My wife tells me that people in the village are pointing out that the Kenway-Potters were very well-placed to remove the warning notice on the footbridge. I consider that my observations are evidence that at least for the first part of the time after they came home that afternoon they did nothing of the kind. I'm prepared to swear to the truth of what I've just told you.'

'But of course,' Pollard went on, 'this doesn't explain why you kept watch in the first place, does it? Edward Tuke was alive and well at the time. I think it is reasonable to ask you why you behaved in such an unusual way, to say the least of it.'

James Fordyce gave a smile of remarkable bitterness.

'I suppose,' he said, 'the psychologists would say I am a masochist. My marriage has been a failure. I was observing their mutual happiness. In short, indulging in envy ... I suppose you'll want me to sign my amended statement?'

'We'll let you know when it's been typed,' Pollard told him. 'Thank you for coming in and putting things straight,' Mr Fordyce. Inspector Toye will see you out.'

When Toye came back he was sitting reflectively at his desk.

'Poor devil,' he said. 'I think I'm dead right about his being in love with the fair Amaryllis, you know. He went about as near as he could to saying so in plain English. And the way he's tensed up suggests that he's got a very strong suspicion—or even knows—that his wife's responsible for the anonymous letters.'

They agreed that James Fordyce's evidence narrowed the critical period for the Kenway-Potters in the late afternoon and early evening of April the twenty-third, but to a very limited extent. The only thing to do at the moment was to go over the depressingly familiar contents of the case file yet again. They had begun to write up the day's notes when Inspector Deeds looked in with a couple of sheets of typescript.

'Nothing likely to tie up with your job, but we thought you'd better have a copy,' he said. 'The forensic lads say the newspapers used to start up the fire at Bridge Cottage were copies of the *Daily Chat*. Only twenty households in Woodcombe take it in regularly, but of course you can pick it up at every newsagent's in Wynford and here. Anyway, here's a list of the Woodcombe regulars.'

'All contributions gratefully received,' Pollard replied. 'In exchange, here's the latest instalment of the Kenway-Potter saga'....

Inspector Deeds listened to the account of the afternoon's interview with close attention.

'You'd have to be a top writer to dream up a yarn like this one,' he commented. 'The way they've both acted all through's been unpredictable from the beginning to the end, wouldn't you say, sir?'

Pollard agreed.

'But my experience over the years is that a lot of people do act in a way you'd never expect,' he said. 'That's one of the things that makes our job so difficult. You've got to have some imagination and be able to get inside the other chap's skin if you can.'

'Imagination's my weak spot,' Inspector Deeds admitted with engaging frankness. 'I was quite hot on maths and science at school, but I never got anywhere with Shakespeare and whatever.'

'Most of the types we deal with are in his plays, you know. You might try another bash at him from this point of view. You've got a lot of what's wanted on the way up: powers of observation and deduction, to start with.'

Patently gratified, Inspector Deeds went off.

'Good chap,' Pollard remarked, returning to his notes.

It had been a strenuous day and he had to make an effort to keep his mind on the job. Some phrase that Deeds had used was lurking irritatingly just outside the threshold of his consciousness. It was not until he was in bed that night that it came back to him: 'from the beginning to the end'. A sonorous phrase reminiscent of the Scriptures ... Mary, Queen of Scots' 'in my end is my beginning' ... T.S. Eliot's 'in my beginning is my end' ... the King of Hearts hectoring the White Rabbit in the Trial Scene: 'Begin at the beginning and go on till you come to the end'... Pollard suddenly found himself very wide awake. Had he really begun at the beginning of the grim and incomprehensible sequence of events at Woodcombe? He had a sudden mental picture of a small boy falling from a tree in Manor Woods, and knew in the same instant that he would go and visit the Westbridges the next day. The decision made, he was soon asleep.

*

The Westbridges had a telephone and Pollard put through a call after breakfast the next morning. A man's voice answered repeating the number.

'Mr Westbridge?' he queried.

'Jim Westbridge speaking. Who is it?'

'Detective-Chief Superintendent Pollard, Mr Westbridge. You probably know that I'm carrying out the investigation into the death of the late Edward Tuke on the twenty-third of April. I think it's just possible that you and your wife might be able to give me some help. Would it be convenient if I came over to see you this morning?'

There was a silence lasting several moments. The suggestion was clearly unwelcome.

'I'd like to know if what you want to see us about is anything to do with the death of our adopted son in 1974. I don't want my wife upset by going over it all again.'

'Yes, it is about the boy's death, Mr Westbridge,' Pollard replied. 'I perfectly understand how you feel about your wife. But if there should turn out to be a link between Robin's death and Edward Tuke's and Leonard Bolling's, the sooner the police get on to it the better, don't you think?'

'I suppose you're right,' Mr Westbridge said unwillingly. 'Though how there can be any link I can't for the life of me imagine. You'd better come over, only don't distress Mrs Westbridge more than you can help, that's all. What time do you want to come?'

Half-past ten was agreed upon and Pollard rang off. He had decided to go alone, and managed to persuade Toye to take some time off and sample Matins at Littlechester Cathedral. He borrowed the report of the inquest on Robin Westbridge from the local police archives once again and studied it very carefully before starting off. One had to admit that it was detailed, straightforward and convincing.

It appeared that the Westbridges lived at the eastern end of the village, and he decided to take a roundabout route and come into Woodcombe by the Marycott road. He felt that it would be as well for the visit to be as inconspicuous as possible. After all, his only grounds for making it at all was a rather odd hunch and it seemed hardly fair to expose the Westbridges to unnecessary local curiosity and gossip on such tenuous grounds. In the event the drive along narrow winding roads virtually free of traffic was pure pleasure. The June hedges were still fresh and green and a riot of Queen Anne's lace, foxgloves and wild roses. He found that the road works had now reached Marycott, and drove on past the place where he had talked to the foreman and got on to the track of the pickaxe and spade 'borrowed' by Leonard Bolling. He

193

parked carefully just out of sight of the drive gates of Woodcombe Manor, and finished his journey on foot.

The Westbridge cottage showed a high standard of external maintenance, and its carefully tended front garden had a fine display of roses and annuals. Pollard's knock was answered by Mr Westbridge, a small man somewhere in his mid-forties, with hair already thinning on the top and an anxious look about him. Mrs Westbridge was a faded blonde who gave an impression of sapped vitality. The atmosphere was defensive to start with, but Pollard exercised his knack of setting people at ease and to his relief they both relaxed. He took the line of enlisting their co-operation over a problem that was greatly disturbing the police. Gradually he worked round to the question of whether they had been satisfied with the verdict of Death by Misadventure at the inquest on Robin's death.

'We've talked it over times out of mind,' Mr Westbridge told him, glancing at his wife who nodded her assent. 'It's this way, if I can make what we feel sound sensible. What the coroner said added up. You couldn't fault it: not one single item. But somehow it didn't add up to Robin. For one thing he climbed like a monkey, didn't he, Millie? He'd quite frighten us the way he'd shin up a tree. We can't somehow believe that he'd've fallen out of that great oak tree with all its solid branches unless something out of the way had happened.'

Pollard's grasp of the evidence given at the inquest and the coroner's summing up clearly impressed the Westbridges. Soon they were talking freely, but in spite of exhaustive questioning on his part little that was new came out. Yes, they agreed, from early on he'd always been happy on his own, but he'd often been rumbustious and naughty like any healthy boy. He got on with other kids and could hold his own. There'd never been any trouble about him being bullied, not even when he moved on to the Middle School in Littlechester. Yes, he'd been

194

quick to read and loved books. Adventure stories were what he'd liked best. They had found some tatty old paperbacks in the box up in the tree house, along with other odds and ends he'd taken up there. A toy pistol and a kid's telescope, and a catapult and so on. Sweets, of course, and pebbles he'd brought back from the seaside. They'd been to Weymouth the year before and out on Chesil Beach.

'We've kept the box just as it was except for the sweets,' Mrs Westbridge said. 'Perhaps you'd like to take a look at it since you're here?'

Pollard accepted the offer, more to keep up the friendly atmosphere that had developed than in any hope of getting useful information. Mr Westbridge fetched a battered square biscuit tin and opened it with some difficulty.

'It got a bit rusty up there in the rain,' he said, handing it over.

Pollard took out the contents one by one, inspecting each carefully. The little room became very quiet. After a protracted pause he looked up to find the Westbridges eyeing him with puzzled expressions.

'I'm going to ask you,' he said, 'to let me take this box away for a time. I shall give you an official receipt for it, and it will be in the care of the police and come back to you exactly as it is now.'

To his surprise it was Mrs Westbridge who reacted first.

'Take it and welcome,' she said, choking back a sob. 'I know it wasn't just an accident ... you see, he came round just for a minute before he died, and he was scared stiff ... struggling in the bed as if he was trying to climb up to get away from something ... please excuse me' ... She broke down and ran out of the room.

'I'm sorry,' Pollard said.

'Best for it to come out if—if there's anything to come,' Mr Westbridge said heavily ... 'It's right, what the wife

195

said. I was there too. We'll never forget that moment when he went, poor little chap' . . .

As Pollard walked into Littlechester police station an hour later he caught sight of Inspector Deeds about to leave the entrance hall and called to him.

'Sir?' Deeds, struck by the urgency in his voice, turned and came towards him with an enquiring expression.

'Where in Manor Woods was the tree that kid West-bridge fell out of and killed himself?'

'I can tell you which tree it actually was, sir. Just before we came to the clearing, we went round the side of a big oak. That was the one.'

Looking at him Pollard saw blank astonishment and intense curiosity on his face, held in check by years of professional training.

'A possible development,' he said. 'Come along and hear about it if you'd care to.'

Chapter Eleven

The Curator of Littlechester Museum who had been called in by Superintendent Martin picked up a handful of pebbles from the biscuit tin and scrutinised them.

'No problem whatever,' he said. 'Most of this lot are water-worn flints. The whole lot have been smoothed and rounded by being bashed against each other and against other stones by wave action. It's been going on through millennia, possibly. These reddish and grey ones may have come from as far west as Devon and Cornwall: there's a steady west-to-east drift along the south coast. It's formed Chesil Bank along with other shingle spits.'

'According to their owner these actually came from Chesil Bank,' Pollard told him. 'I'll now ask you officially what is obviously a damn fool question, Mr Gribble. Could any of these pebbles possibly have originated in the Manor Woods at Woodcombe?'

'Not possibly. If you find any of this type there, well, they were taken there for some reason. The Woodcombe hills are a dark-coloured shaley limestone: grey or greenish. . . The Super here will vouch for my discretion. Is it possible that these pebbles tie up in some way with the extraordinary recent happenings there?'

'As the Super vouches for you, Mr Gribble,' Pollard replied gravely, 'I'll go to the length of saying that I'm not ruling it out of court.'

'That's all you're going to get from the Yard, old man,' the Superintendent told the Curator. 'Come along and have a drink, and leave them to digest your specialised information.'

When the two had gone off, Pollard said suddenly, 'The kid must have been nifty with his fingers... You know,' he went on, returning the catapult to the tin, 'in the light of that old boy's expert evidence I think there's a possible explanation of how Robin Westbridge came to fall out of that tree and break his neck. A lot of country lads have catapults and are good shots with 'em. We know Robin was a bit of a loner and addicted to adventure stories. Trespassing in the Kenway-Potter woods and building a tree house there fits in, doesn't it? I don't think he could have been scared of Old Grim or he wouldn't have dug himself in so near it. But to the average boy with a catapult it would have seemed a perfect target. My guess is that he sat in his tree house peppering it with pebbles and pretending that it was an invader from outer space or a dragon. Or even his teacher, perhaps. And then one day an observer comes along and spots what's going on. Not an outraged antiquarian who says he's going straight to the Manor to tell Rodney Kenway-Potter about it, but someone with an abnormal addiction to the remote past and its beliefs which has become focussed on Old Grim.'

Toye, concentrating intently though puzzled, looked up.

'Mrs Rawlings?'

'Of course.'

Characteristically Toye raised a severely practical issue.

'But how could she have made him fall out of the tree? I don't see her shinning up it and getting hold of him.'

'As I told you, he regained consciousness just as he was dying, and according to the parents he was scared stiff and struggling as if he was trying to escape from somebody or something. It looks as though he was so frightened that his physical control went and he lost his balance, perhaps as he was scrambling up to a higher branch.

'You've no proof of any of this,' Toye protested.

198

'Not a scrap. And it's probably impossible that we could ever prove conclusively that Rawlings was responsible for the kid's death. And she might not have intended it, either. But for my own satisfaction I want the ground round the longstone combed to see if any pebbles like this lot are lying about. We won't tackle it today as it's Sunday and she'll probably be at home. What price that pair of binoculars on her desk and the view of the clearing? The essential thing is not to alert her in any way.'

'But if we could never get up a case against her over the boy's death, what's the point of spending time'—

Toye broke off suddenly and stared at Pollard.

'I see you're working round to it, old chap. Suppose I'm right, and Robin Westbridge came crashing down at her feet because she'd somehow scared the living day-lights out of the poor little blighter? What would have been her reaction? It would depend on how dotty she was at that stage. If she believed that Old Grim was a manifestation of the Devil she'd have been triumphant, I suppose. It was proof that she'd been right all the time about the beastly stone, and a chosen instrument of vengeance for sacrilege... So what price the death of Edward Tuke?'

Toye sat silent struggling to cope with ideas outside his previous experience.

'Let's recap the Tuke affair,' Pollard went on. 'He was alive up to the time that James Fordyce showed him the beginning of the path up to the clearing soon after six on April the twenty-third. We know that Rawlings took evening strolls up to Old Grim. She said in her statement to Deeds that she'd been up on the evening of Tuesday the twenty-second and found the longstone in its usual position. Factual recap over: now I'll dismay you by some further speculation. It's Wednesday evening and she goes up again. Either for a pleasant walk or to do homage to Old Grim or whatever. Or, because after her conversation with Edward Tuke in the Green Man at lunchtime she thinks he may decide to go up to indulge in a spot of vandalism for a rag ... I had a good look at the back premises of the Fordyces' bungalow when I trumped up an excuse to get us into the study the other day. The hedge between their back garden and Rawlings's is close to the study window which would certainly have been open on a warm April evening. She could easily have overheard that Tuke was going up to have a look at Old Grim, slipped out herself and hidden behind the bushes where the path starts and followed him up. She finds him standing and surveying Old Grim prostrate on the ground'. . . .

Toye blinked, and groped for what appeared to be the one substantiated fact which undermined this flow of conjecture.

'But Rawlings has got an alibi for the whole time after she got home from work,' he protested. 'She was gardening out at the back of her place.'

'Has she?' Pollard queried. 'And who provided it?' he demanded bitterly. 'Blind and bloody fool that I am, it dawned on me as I drove back from Woodcombe just now that the alibi rests solely on Eileen Fordyce's word. In short, I've had one of the most disastrous lapses of my career.'

'But why did she do it?' Toye demanded, loyally rallying to Pollard's defence. 'Fordyce, I mean. They weren't buddies. Remember Fordyce saying that they weren't exactly friends. Made out that going in for a cuppa with Rawlings was quite a comedown.'

Pollard pushed his chair back from the table and sat with his arms folded.

'I rather think,' he said, 'that it's been a case of mutual blackmail. We feel it's likely, don't we, that James Fordyce left confidential papers about Tuke's family history lying on his desk when he dashed out after Kenway-Potter's S.O.S. on the Wednesday evening? And also that Fordyce had, in fact, started looking things up for Tuke and got on to the marriage between Tuke's father and Amaryllis K-P. If Eileen Fordyce is responsible for the anonymous letters, this was almost certainly the only chance she would have of getting at the information about the bigamy. The light would have been on in the study at half-past eight on an April evening, and Eileen Fordyce, completely absorbed, perfectly visible from the other side of the hedge. Suppose Rawlings, having spotted her, and curious about James Fordyce dashing off down the road, came round earlier than she admits, waits until she hears Eileen go upstairs to look out of the window, and then slips into the study herself. She files the information in her mind for possible future use, calls up to Eileen to ask if everything is all right and hears the news about Edward Tuke.'

He broke off and glanced at Toye who was listening intently and gave a nod.

'Could've been like that,' he conceded.

'As everybody concluded at first that the football fans had pulled up the warning notices,' Pollard went on, 'it may have been some days before Deeds got round to taking a statement from Rawlings. By that time it would have struck her that an alibi for the evening of the twenty-third might be an advantage. She realised that she'd got Eileen Fordyce by the short hairs and gave her the option of providing the alibi, or having her husband told that she had taken the chance of reading confidential papers that he'd left on his desk that evening. He'd know only too well what the papers had been, of course. And in reverse, so to speak, Eileen Fordyce had got Rawlings by the short hairs in her turn.'

'Funny,' Toye reacted unexpectedly. 'You said something about an unholy alliance before ... Kenway-Potter and Fordyce to protect Mrs K-P when they'd found out about her first marriage ... Do you think Mrs F. knew that her husband was in love with Mrs K-P?'

'I think she probably senses it. Women do. If she does, it helps to explain her vindictiveness.'

'If you're right about Rawlings following Tuke up to the clearing, what do you suppose happened then?'

'I think the impact of finding Tuke contemplating Old Grim flat on the ground sent her irrevocably off balance, leaving her with the quick-wittedness and cunning that often go with insanity. A little friendly chat about football hooligans, advice to Tuke to go up to see the view, and detailed instructions about the handy short cut back to the car park at the Green Man... We've been over all this ground before, haven't we? They part company, and Rawlings nips down and pulls up the notice. Getting back to her cottage is the risky bit, but she pulls it off. No one came forward to report having seen her.'

Toye, having listened with close attention, remained silent. Pollard suddenly grinned at him.

'Come on,' he said. 'I'm waiting for it. Tell me again I've no proof whatever.'

Toye grinned back. Years of working together on a long succession of cases had established an unshakeable rapport between them.

'Now and again I get an idea of the way the wind's blowing,' he said. 'You're working up to the third job, I take it: Bolling's death in the fire? We've got something there that could lead to a solid bit of evidence with a bit of luck. What the fireman saw crouching down by Upper Bridge.'

Pollard saluted him ironically.

'Two minds with but a single thought,' he observed. 'I don't think we've given our full attention to all the gen Littlechester passed over to us on the fire. It's in the file. Let's have a go, and see how it ties in with what we got from Mrs Fordyce'...

The sequence of events after the discovery of the fire seemed to have been clearly established. The 999 call from Woodcombe had reached the fire stations at Wynford and Littlechester at 1.40 am on Wednesday morning. The Wynford brigade reached the scene first.

In a brief statement to Inspector Deeds the officer in charge reported that as the fire engine turned off the main road into the village a woman had come dashing out of the first house on the right into the glare of the headlights, and the driver had slowed and swerved to avoid her. None of the crew had noticed a light in the house or in the one next to it, but their attention had of course been on the fierce glow of the fire at the far end of the village. A Wynford police car arriving about a minute later had contained a constable driver and a sergeant. The latter, well aware of the risk of break-ins when public attention was distracted by a fire, had scrutinised both the Fordyces' bungalow and Mrs Rawlings's cottage in passing, and stated categorically that there had been no lights in any of the windows. By the time the car reached the Green Man people were hurrying out of their doors and running down the village street, and neither of the men noticed a woman apparently on her own.

Pollard hunted in the file and extracted Mrs Fordyce's statement on her actions at the time of the fire.

. . .'I didn't want to be left alone,' he read aloud, 'so I began to grab some clothes, but he wouldn't wait. Just told me to go in next door and see if Mrs Rawlings was all right . . . I saw that her light was on, so I didn't stop. I ran on and the fire engine overtook me' . . .

They agreed that the discrepancies were suggestive but might be difficult to establish conclusively. Toye remarked that people would often tell lies to cover up that they'd made fools of themselves like bursting out of a gate without a thought of traffic. Pollard agreed.

'And she'd want to provide a reason for not going to see if Mrs Rawlings was up and doing,' he said. 'Let's have a go at the Littlechester report.'

Here, in addition to the statement of the fireman who claimed that he had seen somebody crouching down behind the wall at Upper Bridge, or at least something "that looked like a human being", there was agreement between two members of the crew that the two houses at the beginning of the village had been quite dark. Nothing doing in the street, either, until you got past the pub and people were milling about and getting in the way. The occupants of the Littlechester police car which had come along in the wake of the fire engine had noticed no one at the bridge, but confirmed the absence of lights in the windows of the two houses.

Pollard pushed away the sheets of typescript in front of him and sat with his chin cupped in his hands.

'One loose end we must tidy up is this part-time job of Rawlings at the Littlechester City Library. How many days a week does she go in and pick up the Mobile Library van?'

'Posting the anonymous letters?' Toye asked.

'Yea. That'll have to wait till tomorrow. I hate Sundays when I'm up to the neck in a case. Everything in a state of suspended animation. . . . Let's go over to Wynford and see if any of the firemen who came over to Woodcombe are available. We might pick up something. And we could have some grub over there, too.'

By an unexpected stroke of good luck the Wynford fire engine had just returned to base from a small heath fire, and the fire officer they had talked to amid the ruins of Bridge Cottage was available. They bore him off for a drink, in the course of which Pollard was struck by another possibility.

'I suppose,' he asked, 'you didn't notice anyone coming out of the cottage next door to the bungalow that the woman had run out of?'

The fire officer replied that he could say for sure that nobody had been coming out. He'd given a good look, being a bit jittery after that crazy jane had all but landed under the engine. A visit to the Wynford police station produced much the same result. The sergeant who had been in the police car was off duty but located by telephone. He was not only certain that no one was emerging from the cottage as they passed, but had looked back when they reached the Green Man. The ambulance that was following had just turned the corner and its head-lights were lighting up the road into the village, but there was nobody coming along on foot.

Toye agreed over a supper of steak and chips that it did look as though Rawlings hadn't been in her house, at any rate until after the Littlechester brigade and its support had gone through.

Pollard reverted to the fire itself.

'The forensic chaps seem quite definite that the gas explosion wasn't part of the arsonist's original programme,' he said. 'We'll go on assuming for the present that it was the Rawlings woman's scheme to get the ground floor well alight, and practically ensure that Bolling would be suffocated in his bed by fumes and smoke. She would have waited long enough to see things under way and then headed for home.'

'Would she have left her bedroom light on?' Toye asked.

'No, I'm sure she wouldn't. Somebody coming back late from a party or whatever might have noticed it. The great thing for a murderer is to be utterly unnoticeable if possible. But the explosion threw her timetable out. As she lurked behind the wall at Old Bridge I bet she was casting about for some way of showing that she had been in bed when Bridge Cottage blew up, and was hit by the idea of telling Mrs F to say her bedroom light had been on when she—Mrs F—had rushed out to see what was happening at the other end of the village. Knowing Mrs F as we do, she wouldn't have missed out over looking up the aged in case Mrs K-P had already gone into action as Lady of the Manor.'

'I can't say I took to Mrs Fordyce,' Toye observed temperately, 'but would she have agreed to cover up a second successful killing?'

'Rawlings had got her in a cleft stick if she posted the

anonymous letters, knowing what was in 'em.'

They ate in silence for a couple of minutes.

'Even if we find dozens of Chesil Bank pebbles on the ground round Old Grim we've no direct evidence against Rawlings yet,' Pollard said. 'But Mrs F might be tackled on the strength of the firemen's and the police evidence about lights in the cottage. But we've got to co-ordinate with Littlechester. The fire and Bolling's death are still officially their pigeon.'

★

A conference with the Chief Constable, Superintendent Martin and Inspector Deeds was held at nine o'clock on the following morning. After thorough discussion joint action was agreed upon. As a preliminary move a sergeant was sent to the City Library to enquire into the schedules of the Mobile Library vans in connection with alleged complaints of traffic obstruction. He returned with the information that Mrs Rawlings did a round on Mondays, Wednesdays and Fridays. Her Monday round was devoted entirely to villages on the north side of Littlechester.

'All clear for your pebble hunt then, Pollard,' Robert Gregg said. 'You'd better have a spot of help to speed things up... Meanwhile, see if you can get our fire people to send an engine out with the chap on board who says he saw somebody behind that wall, Martin. Deeds, you'd better go along and check for yourself, and take an official statement from the chap.'

Shortly afterwards Pollard and Toye left for Woodcombe. In the back of the Rover was a young constable barely able to conceal his gratification at being chosen to accompany them, and in charge of spades and rakes. Toye parked the car at the pull-in at Upper Bridge and the trio made its way up the path to the clearing. On arrival there Pollard looked around more thoroughly than on his earlier visit when he had been concentrating on Old Grim. The clearing was roughly circular with a diameter of about thirty feet, and looked as though its ragged grass and other plant growth was roughly cut down at intervals. Probably as a result of pressure from the County Archaeological Society, he thought, to make access to the longstone easier.

'Do you reckon we'll find any of those pebbles after all this time, sir?' the constable ventured.

'With luck, my lad,' Pollard replied. 'Fortunately it is not a bare slope where rain could have washed them downhill. Now then, we'll divide the place into three and work outwards from the stone.'

It was already hot and they hung their jackets on branches and raked energetically in shirtsleeves. The search was easier than Pollard had expected as the soil was thin and the plant cover mainly short-rooted. Robin Westbridge had apparently been a good shot with his catapult. Within a comparatively short time a dozen smooth rounded flints and other pebbles had been unearthed near the base of the longstone. As these were discovered Pollard paused to make a rough sketch map and plot the approximate positions of the finds. They moved outwards and located a few more which had considerably overshot or fallen short of the mark, and he decided to call off the operation.

'Let's have a breather in the shade,' he said, subsiding under the oak tree and dusting off his knees. 'We'd be justified in putting in for the price of new trousers, don't you think, Toye?'

After a few minutes the sound of a heavy vehicle starting up and driving off reached them from the road below.

'Could be the fire engine,' Toye suggested. 'Inspector Deeds should be along.'

Footsteps on the path announced the latter's approach soon afterwards. He appeared mopping his brow and asked anxiously if they had had any luck. On being shown the haul of pebbles he raised his eyebrows and gave Pollard a look of unqualified admiration.

'What about you?' Pollard asked. 'Did you get any further with the fireman chap?'

'I did, sir. Very satisfactory. He was a lot more definite seeing the place by daylight. He took up the position behind the wall where he thought he'd spotted somebody, and I got up on the fire engine where he'd been positioned that night. The wall wasn't high enough to give complete cover from anybody at that height.'

Pollard looked up and saw the unspoken question in the younger man's face. The moment of decision appeared to have arrived.

'Well,' he said, 'on the strength of that bit of evidence and our bag of pebbles I'm prepared to tackle Mrs Fordyce on her statement about the alleged light in Mrs Rawlings's cottage on the night of the fire. Would you like to put Superintendent Martin in the picture first?'

'No need, sir. Before I came away he told me to make a decision based on the fireman's evidence and go ahead if you were prepared to. We both feel as you do that Mrs Fordyce is the weak link in the chain. Bust it there, and we'll pull in Rawlings.'

'Right, then, Deeds. Let's go.'

The column started on the descent. Pollard reflected that Deeds would have to take the initiative with Eileen Fordyce as Bolling's death was officially Littlechester's case. He himself must be at the ready to make the right contribution at the psychological moment. He became aware that his spine had begun to tingle slightly as it always did just before an irrevocable move was impending.

When they arrived in the road it was decided that Toye and Smeaton should stay with the cars. Pollard and Deeds crossed Upper Bridge and walked towards the Woodcombe turning. A woman carrying a basket was coming from the direction of Wynford. They bore left, arrived at the gate of the Fordyces' bungalow, went up the short path and rang the front door bell. There was no sound from within and Pollard was suddenly seized with foreboding.

'Excuse me.' The woman with the basket had reached the gate and paused. She had a pleasant middle-aged face, sunburnt and very sketchily made-up. 'If you're looking for the Fordyces I'm afraid they're both out. Mr Fordyce is away on one of his searches and won't be back till tonight. And Mrs Fordyce has gone on a picnic to Great Birdcliff with Mrs Rawlings. I happened to be in the shop earlier on when they came in to buy things for their lunch.'

'Mrs Rawlings isn't working today, then?' Pollard queried with outward composure. 'I thought Monday was one of her library days.'

'So it is as a rule. But she's starting a week's holiday today—Would it help if I ran over here this evening and gave Mrs Fordyce a message?'

Pollard thanked her politely but said that he would ring later in the day. As she moved on he started for the gate with Deeds.

'Christ, that's torn it,' the latter said out of the corner of his mouth. 'They'll have seen the bloody cars at the bridge. Everybody in the village knows 'em by heart by now.'

'Over and above which,' Pollard said grimly, 'the odds are that Rawlings spotted us crawling all over the clearing through her binoculars. She'd got a high-powered pair on her desk, and her sitting room window looks straight across to the woods. Was this picnic a snap decision as a result? Where and what is this Birdcliff place?'

He learnt that it was a stretch of coast formed of high cliffs about fifteen miles north of Littlechester.

'If I get your meaning, sir,' Deeds added, 'it's the sort of place where accidents can happen.'

'Does it mean going back to Littlechester to get there?'

'No need. There's a decent B road branching off from this one which cuts off the corner.'

'You'd better lead.'

Toye and Constable Smeaton, deep in an inspection of the Rover's engine, swung round in astonishment at their superiors' speedy return and dived into their respective cars.

'Tail Deeds,' Pollard told Toye. 'I'll explain as we go along. Where's the map?'

After outlining the situation he studied the route of the B road. It rose gently but steadily to within a short distance of the coast, and then rose sharply to a level platform about fifty yards wide which ran parallel to the shoreline. On the seaward side this ran down steeply to the edge of the cliffs.

Both Toye and Deeds were superb drivers who seemed to have slipped effortlessly into perfect synchronisation. There was little traffic on the road and the distance was covered in what seemed an incredibly short time. As they approached the final rise Deeds flicked out his nearside indicator and drew in to a layby. A few moments later Toye pulled in behind him. Deeds appeared at the passenger window of the Rover as the car came to a halt.

'There's quite good cover, sir,' he told Pollard. 'Clumps of big gorse bushes. As Smeaton's the only one of us those women wouldn't recognise, how about sending him up on a recce? Pity we don't know the car.'

'Grey Mini. 88Z 123,' Toye contributed.

Deeds stared at him dumbfounded.

'Cars are his thing,' Pollard told him with a grin. 'We'll never know what he suffered playing second fiddle on this run ... Yes, you're dead right. Let's brief Smeaton and send him up' ....

Smeaton, pink with excitement at the company he was keeping and the importance of his mission, set off briskly up the hill.

'Try to look like a ruddy birdwatcher,' Deeds called

after him.

They locked the cars and followed, stopping just short of the top of the rise in the lee of a hedge and waited.

After what seemed an eternity, Smeaton returned.

'They've driven along the top to the right,' he reported to Deeds. 'The car's between two big gorse clumps: I didn't spot it at first. Then I saw nobody was in it and slipped round to have a look. The brake's on, but she's in neutral, although the ground's started falling away down to the cliffs. No other cars anywhere near, and two women are walking back towards the car from further along like as if they'd been for a stroll.'

'O.K. Good work.'

There was a short consultation at the end of which Pollard started off with Smeaton. On reaching the top they stood contemplating the sea for a few moments.

'Push on now,' Pollard said.

Guided by Smeaton they wandered in a leisurely way through the gorse, finally arriving behind the large clump concealing the Mini. The sun beat down powerfully, and the fragrance from the mass of golden flowers was almost overpowering. With the surface layer of his mind Pollard identified it with the aroma of Jane's coconut buns just out of the oven. . . .

Women's voices, distant at first, became audible. He could hear Eileen Fordyce saying something about being hungry.

'Better to eat in the car. More comfortable, and cooler, too, with all the windows open. There's quite a breeze. You get in and I'll fetch the basket out of the boot'. . . .

A car door opened. Someone, presumably Eileen Fordyce, could be heard getting in and releasing a deep breath of satisfaction. Pollard was aware of Deeds and Toye arriving close to him.

Another car door opened.

'Take the thermos, will you, while I get out the eats?' Ella Rawlings said.

There was an interval, surprisingly protracted, and unidentifiable sounds of things being moved in the boot.

Without warning a terrified scream rent the air.

'The car's moving downhill! Stop it! Stop it!'

Without conscious thought Pollard found himself seizing the woman at the back of the car who was pushing it forward with all her strength. He wrenched her away from it and swung her round. His heart missed a beat. He was looking down into an horrific face—frenzied, ravenous, sprouting greenery from eyes and mouth...

With uncharacteristic violence he tore off the mask Ella Rawlings was wearing, and knew what had happened to Robin Westbridge.

As she slumped to the ground he was aware that the car had stopped moving but that the screaming was still going on: an hysterical insistence that alibis had been given in all innocence out of loyalty to a friend.

'She must have managed to take the brake off when she passed in the thermos,' Toye was remarking prosaically at his side.

*

When the legal preliminaries in the Rawlings and Fordyce cases had been completed Pollard and Toye returned to the Yard. Pollard finished his lengthy report on the Woodcombe investigation as a whole and sent it in to his Assistant Commissioner. After a few days had elapsed he was notified of an appointment with the latter, and duly presented himself.

'Morning, Pollard,' the A.C. said, giving him a searching and slightly sardonic look. 'So you've pulled it off, apparently. The best feature to my mind is that the Rawlings woman has been pronounced unfit to plead, so you won't be tied up in a trial dragging out for God knows how long. What's going to happen to the other one?'

'Eileen Fordyce, sir? I gather that in the light of the evidence she's been advised to plead guilty.'

'Good. That'll cut down the length of the trial.... I suppose you're kicking yourself for not getting on to Rawlings sooner?'

'Yes, I am, sir,' Pollard replied frankly. 'On the other hand I don't see how I could have taken a different course. As I said to you earlier on, the whole affair was stiff with motives: Kenway-Potter back history, Bolling's anti-Kenway-Potter obsession, Eileen Fordyce's fixation on social status, and her husband's frustration. In the midst of all this gaggle Rawlings seemed to be a cultural nut with no personal involvement with anybody. But I admit, of course, that I made a fatal mistake over not spotting how inadequately her alibi for the evening of Tuke's death was supported.'

'Hardly a fatal mistake,' the A.C. commented. 'Don't dramatise yourself, Pollard. At least an insane woman with homicidal tendencies is under lock and key. Eileen Fordyce will get a short stretch, I imagine. What will happen to her when she comes out?'

'My guess is that her husband will get a divorce, but continue to provide for her, being the sort of chap who takes his commitments seriously. I think he might have swallowed the anonymous letters to the police and even to the Press, but not the ones she sent to Amaryllis Kenway-Potter.'

The A.C. sniffed.

'Lord, what fools these mortals be ... By the way, the Registrar-General doesn't propose to take any action in connection with Amaryllis Kenway-Potter's bigamy in 1950, in view of the death of the chap involved twenty-eight years ago ... And you've doubtless seen the recent headlines in the Press? "Archaeological Outrage", "Doom Stone Disappears", "Grim Goings-On". No prize is offered for allotting them to their respective newspapers.'

'Yes, sir, I've seen them,' Pollard replied guardedly.

'I can't wait for the impassioned correspondence that will break out in *The Times*...You know where the damned thing is, I suppose?'

'I can hazard a guess, sir. Somewhere where, according to a Woodcombe local, "us won't niver 'ave any more trouble with 'ee"?'

'It's Kenway-Potter's legal property. How's he reacting to its disappearance?'

'I wouldn't know, sir. He and his wife are on holiday in British Columbia.'

The A.C. gave a short bark of laughter.

'Well, if you're determined to compound a felony Pollard, for God's sake keep your mouth shut... That's about all, I think.'